Saxon Slayer

Book 5 in the
Wolf Brethren Series
By
Griff Hosker

Published by Sword Books Ltd 2013
Copyright © Griff Hosker First Edition

The author has asserted their moral right under the Copyright, Designs and Patents Act, 1988, to be identified as the author of this work.

All Rights reserved. No part of this publication may be reproduced, copied, stored in a retrieval system, or transmitted, in any form or by any means, without the prior written consent of the copyright holder, nor be otherwise circulated in any form of binding or cover other than that in which it is published and without a similar condition being imposed on the subsequent purchaser.

A CIP catalogue record for this title is available from the British Library.

Chapter 1

Mona 604 AD

It was a pleasant morning to be riding across Mona with my son Hogan, the Prince of Gwynedd, Cadfan, and my squire Lann Aelle. A couple of years ago I would have needed my horsemen as an escort but since the dark times when the Welsh and the Irish attacked us we had secured our land. The treacherous attempt to attack from within by the Saxon spies had been thwarted and my land was at peace once more. We had paid a heavy price with some brave warriors perishing. I thought of those men as we travelled over the old Roman Road towards the Narrows and the land of Prince Pasgen. He was a potent reminder of our past and a symbol of the power that we had once possessed. He was the last of the true kings of Rheged. He was the last of the Romans. I smiled to myself. I was now, by the grace of the Roman Emperor, Dux Britannica. I was the last Roman lord of the province of Britannia. That in itself was a cause for mirth as the only parts under my direct control were the island of Mona and the peninsula below Wyddfa. It was a start and in a year or so we could begin to expand our control.

I glanced over to the young Welsh prince who had sought sanctuary in my land. His father was King Iago. He had betrayed me and even had his own son, Cadfan, imprisoned at the behest of his step mother. Prince Cadfan would be a better king than his father when I had wrested Gwynedd from the tyrant. I would never be a king. I did not want to be king. I was happy with the title, Warlord, bestowed on me by King Urien of Rheged, I would never stop fighting the Saxons although I knew we could never defeat them; there were too many of them. They grew like weeds.

The young prince was engaged in a lively conversation with Hogan Lann, my son and heir. It would be about weaponry and wars for both were powerful warriors. My son had grown immeasurably both physically and mentally after he and Pol had visited Constantinopolis and the Emperor of the Eastern Empire. He was now a full-grown man. Many said that the only one who could best him in combat was me, his father. That would never happen. I would never fight my son but it was a measure of his standing amongst the finest warriors in the whole of Britannia.

Glancing behind me I saw Lann Aelle taking in every word of two of the three men he admired most. Those three were Hogan, Prince Cadfan and Pol my former squire and the warrior who had trained both my son and Lann Aelle. Lann Aelle was also my nephew which made him even more special to me.

"You are quiet father. Do you yearn for war again?"

I shook my head. "I may be Warlord and Dux Britannica but I never yearn for war. I am happy that we have the time to prepare for war. There is little point in fighting unless you can win and with a strong army and well trained warriors, we will win."

"There Cadfan, that is how a Warlord thinks."

I heard Cadfan laugh, "That is how a wise man thinks. He does not rashly rush into war without thinking of the consequences."

If there was a bitter note to his words it was understandable. His father, King Iago had launched a sneak attack on our fort and he had lost many of his warriors. The king had blamed his son for the defeat but it had been a bad plan and been badly led by the king. It was why we now had Prince Pasgen on the mainland with a solid fort and defences. He protected our pontoon bridge across the Narrows which guaranteed our safety. We would be crossing it soon to help Prince Pasgen and his men begin the building of the monastery I had promised Bishop Stephen. He was bishop of the monastery of St Asaph and there were many acolytes who wished to be monks. Bishop Stephen was a wise man and knew that the monastery at St Asaph could be raided and attacked by many enemies. His new monastery, St. David, would be within the protective wall of Prince Pasgen's defences. I was not a Christian, nor was Pasgen but we tolerated them for they were kind to us and they did not try to convert our warriors. I was not certain how a warrior could be a Christian for the religion promoted turning the other cheek. The thought made me ask a question of my son. The question had been rolling around my head for some time.

"Hogan, are the warriors of the Emperor Phocas, Christian?"

"Yes father, why?"

"I wondered how they reconciled the teaching of the White Christ and the need to kill the Emperor's enemies."

Hogan and Pol had spent some time in the east with the Emperor and they had studied the military theories in the schools there. They had both come back full of ideas and it was they who had created our own Cataphractoi. "They have dispensation to fight the enemies of the Empire although they are not supposed to fight other Christians."

"But they do."

"Yes father, they do."

"Their belief is not as strong as ours then?"

"I think they are, what was the word Andronikos used? Ah yes I remember. They are pragmatic."

I laughed, "Which is a way of saying that they ignore the tenets of their religion when it is inconvenient. Now I understand."

We reached Mungo's Burg which was the first fort we had built on the island of Mona. Mungo led the men of Strathclyde who had fled the Saxons who invaded their land. He was a doughty warrior and I knew my front door was safe. He came with us across the waters to the mainland where Prince Pasgen met us with his equites. Since he had come south the prince had become his old self and regained some of the confidence he had lost when his brother, the king, had betrayed him to the Saxons.

"Welcome Warlord." He waved his arm at his equites. "The new warriors are coming on are they not?"

Hogan was the expert in horsemen and he answered for me, "They are Prince Pasgen and they are a credit to you."

"Ah, Hogan Lann, would that I had the armour you brought back from Constantinopolis then my men would truly be invincible."

My son and Pol had the full armour and weapons of the Cataphractoi. We had bred horses which could also carry the armour and my son and Pol were building up a powerful force of equites who would soon number ten. The lack of the expensive armour was the only thing which limited their numbers but Ralph, our blacksmith, was producing better armour each month as he learned the techniques after studying the new armour.

"Your men are a credit to you and there is no force of men on the mainland who could stand against you." I saw my son nod approval at my comment. He was becoming a wise leader. It had been the right thing to say to Pasgen for he still needed reassurance that he and his men were successful. When he had come south with me he had been the leader of a defeated and demoralised force.

We did not have far to travel and when we reached the site Bishop Stephen and his monks were already there labouring away. These were not aesthetes, these were working monks. They stopped their work at our approach,

"You do not need to toil, Bishop Stephen. I told you that my men would aid your monks."

He shook his head. "It helps me to work with my monks and stops me getting above myself. God made us all equal and I like to think that we are still equal in his eyes. This teaches me humility."

That was where I disagreed with the bishop. If all men were made equal then we would not have kings who tried to take the land of others but this was not the place for that debate. "Are you happy with the land we have given to you?"

"It is a good place. There is a stream and the lord has seen fit to give us these stones." He pointed to the stones which littered the base of the mountain. Again, I would have disagreed with him, as would Myrddyn my adviser and wizard. We believed that the mountain and the Mother had given us the rocks but the bishop believed that everything good came from God.

Just then a rider from Pasgen's fort galloped up. "My lord, the prince has sent me; a ship has come for you from Caer Gybi."

A sudden shock of fear raced up my spine. Had something untoward happened at my home? Were my family safe? Perhaps the Irish had raided again. Hogan saw my fear. "Let us return to the fort father and we can find out if this is a cause for concern or not."

"I am sorry I could not stay longer, Bishop Stephen."

"It was good of you to come. May the lord watch over you and your family." He made the sign of the cross which seemed to be the way the Christians had of casting a spell.

I knew he meant well and was being kind. "Thank you, bishop. I look forwards to seeing the building take shape."

When we reached the fort I saw 'The Wolf', one of our four ships. Brother Oswald was on board. He was the cleric who administered my lands. He was a good engineer and a wise man but his presence put my mind at rest. If there had been danger at home then he would not have left. He was waiting patiently for me. "I am sorry to drag you away from the bishop Warlord but a ship has come from Constantinopolis. It is the strategos, Andronikos and he wishes to speak with you. I thought a ship would be quicker than a horse."

"And you are right. Come let us get aboard." I turned to Prince Pasgen. "If you could send a couple of riders with our horses back to Caer Gybi."

Prince Pasgen nodded and then smiled, "Perhaps Hogan Lann might send back a couple of the new maces for my men to try; if he has any to spare of course."

Hogan laughed, "I think we can find a couple. You should have been a horse trader Prince!" They clasped hands and we boarded.

With a favourable wind we could be home within a few hours for the ship could drop us at Castle Cam and we would save a journey from the port. The priest had no idea why the strategos had come but he told us that it was an Imperial ship and not a cargo ship. I wondered what had brought Andronikos all the way from Constantinopolis. He was an important man and an adviser to Emperor Phocas. I asked Hogan for he was wise beyond his years and knew the strategos better than I did.

"It has me interested too. He rarely leaves the palace. When we initially saw him, it was his first mission for the new Emperor. He is one of the few strategoi who is trusted by Emperor Phocas."

"You see that I cannot understand. I trust all of my captains and all of my leaders. If I did not then I would rid myself of them."

"And therein is the fundamental difference between us and them. In Constantinopolis there are factions and plotters all vying for position. Men smile but not with their eyes. It is a very dangerous place. The Emperor is not a popular man. He has to keep a tight rein on all of those around him. He came to power through the military and he ended the reign of a line of families."

I suddenly saw a similarity. "So in many ways he is like me."

Hogan said, slowly, "Yes, I suppose so but he is more than a king. He rules vast lands which are far bigger than you can imagine."

I laughed, "I was not getting above myself son. I was thinking of our backgrounds. Mine is military as is his."

"Yes but you are a warrior, he is not. He was a leader but he could not understand you standing next to your men and fighting alongside them. You piqued his curiosity."

My curiosity was also aroused by this visit. It had come at an unusually quiet time for us. The Saxons were busy with minor wars between themselves and King Iago was trying to subjugate the other kings, Cloten and Arthlwys. As for the Irish, we had beaten them twice and soundly both times. I think they were wary of us. If the chance came and someone invaded us then, like the wild dogs that they are, they would fall upon the bleeding carcass but until then we were safe.

My stronghold, Castle Cam, hove into view. We had named it Castle Calm but the people pronounced it Cam and it had stuck. We headed towards the beach. There were small boats drawn up on the sand and I saw men rushing to row out to us. Soon we would discover what had prompted this visit. Garth, the captain of my garrison, was there to meet us as we stepped ashore.

"I am sorry to have cut short your visit to the bishop Warlord but Lord Andronikos seemed quite keen to speak with you."

"There is no problem, Garth, besides I am interested in what he has to say to me that brings him from the other side of the world. I assume that my wife has made him comfortable?"

"She has, Warlord, and don't we know it!"

My wife was not backwards at coming forwards. Title and position meant nothing to her and if a guest were to come then she would want everything to be perfect. I suspected that Garth was more than glad to have me back. The men at the gates saluted as we entered and I saw my wife with son Gawan in her arms and Nanna, my daughter holding her hand. Behind the three of them stood my wizard, Myrddyn, and Andronikos the strategos from Constantinopolis. Nanna ran to me as I walked towards her and threw herself into my arms.

"You said you would be away tonight!"

I kissed her, "Well I couldn't bear to be away from you so I came back."

"I'm glad. I missed you." She pointed at Andronikos. "We have a visitor." She leaned in and whispered in my ear. "He smells like mother when she has bathed and put on perfume and he has a slippery beard."

I whispered back. "Thank you for telling me but it would be rude to mention it to him."

She nodded, "I won't say a word." She saw Hogan behind me and squealed to be put down. "Hogan!" She threw herself into his arms. I was lucky with my family and I knew it.

Myfanwy hugged me and whispered, "Why is he here?"

I murmured back, "I have no idea."

Andronikos dropped to one knee. "Warlord, the Emperor sends his greetings and congratulations on your great victory over three enemies!"

"I thank the Emperor. We will go inside so that we can talk more freely."

We went to my solar. It was the place I felt the most comfortable and the most protected. There was but one door in and a guard stood outside at all times. He was there to protect my privacy, rather than my life. Myrddyn joined us, unasked. He was my adviser and I trusted him in all things. I knew that my wife and Brother Oswald would deal with the feast but this was more important. This was statecraft. We had settled into the chairs when there was a knock on the door. The guard peered in and looked embarrassed. "Warlord, it is your son. He seeks admission."

What did Hogan want? "Admit him and thank you."

I threw a questioning glance in my son's direction. His eyes pleaded with me. "I was anxious, Warlord, to hear what the Emperor's envoy had to say."

I looked over to the strategos. "Will it be a problem if my son sits in on this conversation?"

Andronikos smiled, after my son's comments aboard 'The Wolf', I wondered if this was Byzantine politics. "He is more than welcome, Warlord, and he may even aid our discussions."

"Then you may stay." I noticed the hint of a smile on Myrddyn's lips.

There was a silence which could have been awkward but my son and my wizard's smile made it just seem like the preparation for a discussion. Andronikos looked me squarely in the eye. "Emperor Phocas would like you to come to Constantinopolis."

I think that took everyone by surprise. Even Myrddyn looked, albeit briefly, shocked but he quickly regained his composure. Hogan's face lit up like a winter bonfire. I was more cautious. "I am honoured by the invitation but I wonder what prompts it?"

"You, Warlord, are the talk of the capital. You defeated three enemies, all of whom greatly outnumbered you in a very short space of time. Everyone wants to know how you did it." I remained impassively silent. "You are the ally of the Emperor. You have had success more than any other and he is anxious to meet with you and learn from you. He, like you, is a warrior and he feels a face to face meeting will profit both of you."

I remembered my son's words and wondered how much was the truth and how much was lies. "It is an honour but I am needed here on my island. We have a perilous hold on the land and our enemies could return at any time."

I saw the pleading look in Hogan's eyes once more. "Warlord, your enemies will not return for a year or more and the Emperor Phocas will only keep you away from your home for a short time. Two sea voyages and a month in Constantinopolis are all that he asks from you."

Hogan could not keep silent any longer, "Father it will be a wonderful opportunity for you. You will see the greatest city in the whole world!"

"But what of my home, my son? What of your brother and sister? What of my wife? There is much to consider here."

I glanced over to Myrddyn who had kept a stony and impassive face throughout the conversation and discussion. Androniknos saw the glance and smiled, "The Emperor is also keen to meet this famed wizard." Myrddyn merely looked at the strategos and gave him a polite smile. "The stories of your magic abound in the east and the Emperor and his holy men are keen to speak with you. We are not as intolerant of other cults and religions as the Western Empire."

The wizard spoke for the first time. "I am flattered but I fear that I would be a great disappointment. However I can see that the Warlord might benefit from such a visit."

I looked at him in surprise. I had expected him to reject the offer. "You are correct in that our enemies are cowed at the moment but that could change. Who would defend my people against these enemies if I was absent?"

"I would." Hogan looked at me. "Or do you not think I could defend our home, our family and our people?"

There was an edge to his voice and I could see a chasm opening before me; if I said the wrong thing then I would fall into it and there would be a rift between my son and me. I would be doing as Iago had done. Andronikos' eyes flashed between us. "The Emperor also sent another inducement. In the hold of the ship are twenty sets of Cataphractoi armour for man and horse."

Hogan almost leapt from the chair and his eyes lit up in excitement. "That would make us invincible!"

I held up my hand. "The Emperor is a generous man and I am tempted by this extremely attractive offer, however, Andronikos, Stategos of the Empire, you would not expect an answer before I have consulted my advisers and my wife."

He nodded his head slightly. "Of course Warlord but my ship and I must sail on tomorrow night's tide."

I had an ultimatum then and only a short time to make my mind up. "I will meet with my advisers after the feast this evening and you shall have your answer by morning."

The strategos nodded. "I will spend the time with Brother Osric's papers. I am grateful for the copies you sent to me but Brother Oswald has found some more and I was most interested in them. They give an insight into how the

Saxons succeeded in conquering so much of this land and we Romans can learn from them."

As I walked back to my quarters Myrddyn and Hogan accompanied me. I noticed Hogan glancing at Myrddyn and I smiled. "Hogan, speak your mind. There are no secrets between Myrddyn and me."

He grinned, "Sorry Myrddyn, I forgot. " He became more serious. "Father when you sent me to Constantinopolis it was to learn how to become a leader. Since I have returned, have I disappointed you?"

"No, of course you haven't but…"

"And when you were my age did not King Urien give you Castle Perilous with orders to protect his borders? Didn't you control a larger piece of land than Mona?"

He had me there and I heard Myrddyn chuckle, "He is right my lord. In fact you were younger than he is."

I turned and faced both of them. "I have heard your arguments but I have not yet heard the advice either of my other leaders or of my wife. When I have all the information then I will decide." I smiled at Myrddyn. "You of all people should know that it is best to sleep on decisions such as this. The dream world has yet to be consulted."

Myrddyn nodded and smiled. "Some of my wisdom must have brushed off on you Warlord. You sometimes think like a wizard now and not always as a warrior."

As I entered my quarters and changed from my mail I pondered their words. Hogan was, of course, correct. I had commanded a larger land and more warriors when I was younger than he was. I was proud of him and I could trust him. He was the best leader I had and superior even to Garth and Prince Pasgen. What was stopping me? As I changed into my clothes for the feast I knew the reason; it was my young family. I was loath to leave them. I had missed Hogan growing up and my first daughter had died with Aideen my wife. I wanted to watch Nanna and her brother becoming children. I had time for that now. It was a dilemma.

The door opened and Myfanwy came in. She handed my son to a servant and closed the door. She embraced me and kissed me. "You look good out of armour, my husband."

"Thank you and you look good all the time!"

"Flatterer." She began to dress for the feast. "Well, have you made up your mind yet?"

I threw her a look. "Hogan spoke with you."

"Of course he did. Am I like Cadfan's stepmother to be feared? No, your son does me the honour of treating me as his mother and I think of him as my son. Would he talk to someone else perhaps?"

I laughed, "No. As usual you are right and I am pleased that you are close but I hope he did not worry you?"

She snorted. "Of course not. But he is ready to lead the people. You know that as well, if not better, than me. That is not the reason you hesitate is it?"

"No. I have yet to consult the other warrior leaders."

"Hah! Do not try to deceive me husband. We both know that they will go along with whatever you say. What is the real reason?" I remained silent and pretended that I was fiddling with the laces on my tunic. Her voice became softer as she came over to tie them for me. "I know that it is the children and me who stop you going. That makes me love you all the more but it is not the reason you should not go. We will be safe here. Hogan will protect us and we will be here when you return. Now if you are afraid of a sea voyage then that is another matter and I can understand that."

I laughed and picked her up. "You know me too well." I threw her on the bed and we kissed. "I do not want to miss the children growing up."

She pretended to be outraged. "So, you would not miss me. That is a fine thing to say to your wife."

"Of course I would miss you." I suddenly had an idea, "Come with me! Bring the children."

She stood and straightened her dress. "You may not be afraid of sea monsters and falling off the edge of the world but your wife is and besides your son is too young to spend a month at sea." She kissed me and said, gently, "You go. We will miss you but you know you would regret not going and I would hate to be the cause of regret. It is less than a year you will be away and you will see a change in the children when you return." I nodded. "Will you tell Andronikos now?"

"No, I will consult with my leaders and tell him tomorrow. I would not have the Emperor and his strategoi thinking that I dance to their tune."

She nodded her approval. "You have grown my husband and you are now wise." She nudged me in the ribs, playfully, "See what having a clever wife does for you?"

The feast was well organised as I had come to expect from my wife and Brother Oswald. I could see that Andronikos was desperate for an answer and his silences were eloquent. Hogan too merely picked at his food. I suppose I could have told Hogan before the feast but I thought it would do him good to wonder. As the last platters were cleared Myfanwy said, "Well strategos would you care to watch the sun set from the cliffs? It is particularly beautiful at this time of year."

"Of course. I would be delighted." He took my wife's arm. She smiled at me over her shoulder as she left.

When they had left we emptied the hall of servants, I asked Lann Aelle to stand guard at one door while Pol stood at the other. I explained to the assembled captains of the offer of the Emperor and asked for their opinion. Hogan began to rise. I held up my hand. "No, my son, I already know your opinion. Allow others to speak first."

Garth began. "I cannot see how we can benefit, Warlord. Hogan and Pol have already given us much knowledge and Miach's son has brought back better bows." He shrugged. "Why go? What is in it for us?"

Tuanthal smiled, "Twenty suits of armour are a nice bribe, Garth." The horseman wanted to get his hands on the Imperial weaponry.

A silence descended. "Myrddyn, you have yet to speak. You are a wise wizard; can you not give us some advice?"

"The problem is, Warlord, that I am torn. I would dearly love to see the greatest city on earth and learn of its secrets but I worry about the motives of both the strategos and the Emperor. I could not give you honest advice." He looked at me with his keen, sharp eyes, "This will be your decision."

Ridwyn spoke. "If you do go my lord how many bodyguards would you take with you?"

"None."

Ridwyn was shocked, "But how would your life be protected?"

I looked over at my son. "Hogan, how many warriors are in the Emperor's palace?"

"A thousand bodyguards and another five thousand protect the city."

"I think I would be safe, Ridwyn."

"But suppose the Emperor had you murdered?"

I laughed. "I know you and the warriors you command are good but do you honestly believe that fifty of you could protect me from the Emperor's guards? If he wanted me dead I would have been murdered here but I do not think he wishes my death."

"But he does have an ulterior motive, Warlord."

"You may be right, Myrddyn, which is why I am glad that you and your wisdom will be with me."

Hogan let out a shout and slapped the table. "You are going? What about Myfanwy?"

They all looked at me expectantly. "I have already spoken with my wife and she approves."

Lann Aelle suddenly burst in. "You will take me too my lord!"

I laughed. "Yes I will take you and I will leave my son Hogan as Warlord in my place until I return and you will all obey him as you would me."

They all chorused, "Aye my lord."

With that the decision was made and I would sail to the other side of the world to visit the centre of the greatest Empire known to man.

Chapter 2

Andronikos was delighted when he heard of my decision. Having made it I realised what a short time I had to prepare things. Myfanwy, Hogan and Brother Oswald all took charge of the various parts of my life and made it much easier for me. It allowed me the morning and afternoon to play with my children. My brother, Aelle, did not live far away and he could easily ride to see us off. I had sent messengers to my brothers, Prince Pasgen and Mungo to let them know of my orders regarding the defence of my land. Aelle and his wife rode over to say goodbye to their eldest son.

Lann Aelle had grown both in size and in his maturity since he had become my squire. He was now a confident young warrior and not the nervous youth who had come to me to be trained. I was happy that he would be accompanying me but I knew what his parents would be going through. It was the same as my own feelings for my son and daughter. They spent the afternoon together. We all travelled to Caer Gybi in the middle of the afternoon. Hogan, Pol and Tuanthal were anxious to see the suits of armour which were being unloaded. Myfanwy wanted to make sure that my chests were stored to her satisfaction. We made quite a cavalcade as we headed to the Imperial ship, 'Augustus'; it dwarfed every other ship in the small harbour. Andronikos went aboard to arrange the landing of the cargo and we stood on the quayside. It was both sad and exciting. Nanna was excited about seeing the huge ship but she clung to my hand as though she knew that something was going to change. Children do not like change; I had learned that much already.

While Myfanwy was on board Aelle took a package from the horse he had brought with him. He handed it to Lann Aelle. "This, my son, is my gift to you. It is the sword I was given after your uncle killed King Aella of the Saxons. I used it rarely but it is a symbol of our victory and it is our family's sword. You are now a man and need a man's weapon. Wear it with honour."

He handed it over and Lann Aelle unwrapped the sheepskin in which it was protected. I had not seen the sword for many years and it was magnificent. It was not Saxon Slayer but it was a weapon worthy of a king. The blade was as long as the Slayer and the hilt had the warrior rings won by King Aella. My brother had left them there, even though he had not earned them. He felt that our defeat of the Saxons had earned us the right to display them.

I worried that Lann Aelle would break down and weep in front of all the people. There was nothing wrong with tears but I knew that he would feel embarrassment later on. He held them back and embraced his father and then his mother. "I swear that I will wield this sword with honour and prove to be a worthy heir to the great Lord Aelle of Glanibanta."

His mother could not hold back the tears and they flooded from her eyes. Nanna whispered to me, "Why is Lann's mother upset? Has she hurt herself?"

I picked her up and hugged her. "No, my pet, Lann Aelle is going away and his mother will not see him for some time. She will miss him."

"I will miss him too." She suddenly looked at me. There was fear in her eyes. "You are not going with him are you?"

"Well my brave little girl, we cannot let your cousin go there all alone can we?"

She burst into tears and threw her arms around me. "No! You have to stay! Please don't go!"

Myfanwy came down the gangplank, having supervised my chests. She shook her head, "I see you have told her then?"

Nanna looked at her mother. "Don't let him go please!"

My wife prised her away from me. "Well, my sweet. He is going to a beautiful city and he has promised that he will bring us some wonderful presents back. How would you like that?"

She sniffed, "Can't we go with him?"

She whispered in Nanna's ear. "We wouldn't like it my pet. It is a bit dirty and smelly. It is fine for men but not for ladies like us. Hogan is staying and he will look after us."

My daughter looked over at her brother and he nodded. "I will be here little sister and father will not be away long. Now hide those tears and give him and your cousin a kiss for I can see the captain needs to go."

My son was now a man. Nanna nodded and rushed over to me, "I love you. Come back soon." As she kissed me I fought back my own tears.

My wife grabbed me and kissed me. "And that goes double for me. Keep safe. You are too good a man to lose to the sea."

I could not speak. I turned and gave a wave. Myrddyn put his arm around my side and helped me aboard. "Do not worry Nanna, Lann Aelle and I will look after him. Farewell."

Andronikos stood awaiting us. "It will not be long, Warlord, and you will have much to tell your children when you return."

I looked to the land as the gangplank was hauled on board. My family seemed so small and vulnerable as the captain gave orders to cast off. The last time I had said goodbye to a family was when I had buried my mother and father. This felt worse. I was slightly comforted by the sight of Hogan with his arm around his stepmother whilst holding his little sister. My family were in safe hands, my family was in the hands of the next Warlord.

The ship we were travelling in had huge sails but in the tricky and narrow waters of the harbour the captain was relying on the oars of the rowers. This was an Imperial ship and was fully manned. With every rower rowing, the ship would, I imagined, fly across the water. It was a worrying thought that there were more rowers chained below than there were in the rest of the crew. When I mentioned this to Andronikos he smiled, "We have thirty Imperial troops on board as well as thirty crew members. We can deal with the rowers. You just enjoy the voyage. I think that you will find it illuminating."

I saw that Myrddyn and Lann Aelle were already exploring the huge ship which was twice the size of 'The Wolf'. I wanted to explore the ship but I needed to watch my island, my Mona, disappear behind me. I wanted to keep the link with my family even though I could no longer see them now as we headed south through the darkening waters. The sun slowly set and I stood at the stern watching the darkening waters spread like blood behind me. I wondered if it was an omen.

Andronikos came to find me. "Warlord, come with me and I will show you your cabin. Myrddyn and Lann are both there." He put his arm around my shoulder and I was struck by the strong smell of perfume. "Your family will be safe. Your son is a good man. I got to know him well and I would trust him with my life."

I shook myself free from the trance that was Mona. "You are right and I am behaving like a woman. Take me to my cabin. I will explore the ship tomorrow."

"Yes we have many days at sea although the next few days will be interesting for you as we sail around your island. You will see parts of Britannia you have never seen before."

When we ate our first meal on the ship Lann Aelle was full of excitement and Myrddyn was full of questions. People have often asked me what a wizard is. I suppose the honest answer is a very clever man. That was Myrddyn. He always wanted to understand how things functioned. Once he knew that he could begin to think of ways of making them better. He also had an insatiable appetite for knowledge.

Lann Aelle was just excited. He was on the cusp of being a man. His body was almost there as was his mind but he still had the wonder of a child at seeing new things and I was pleased that I had brought him. He would return as rounded as Pol and Hogan had from the exotic experience.

As for me, I sat silently through the meal. I did not even taste the food. My mind was torn between my family and the new land to which I would be going. I was seeking a reason for my summons from the Emperor. He was a great and powerful man. He could have just sent me a message but he wanted to meet and speak with me and I wondered why. My dealings with treacherous leaders such as Morcant Bulc and Iago ap Beli had made me wary of a smiling face. True, I had met noble and honest kings like King Urien and Rhydderch Hael but I had learned to wait until I knew them to offer a judgement.

"You are quiet Warlord. Was the food not to your liking?"

"I am sorry Andronikos. The food was delicious it is just that this is the start of an adventure and I am pondering its direction."

Lann Aelle said innocently, "East?"

I laughed and it broke the mood. "Of course nephew. Your uncle must be losing his mind. Go and fetch your new sword. I know that the strategos would be interested in the blade."

When he left Andronikos leaned forward. "Your son and Pol enjoyed reading in the libraries of Constantinopolis about the story of famous swords. One of the librarians thought that he had a reference to your sword from some writings of the Emperors Claudius and Hadrian."

I was intrigued and I could see that Myrddyn was. "Then we must meet this librarian for that fascinates me."

Lann Aelle returned with the sword, still wrapped in the sheepskin. "Well done, squire, you need to protect the blade from the salt air."

He grinned, "I learned that lesson from Pol at the expense of many a cuffed ear."

It was my turn to smile. "Much as I cuffed your father when we were growing up."

He withdrew the blade and placed it on the gently swaying table which was suspended from the wooden ceiling. The glow from the oil lamps picked out intricate detail on its blade. There were runes on the steel and Myrddyn peered at them. "These runes say that the blade was forged in the mountains for a leader called The Bear Killer."

Lann Aelle ran his fingers over the runes as though he would be able to read them too. "What are these rings around the hilt uncle?"

"When a warrior wins a single combat against a formidable foe he is allowed to put a ring around the hilt. There are many rings here."

"Does that mean Aella was a mighty warrior?"

"He was a good warrior but some of these are old and it may have been that the king did not remove the old ones." I shrugged, "Not all men have honour."

"Should I remove them?"

"If you do then you will need to put new bindings on the hilt as the removal will weaken it."

"Thank you Myrddyn."

"May I?" Andronikos held his hand out for the sword. He balanced it on his hand. "This has a fine balance." He stood away from the table and swung it in a horizontal plane. It made a humming noise. "Do you hear how it sings? This is a fine sword. The best swords always sing. If you like we can have the rings removed and the hilt strengthened at the palace. The Emperor has his own blacksmith and he is highly skilled. He would be honoured to work on such an ancient sword. And we can find out the history of this blade too."

When Lann took back the sword I could see the wonder in his eyes. This was no longer a weapon given to him by his father; this was a mystical weapon from another culture. He now had his own Saxon Slayer. "You should name it Lann."

Myrddyn smiled, "It already has a name Warlord. It is called Bear Killer. It is not wise to rename a sword. What think you to that name?"

Lann nodded, "I like it. Bear Killer it is."

Andronikos shook his head. "I understand how you appreciate a fine weapon but this naming of a weapon makes no sense."

Myrddyn explained as though to a child, "The name means that the weapon becomes alive. The name lives on after the warrior who died using it. The power of the sword grows as each successive warrior adds his skill and power to it."

"Does that not depend upon the warrior?"

"That is where we will have to disagree, Christian, for we believe that the weapon and the warrior become one. The weapon has a life of its own." Myrddyn pointed to me. "Until he found the sword he was not a great warrior but the moment it touched his hand then his life changed. This warrior and his sword almost saved Rheged and they have saved a part of Roman Britain. Would this have happened without the sword?"

"You have given me much to ponder. And now I think I will retire. Sleep well."

I had slept on boats before. I did not find the motion uncomfortable. As we had the wind with us the rowers were not used and we sailed gently south. Each mile took me further from my home but, that night, I dreamt my last dream for a while.

My mother came to me and lifted me from the ship we flew high in the sky and we became hawks. Below me were crows and magpies. I was suddenly alone for my mother had gone. I plunged down to seize a crow and I was flying with the dead bird in my talon. Suddenly I found myself being attacked by something I couldn't see and, as I dropped my catch, I glimpsed an eagle tearing at me. Then I was falling and spiralling down to earth.

"My lord!"

I looked up and saw Lann Aelle above me. "What is it Lann?"

"You were shouting in your sleep. I was worried."

Myrddyn's voice sent shivers down my spine. "He was dreaming, Lann, and his mother came to him." I looked over to him, the question on my face. He nodded, "Yes, Warlord, I dreamed your dream too."

"What does it mean?"

He came over to me and spoke quietly. "It means that we must be on our guard, both here and in Constantinopolis." He put his arm around Lann. "That means all of us."

Lann's eyes were wide, "Yes, Myrddyn. I will be careful." He had his sword in his hand, albeit in its scabbard, "I swear by Bear Killer." In that moment, I saw my nephew become a man.

When we had eaten we went to the main deck where we joined Andronikos and the captain. It was obvious that the captain could do without the strategos and us watching his every move. I felt sorry for him. He had a hard enough job sailing the huge behemoth, without visitors on his deck. Andronikos pointed to the land on the left. "The captain will be pleased when we have navigated this section. The cliffs are littered with savage rocks and to the south are a string of ragged rocks which have torn the bottoms out of many ships."

Myrddyn showed his wisdom and his understanding of the dilemma of the captain. "Then let us leave the man to steer the ship for we can go forrard and see this land which is so fearsome." I saw the grateful nod from the portly captain.

"This is the land of the Britons. They are, like you, the last peoples to fight the Saxons."

"And are they allies of the Emperor like us?"

He shook his head. "I fear they are not as civilised as you. They killed the last envoy and destroyed his ship. The Emperor hopes that, in time, you may be able to reconcile them to the way of Rome."

I realised then that the Emperor had not just gambled on me. He had others with whom he hoped to regain his provinces. I stored that information away for the future. "Tell me strategos, do you not worry about pirates? I know that we have passed beyond the land of the Hibernians, but here are others who would prey upon such valuable prizes."

In answer he pointed to the bolt throwers. There were two at the prow, two at the stern and two in the mid deck area. "The bolt throwers are, as I know you have found out, effective. We are too big for most pirates to attack."

I glanced at Myrddyn. I had already worked out how such a ship could be taken and the knowing look from Myrddyn showed me that he, too, had worked it out. "And how long to reach our destination?"

"That depends upon the wind. If we had to row the whole way it would take a long time but the winds are generally in our favour until we reach the Pillars of Hercules. However the weather is also unpredictable. We may be there in under a month or it could take us two months. We are in God's hands."

I wondered about that as we headed east. There were still free people on the island of Britannia who had not been defeated by the Saxons. Perhaps there was hope for us. The people of Cymri still held out and with good leadership we could begin to claw back some of the lands stolen from us by the invaders who sought to reap the benefit of the work of the Romans and the Britons. I determined, as the coastline slid by behind us, that I would rid the land of these parasites that did nothing constructive themselves but took the hard work of others. If nothing else this journey to Constantinopolis had hardened my resolve and given me purpose.

The day turned grey and stormy as we headed towards the coastline of the land of the Gauls. Once Roman, it was now a land of the old tribes fighting amongst themselves; as they had done before the Romans came. As Myrddyn and Lann wandered the ship with Andronikos I went to the stern to talk with the captain. "Is there no trade with the people of these lands?"

The portly captain nodded to the helmsman to keep on the same course and joined me. "No, Warlord, for they are unpredictable. Their leaders change frequently and the new ones just want something for nothing. Many of my friends have lost their ships and their lives because they cannot predict what the natives will do. We avoid it now and it means that they do not enjoy the benefits of trade. They live primitive lives. Your land has benefited from trade and it prospers. These people just take what they can and live hand to mouth. Your land is a haven for traders such as us."

Suddenly a squall came from nowhere. "You must go below decks, Warlord; this will get worse before it gets better."

I heeded the advice of the captain and returned to our cabin. The others soon joined me and they were soaked to the skin. Lann Aelle was laughing. "This is a strange way to live my lord. There was sunshine and then, within a heartbeat, there was rain. Have we upset the gods in some way?"

I looked at Myrddyn who gave the hint of a smile. He had wondered why we had not appeased the gods before we left Britannia. Andronikos shook his head, "It is just the weather. God does not punish men for sailing his seas. The wind will abate and the rain will stop. We must be patient."

He was right although it took two days for the winds to blow themselves out. Lann Aelle was sick for most of those two days as was Andronikos. Myrddyn and I did not seem to suffer. We ate and slept as we normally did. When the wind ceased we assessed the damage.

The captain approached Andronikos. "As far as I can see we are quite close to the Pillars of Hercules and we have reached here sooner than we thought but the ship has suffered damage. We have lost four men overboard. Many oars were destroyed and the sail needs replacing." He pointed to the mid ships area. "And we have lost two bolt throwers. We will need to repair for half a day." He pointed to the south. "We must keep a good watch. There are many pirates here. Africa is a hotbed of brigands, bandits and pirates. I would arm yourselves."

When he had gone I looked out at the now placid sea. "It looks so peaceful."

"True but like the storm which came from nowhere it can change in a moment. I would suggest you do as he says. We are helpless here until we have repaired the ship."

As we went below I saw the Imperial troops building a new bolt thrower. They worked so feverishly that I knew it was a serious situation. "When we are armed we will get out bows, Lann Aelle. I have a feeling that we will need them soon."

I wondered if I was right as we saw the ship transformed before our eyes from a semi wrecked hulk to a working ship once more. The sailors knew their jobs. The ship obviously kept spares for just such an occasion and the vessel began to heal itself with the aid of the mariners. The hardest and the longest task was the sail. The old one had to be taken down and manhandled below for repair while the new one, stiff and unyielding, was brought up to be hoisted.

It was when we were in the middle of this delicate operation that the three pirate ships appeared. They came from the south. One headed for our bows whilst the other two each took a quarter of the ship. As we had no sail we were relatively immobile although the captain ordered the rowers to their stations despite their tiredness. They were happy to be at their benches for the prospect of capture by the pirates was not an attractive one. The five bolt throwers were manned and the Imperial troops formed themselves into three lines. The first one was armed with shield and spear while the rear two had bows. Andronikos and his servant appeared, both in the armour of Cataphractoi.

He stood by the three of us. "Interesting is it not Warlord." He pointed at the decks of the three ships which approached us; they teemed with half naked savages who were waving weapons in the air. I could not see the weapons but I assumed they would be primitive yet effective. "We can beat any of their ships one on one. We can defeat all of the warriors in any one ship but if they attack us at the same time then they will win."

"You do not seem worried strategos?"

He shrugged, "Worry would not win the battle and might even lose it for us. We will try to defeat each attack they make and adapt." He smiled. "It usually works and we have the best trained men on board." He pointed to Saxon Slayer. "However as you have never lost whilst using your mystical weapon perhaps we need not fear."

"I wish it were that easy, strategos. Where would you like us?"

"Go with the archers and loose when they do. Wizard, perhaps if you could make their ships fill with water…?"

Myrddyn had the good grace to smile. "As this is my first sea battle then I shall watch and come up with a stratagem for the next time."

Lann and I joined Andronikos at the prow with his men. I could see the centre ship heading directly for us. She was making herself a small target. I looked at the mast head and saw the pennant fluttering in the wind. "It is a pity we do not have the sail hoisted for the wind is with us."

"Yes, Warlord and at that moment that aids us for they have to tack into the wind to reach us but once they are upwind of us they can pick us off at will." He tapped his captain of artillery on the shoulder. "Whenever you are ready."

The two bolts hurtled towards the ship. One of them struck the bow and stayed there. The other bounced off the side. Andronikos seemed pleased. "Not bad for a first attempt."

They fired a second time and this time one struck the mast, which visibly shivered and the other struck the bow. I drew back my bow. I aimed for the mast, and I hoped that my arrow would fly over, and strike somewhere close to the rudder. In my experience, missiles raining down on men who thought they were safe had a sobering effect. I watched it climb and then plunge down. I loosed a second and a third. The bolts were still striking the African ship but did not appear to be slowing it down. Suddenly the ship yawed to the left and the next two bolts hit home close to the waterline. The early bolts had caused holes and the sudden turn must have caused water to begin to enter the boat. It began to sink. There was no cheering but the men from the bolt thrower went to the mid ships. On one side the one bolt thrower was having little effect whilst on the other there was no bolt thrower. The ship on that side was much closer. Andronikos led us there and we all loosed our arrows as fast as we could. Men began to fall over the side but still the ship came on. I was acutely aware that the pirate on the other side would be closing and there would be no diminishing of the men on her decks. When she reached us she would be fully laden.

Andronikos turned to me. "Take your nephew and try to thin out the men on the other ship. We will join you when this one is destroyed."

I admired his confidence. When we reached the other side we could see that the approaching vessel had been hit below the water line and was moving more sluggishly but she was still approaching at a reasonable speed. As we crossed I noticed Myrddyn hauling, with the sailors, on the rope attached to the sail. I could not remember the wizard resorting to physical labour. Perhaps he had foreseen our end. "Aim at the leaders, Lann. You stop only when you are out of arrows and then we will try your new sword."

I saw a huge warrior with a fine helmet and scimitar. He was at the prow exhorting his men to attack us. He had no armour and my arrow threw him backwards into the sea. I loosed a second as another man took his place. The effect was like emptying a beach by picking up each grain of sand; in the long run they would overwhelm us. I remembered Andronikos' words. I stopped worrying about the outcome and concentrated on killing as many as I could. They were less than forty paces from the side of our ship. The sail was almost hoisted but it would not save us. I shouted, without turning. "They are almost upon us." I loosed my last arrow and looked down at Lann who showed me his empty quiver. "Get your shield then." I decided not to use a shield and took out my small axe instead. There would be no arrows coming in my direction and I wanted two hands to kill as many as I could. I settled my helmet firmly on my head. "Lann, stay to my right and guard my back."

I heard the bump as the ship struck us and I strode to the side. The Africans attached grappling hooks to the ship and began to swarm up the sides. I swung Saxon Slayer in a wide arc. I felt it strike flesh and heard the screams as it bit into men's flesh. Others fell backwards as its deadly blade came towards them. "Well done my lord!"

"They will spread out Lann. Watch for them along the side." I was praying that Andronikos and the men on the other side would have succeeded and be able to come to assist us.

I kept swinging and was gratified to hear the death screams of the pirates until Lann shouted. "They are on both sides of us."

"Then stand to my back and let them taste our steel." I saw that there were forty men who had made the ship. We would never kill that many. I swung my sword around my head and one of them threw a knife at me. It clanked off my helmet and made them pause.

Suddenly I heard Myrddyn's voice, "Lann, Warlord. Drop to the deck. Now!"

I trusted Myrddyn but I knew not what he was up to. "Lann, drop now!"

As we dropped the surprised Africans ran towards our defenceless bodies. Then the four bolts fired from the prow and the stern, ripped through them. Before the survivors had chance to recover Andronikos and the Imperial warriors leapt at them and cut them to pieces. Then we stood and found a deck slippery with blood and dead pirates. The last ship was limping away while the sharks ripped and tore the survivors from the first ship who were clinging to the wreckage. Lann and I went to the side and we watched, with morbid fascination, as the pirates were slaughtered by the terrors of the deep. Myfanwy's sea monsters were real. When I heard the cheer I knew that the sail had been hoisted and we had been saved.

Myrddyn made his way from the stern. He smiled at Andronikos. "Not quite magic but effective, wouldn't you say?"

Chapter 3

I looked at the bodies floating in the waters as the Augustus got under way and we headed east to the Pillars of Hercules. "They were brave warriors. Do none of them possess armour?"

Andronikos shook his head. "There are many of them. For these people the risks are worth it. They hope to overwhelm us with numbers. It was close this time." He patted Myrddyn on the back. "A clever tactic wizard but you risked your Warlord."

"No strategos. I knew he would heed my words and I had aimed the bolt throwers myself. But I think you need something smaller on the decks for just such an occasion."

"It is rare that they would get close." He pointed to the clearing skies. "If the storm had not struck us then we would have sailed by without them getting close."

Myrddyn and I smiled at each other and Lann Aelle said, "*Wyrd*!"

"What is this *wyrd*? Hogan and Pol said it on a number of occasions."

"It is fate, happenstance, those things shaped by the gods to spoil our plans or to shape our world." Myrddyn pointed to me. "He is the living embodiment of it. He found the armour and the sword before the Saxons came to his people. He was away from the village when it was raided and he ran towards King Urien even though he did not know that he would be there. That is *Wyrd*."

"Merely accidents. There are clever men in Athens and Constantinopolis who will explain how these things work."

"If they had happened to the Warlord once only then I might have accepted your argument but there is something shaping his destiny and it is not of this world."

Andronikos smiled, "Then he need do nothing and he will still garner success."

"It does not work that way. The gods help those who help themselves." I thought of the times that our interventions had saved us and I was convinced that it made the gods help us more.

"Your religion does not follow the same rules as ours."

"True. In fact ours has no rules. We try to live in harmony with our land and our people." I grinned, "We have never gone to war for religion. I believe the Roman Empire has torn itself apart before now over religion differences."

"Hm, an interesting idea; I can see some of our priests will enjoy talking with you." He pointed to the east. "Soon you will sail between the land of Africa and what was the Western Roman Empire. You will sail through the Pillars of Hercules and enter the waters which we control. The sea will be calmer and you will no longer need your wolf skin Warlord."

Before he had spoken I had noticed how warm it was becoming. I had put that down to the aftermath of the storm but perhaps it was something else. "Will we stop again?"

"The captain will need to replenish some of his stores. We will call at Ostia. It was the main port for Rome in the old days and it has good supplies." He shrugged, "It is not as civilised as it once was but it is safe enough."

As we headed west towards the two promontories which seemed to be almost close enough to touch, Myrddyn and I checked that Lann Aelle had survived without injury. "You seem well enough but there were many warriors."

"Aye Myrddyn but they had no armour and Bear Killer was sharp and deadly."

"Aye but I think we need to get you a shield such as these Romans use, one which is easier to manage." I had noticed that the shields they used on the ship covered more of their body but were lighter than the ones we used. Lann Aelle was growing stronger day by day but the heavy round shields we used were difficult to manage. I was a strong man and I knew when I had been in a battle. Their shields were elongated and had a slight point at the bottom. The tops of their shields were rounded as were ours. I would ask Andronikos about them later but I could see that he and the captain had more pressing matters to deal with. Some of the crew had died in the storm and in the battle. They would need burying.

When we entered the Mare Nostrum I felt a sudden change. It was as though we had entered a different world. The sea changed colour from a slate grey to a deep blue and, in places almost a bright, azure blue. The air became warmer and I could smell strangely exotic and powerful aromas which I assumed came from the plants and trees. Myrddyn, too, was much taken by the differences. We could see mountains away to the south and there was snow on the tops. "It is warm Warlord, and yet there is snow. I wonder how that can be."

"A question which Myrddyn does not know the answer to; this is indeed a new world."

Myrddyn affected a smug smile. "The main reason I came was to seek answers to questions I have not yet asked. I do not know everything, Warlord; at least not yet!"

We asked Andronikos all of our questions during the meals. He apologised for our slow voyage but explained that the storm and the injuries had made us less efficient. "I am just pleased that the storm did not happen further north. Many of our ships have perished off the Gallic and Lusitanian coasts. They are a graveyard of mariners. But at least I can try to answer all your questions."

When I had asked him about a shield he had found a spare from one of the dead soldiers and he gave it as a present to my nephew. Lann Aelle spent some of the time aboard painting a bear on it. He had seen my wolf emblem and wanted one of his own.

It was almost six days after we had entered the Mare Nostrum that we reached Ostia. Andronikos apologised for its condition but it was colossal in my eyes. Civitas Carvetiorum, Caer Gybi and Eboracum would have all fitted into the harbour. I had never seen so much stone, at least not on any structure other than a castle. Myrddyn and I were desperate to go ashore but Andronikos shook his head. "This is no longer the Roman Empire. It is as dangerous as a Saxon camp." He pointed to the gangplank where the captain had placed ten of his biggest soldiers. "Time was that the legions would have protected visitors now they would have the coins from a dead man's eyes. Besides this is nothing compared with Constantinopolis and we will be there in seven days, if the winds are favourable."

We were disappointed but I understood his caution. The Emperor would not have looked kindly on the man who lost his guests this close to home. As the weather had become warmer, even hot, Andronikos had given us some lighter clothes to wear. At first they felt strange but the cool fabric made us much more comfortable and we soon used them daily. I watched as my companions changed colour before my eyes. They both became red and angry and then, gradually, almost imperceptibly, they became brown until Lann looked the colour of Hogan. When I commented they both laughed. "Well Warlord, you look the same as we do. Myfanwy will not recognise you."

Andronikos also expressed regret for the lack of a bath. "The worst side to these journeys is that one ends up smelling like a horse. As soon as we land you will enjoy the finest baths in the world. Once you have had one you will wonder how you survived without them."

Hogan and Pol had confirmed that fact and Brother Oswald had been tasked with building one. I suspected that as the temporary Warlord he would have initiated the work already The beautiful Greek islands, like jewels in the clear blue water suddenly made me realise that I had not thought of my family as much. I worked out that the last time was when we had entered the Marie Nostrum and we had been given our new clothes to wear. It was as though we were being changed. The Pillars of Hercules were like a portal into a different world. I mentioned this to Myrddyn who nodded. "I have thought this too Warlord. I have wondered why we were summoned. I believe that the Emperor wants to make you truly Roman in dress, smell and attitude. He wants you to think as a Roman." He spread his arms. "These clothes were ready for us. They were not just here by happenstance. I think that they will try to school us and impress us in their city. Remember Pol and Hogan? They were overwhelmed by Constantinopolis. He intends to do that with us too."

"Yes, old friend, but we are not impressionable young men and we can think for ourselves."

"Yes Warlord, but we will need to keep our counsel too and guard our tongues." He nodded at Lann Aelle who was busily adding detail to his shield. "We must impress on young Lann the need for discretion."

"You are right but it will be hard for the boy."

"No, Lord Lann, it will not be hard for he dotes on you. He may emulate the actions of Hogan and Pol, but he would be you if he could and he will heed your words. Of that I have no doubt."

We knew when we were approaching the great city. For two days the captain had every available crew member cleaning from dawn until dusk. Every rope was neatly coiled and, on the day we began to head north to the Harbour of Theodosius, everyone was dressed in their finest clothes.

Andronikos beckoned us over and looked at us apologetically. "I realise that it is an imposition but the Emperor and the courtiers will expect to see the Warlord of Rheged when you step from the ship."

I was puzzled. "I thought I was the Warlord of Rheged?"

"You are but you should look like him. If you and Lann Aelle could don your armour then I would be grateful." He looked embarrassed and a little worried. "I know it is an imposition but it will not be for long."

Myrddyn smiled. "Come along Lord Lann." There was a mischievous glint in his eye. "You said you wanted to be yourself. This is your chance. Let the Imperial court see the fierce barbarian and slayer of Saxons!"

Andronikos looked in shock at the insolence of the wizard but I just smiled. "Well in that case you can wear the clothes you wore when we boarded and look like the magical and mystical Myrddyn about whom they have heard so much."

The ship seemed to take an age to dock but I would not have liked to attempt it. There were vast numbers of ships ranging from tiny dories to huge ships such as ours. I also suspected that there were imperial eyes upon us. I saw Andronikos cast an anxious glance to a palace rising high on a hill to the east of the city and I assumed that would be where the Emperor would be watching us. Myrddyn pointed to the quayside. "It looks like we were expected Warlord."

There were two lines of immaculately turned out guardsmen. They all had the same oval shield decorated with a six armed cross against a green background. They had red plumes in their conical helmets and all wore mail. There was a wide gap between the two lines and, waiting on the steps at the end were three men in white robes.

Andronikos materialised at my side. "The three men are advisers to the Emperor; they are also priests and I daresay there will be some sort of ceremony before we are taken to the palace." He looked at me apologetically. "It will seem tedious to a fighting man such as you but…"

"I know we must bend to the will of the politicians." I turned to Lann Aelle. "Make sure you are presentable or I will have your mother to answer to when we return to Mona."

He grinned. It was all an adventure to him. "It is all right my lord; I won't tell her."

When the boat was tied up the captain came down and gave a half bow. "Thank you captain. You are a good seaman and you have a good crew."

"Thank you Warlord and you have been excellent passengers." He threw a rueful look at Andronikos. "Sometimes we have passengers who make the most ridiculous demands on the crew. I wanted to thank the three of you. I am not sure we could have defeated the pirates had you three not fought so well. My men and I appreciated it."

"It was our pleasure."

As we descended the gang plank Andronikos said, "That was almost emotional for the captain. He is normally a dour sort. You have made an impact on him." I didn't know how, I had merely behaved the way I always did. I treated all men well until they let me down and then they would risk my wrath. I noticed too, as we descended the gang plank, the large crowds which had gathered to stare at us. It felt strange for they were not looking, as my people did, to admire and to cheer. These were just looking at something which was different; a freak show. It was the first of many such experiences.

The three men at the end bowed and began to speak in, what I assumed was Greek. I could converse a little in Latin but this was beyond me. I watched Andronikos and saw that he kept an impassive face. I did the same. The ceremony seemed to be interminable but eventually they bowed and opened a gap for us.

"We can go now. I would suggest a closed carriage. If not we shall have to walk and there will be many people trying to get a glimpse of the king killer."

I was shocked. "Me?"

"I am afraid that you have a reputation, fuelled by the Emperor's people but they believe it."

"I will be guided by you strategos."

When we reached the main street, there were four closed carriages awaiting us. Besides each of them stood six huge Nubian slaves. Lann looked a little worried as was I but I was Warlord and could not show fear at something as innocuous as a closed carriage. "Do not fear Lann. Climb inside and enjoy the experience." I set the example and sank into the sumptuous cushions. The curtain was lowered. After a few moments the whole contraption rose in the air. It was a very smooth, albeit disconcerting, motion. I felt sympathy for the slaves. They were carrying a very large man and armour but we seemed to be moving swiftly and smoothly. I was tempted to peer from the curtain but decided against that. It would not look dignified. I could hear the babble of many tongues outside and, from the occasional shouts from our guards, realised that there were some hold-ups which required clearing.

Suddenly we stopped and it was quiet and peaceful. Without a command I was lowered to the ground. The curtain was drawn and there was a smiling Andronikos. "I hope it was not too unpleasant for you. We will use horses next time we travel."

I saw that our chests were already being carried in even as we stepped from our carriages. Lann looked in awe and Myrddyn looked bemused as they joined me. "What a curious sensation."

"We have one more thing to do before we can have the bath I promised you, we must meet the Emperor."

I looked at him curiously, "Surely we are too dirty from our journey. Would he not wish to see us freshen up and in clean clothes?"

The strategos leaned in to, almost, whisper in my ear. "He was quite clear that he wished to see you as you were when you arrived." He shrugged and I saw it was fear which prompted his words, "I am sorry but I have my orders."

I smiled. It mattered not to me. If the Emperor could stand our smell then I would not delay our meeting. "Very well strategos, lead on."

Constantinopolis is built, like Rome, on hills and the palace was on a hill at one end from the acropolis. There were many steps leading up to the entrance and I knew I had climbed when I reached the top. The same guards from the harbour were there and they kept an impassive stare as we passed although they did give a slight nod of the head as Andronikos passed. The corridors were cool after the heat outside and everywhere there were marble statues. At every junction there were more guards. Security was important to these people. At home we only kept sentries on the walls not inside the castle. I wished that I could speak with Myrddyn but I was aware of the silence; our words would be heard.

We approached a pair of double doors guarded by four warriors. Andronikos held up his hand and gave an apologetic smile. Suddenly the doors opened. I could see Myrddyn looking for the secret spy hole which told someone inside that we were there. I was too busy preparing for my meeting with the most powerful man in the world.

The court was filled but the area around the throne was clear and the Emperor sat alone. There was a clear military presence and the sentries looked both alert and efficient. This was a man who took threats seriously. He beckoned us forwards and we walked towards him. I was acutely aware of the stares, whispers and nudges from the courtiers. I wondered if this was the reason we had been told to come directly from the ship he wanted to cause a stir. I felt Lann so close to me as to almost be my shadow. I glanced at Myrddyn and you would have thought he met Emperors every day of his life. He was calmness personified.

Andronikos halted ten paces from the Emperor. "Your Imperial Highness may I present Lord Lann, Warlord of Rheged and Dux Britannica, his wizard Myrddyn of Mona and his squire Lann Aelle."

The Emperor stood. He was not tall and he was slight but he looked to be without any fat at all. He had a lean and hungry look. The most prominent feature was his eyes; he looked like a hawk and this was accentuated by a sharp beak of a nose. He smiled as he approached me and it was the kind of smile which makes you wonder if the person ever smiles normally.

He spoke in Latin, "I am most pleased you have accepted our invitation." His voice was both smooth and commanding; a powerful combination. He placed a hand upon my shoulder. "This is a warrior! This is a man who has fought and killed kings and this is a strategos who has never lost a battle. Welcome Dux Britannica."

I was at a loss for words and I just mumbled, "Thank you, your Imperial Highness you do me great honour by inviting a humble soldier to your magnificent palace."

I caught the faintest of nods from Myrddyn and a smile of relief from Andronikos. "It is we who are honoured and I understand that you had to fight pirates on your way here." I was aware that he was speaking with the rest of the court. "And that you and your young squire faced fifty armed pirates." He did not wait for an answer. "And you defeated them! You are truly a Hercules reborn!" The whole of the court cheered. It was a lie, of course, Myrddyn had defeated them but they did not want to hear that. They wanted the myth that a man and a boy could stand and beat three pirate crews. "However I am aware that you have travelled far and need to rest before our feast. Strategos take our honoured visitors to their quarters." He stepped back to the throne so that he was above me again. "Before you go would you show my court this sword called Saxon Slayer that we may all witness its power?"

To say I felt foolish would be an understatement but I was beginning to understand this Emperor who was trying to achieve glory through association. I slowly drew the sword. By some accident of the hour a shaft of sunlight suddenly struck the blade and its jewels and there was an audible gasp from the court. The blade looked to have been made by the gods. I could see that the Emperor did not need to feign a smile; he positively beamed. Even the guards looked to be entranced as I sheathed the sword and followed Andronikos out. As the door closed behind us I heard Myrddyn murmur, "You should have been an actor Warlord for that was a powerful performance worthy of Myrddyn the magician!"

Our quarters were a suite of rooms all interconnected. There was a guard on the door and he nodded and stepped aside as Andronikos approached. Once we were inside I turned to speak but Andronikos held his finger up to his lips. He smiled and said loudly. "If you take off you armour and put on your lighter clothes." I noticed that our chests had been brought up and the items unpacked. "I will await you outside and we will visit the Imperial bath. I think you will enjoy the experience."

Myrddyn had got the message too but I could see that Lann Aelle was both bemused and confused. I smiled. "It is all strange to us too Lann. Let us have a couple of days to become used to things first."

Lann shook his head, "What was the Emperor saying? I didn't understand a word of it."

I laughed. Of course Lann could not speak Latin it would have been incomprehensible to him. "The Emperor welcomed us and praised us for defeating the pirates. He asked to see Saxon Slayer."

Lann looked relieved, "Ah that explains it. I wondered why they were all cheering and why you were waving the sword around." He looked up at the huge room. "Are all the rooms as big as this I wonder?"

"We will find out, nephew. Now come I am ready to see these magnificent baths."

The baths did not disappoint. Even before we reached the water the white marble floor was highlighted by mosaic murals on the ceilings and walls. Statues adorned every niche and cranny. We were taken into a room where slaves disrobed us. I found it disconcerting but the look of horror on Lann's face as two men undressed him, made my ordeal less painful. They wrapped towels around us and then we were taken to a room with gleaming white benches surrounded by shallow pools of water. More servants bathed our feet and then we were led by Andronikos towards a room with steam emanating from it. There was a bath big enough to contain my shield wall, all one hundred of them! The lighting was discreet and there were torches lighting up more murals on the ceiling. The water was a bright blue. There were steps leading down to the water and a slave took away our towels as we entered the wonderfully warm water.

Andronikos had a justifiably smug smile upon his face. "This is worth travelling half way around the world for is it not?"

He led us to places where we could lie with our heads above the water. Lann was just beyond amazed. He had entered the world of dreams. Myrddyn was working out how the whole thing functioned and I could see him formulating questions for Andronikos. Slaves brought us iced wine. I was too enraptured by my surroundings to talk and I lay with a pillow, discreetly brought by a slave, sipping the wine and taking in the colours, sights and smells of this most fantastic place. No wonder Hogan had been impressed.

I almost fell asleep I was so relaxed but Andronikos stood and said. "We have more to experience yet."

We rose and were towelled dry and then led to another room with benches. There, slaves laid us on towels and began to oil our bodies. They used a stick, called a strigil and began to scrape the oil off. I was amazed at how much dirt came off. My slave said something and Andronikos laughed. "What did he say?"

"He wonders how much would come off if you had the hairs on your body shaved."

It was only then that I noticed that Andronikos had a completely hairless body. "Do many men have their bodies shaved?"

There was a pause and he said, "All of them!"

I did not know if I would go as far as that. When they had finished we were taken to a room with six baths in and we were lowered into chillingly cold water. I shivered. "Is that supposed to be good?"

"Wait until we have finished the whole process and then you can decide for yourself. After the cold bath we were taken to a bath the same size as the first one but this one had water which was warm rather than hot. After the icy water it felt wonderful and this time I did fall asleep. I was woken by Myrddyn, "I think we need to dress. It is time for the feast."

I did not know what to expect at the feast. The baths had been beyond my comprehension; how much more fantastic would the food be? It was Myrddyn who noticed that we had been perfumed. "We now smell as your son and Pol did when they returned from this land." He sniffed himself. "I am not sure I approve. The smell of the earth is more natural."

"Let us just live as they do whilst we are here. The last thing we want is to stand out more than we have to." I looked around the room. "Let us use only Saxon while we are in here but save meaningful conversations for when we are outside and alone. I would not be overheard in case we offend someone."

We had discussed this on the boat and, now that we were here, it made even more sense. There was an air and atmosphere of intrigue. I would find the time to talk with Myrddyn for I was sure he had deduced how they were listening to conversations and spying on people. I looked at the other two, "Ready?" They both nodded and I felt better that I had two people sharing my ordeal.

We did not sit at a table as I had expected but we lay on couches with low tables before us. Plates and platters of food kept appearing. There were many oohs and aahs and I suppose that meant it was supposed to be wonderful food but I found most of it too insubstantial. The dormice were supposed to be a delicacy but I could taste little and they seemed to be all bone. I enjoyed some of the spicy food and the wine was excellent but I moderated my intake and watched what the others did and said. The latter was difficult as most of the talk was in Greek but I learned to watch their bodies and they way that they looked. Suddenly I was aware that Phocas, the Emperor was watching me. He raised his goblet in a toast to me and I reciprocated. I sensed that he too was watching his alcohol intake. He struck me as a very careful and calculating man.

I had expected that I would be summoned to speak with him at some point but it did not happen. I looked up late in the evening and he had gone. It was then that the other guests began to drift away. I turned to Andronikos, "Do we leave now too?"

He had not been watching his drink. I saw, for the first time since I had met him, that he was a little drunk. "You can stay or you can leave. You just don't leave before the Emperor; that would never do." He leaned in to me, his breath sweet with the strong wine he had been drinking. "The Emperor is very pleased with me and with you. He has high hopes and great plans for you!" He tapped his nose. "We will talk in the morning."

Myrddyn stretched. "We might as well retire. I have seen sufficient tonight to keep my mind working until dawn."

Chapter 4

We were summoned early the next morning. I was glad that I had watched what I drank for I knew that I would need a clear head. This time we were taken to a small courtyard which overlooked the Hippodrome. There were chariots practising already in the cool morning air.

There were bowls of fruit and jugs with juice on the low table. Emperor Phocas waved an airy hand indicating that we should eat. Lann looked eagerly at the fruit but then he glanced at me for approval. "Eat Lann. It is there for us I am sure."

My squire eagerly fell upon the fruit most of which we did not recognise. We had seen people eating them the night before and I knew Lann was eager to try new tastes. While he ate I drank a goblet of the sharp juice before me. It was refreshing and delicious at the same time.

"You are a careful man Lord Lann." It was not a question and so I smiled and nodded, "I watched you last night. You drank less than all but me and you listened more than you spoke. Those are traits I admire." He suddenly sat up, "You know my story do you?"

"Your story you highness?"

"I was a strategos. Andronikos and I were the two best generals but we tired, or at least, I tired of Emperor Maurice and his failure to hold back the enemies of our Empire. I took the Empire by force and I have been making her stronger ever since. Our stories are similar. You are the one who held together Rheged and you are the only hope the people have against the Saxons. It is the same for me and that is why I wished to meet with you. I think we can learn much from each other."

I shook my head, "With respect, Highness, I rule a tiny island and you rule a vast Empire."

"You keep all your enemies at bay. You do not lose land you gain it. You have warriors who flock to serve you. They are great achievements. Now come, tell me how you rule your lands."

We spent the morning talking of how we operated. I could see, from within the first moments, how we differed. Phocas demanded total control. He trusted no-one. I could see that Andronikos was the only leader in whom he had faith. Andronikos' fear showed that it was not a good relationship. After an hour he waved Myrddyn over. I knew that my wizard had been eager to join in.

"You are a wizard?" Myrddyn nodded. "We do not have wizards in this land."

"You have men who study in your libraries and you have engineers. Picture me as a mix of the two."

Phocas laughed and it was one of the first genuine laughs I had seen. "Then you do not use magic?"

"What is magic highness? It is that which men do not understand. If you are a man who studies then you can understand more than those who do not study and you can use that knowledge. To the tribes who live in caves in your far regions your bolt throwers, your Greek Fire, even your Cataphractoi will seem as magic will they not?"

The Emperor rubbed his chin. "I can see how you two work so well together." He leaned forwards. "Even though I have heard it before I would like to hear your stories, from the beginning." He gestured at the four clerks who sat in the corner. I had not noticed them. "My scribes will write down your words and then they will be placed in my library."

And so we told our tales and they were written down. We did not see the finished versions before we left for home but I have met people who have read them. They are versions of the truth. There are others who heard the stories and retold them. They are not the truth. Many of the story tellers earned a living telling the tales and I do not blame them but they are not the truth. I did not find a hand coming from a lake holding my sword nor did I pull it from a rock in a cave guarded by a dragon. Morcant Bulc, or Mordant as he is often named, was not the king's illegitimate son and he did not slay the king on the battlefield. I did not fly with my wizard into the high tower of Din Guardi to kill the king's murderer. I did not disappear into the underworld and visit the world of the dead.

When Myrddyn heard the stories he was amused but I was not. We had told our tale truthfully and it had been changed into a story of fantasy and romance.

When we had finished the Emperor dismissed his scribes. He gestured for Andronikos who had been seated in the corner all morning, to join us. "My good friend and strategos, Andronikos has been watching you Lord Lann and reporting to me. I like what I hear. Having heard your story from your own lips it has confirmed an idea I have had for some time." He paused and peered keenly into my eyes. "I would like you and Myrddyn here to become the leaders of my army and reconquer the lands lost by Maurice."

I looked at Myrddyn in shock. This could not be happening. When I glanced at Andronikos I could see an embarrassed expression on his face. He had known. "I am flattered, your Highness, but I have a family at home and people who need me."

"Bring your family here and as for your people I believe that your son Hogan will make a good leader. We invested much time in him and his companions last year so that they would be able to rule your lands."

This had been planned. Now I understood the subtle changes in Hogan. Now I knew why he had been so keen for me to visit. I became angry. Myrddyn knew me better than any man alive and he gave a slight shake of the head and I kept my anger cold and within and not hot and without. I took a deep breath.

"You do me great honour but this is a surprise. If you value me at all you will know that such a decision needs thought and reflection."

"Of course. Take all the time you need. The ship which brought you is ready to take your squire home to return with your family. Now please, go with my strategos and explore our city. I am sure it will help you to reach a decision."

I was seething with rage as we left but I kept a smile on my face and my thoughts to myself. Myrddyn had trained me well. Andronikos was eager to please and behaved like a young puppy offering various suggestions.

I had my own ideas and my own plan. "I think that I would like to ride beyond the city to see its fabled walls. How about you Myrddyn?"

Myrddyn could almost read my mind. "I think a ride would be an excellent idea." Lann, of course, just wanted to be wherever we were.

"Very well I will just get some guards…"

"We need guards? I thought that this was the most civilised city in the world and yet we cannot travel twenty paces from its walls?"

"It is not that. I just did not want you to be mobbed by the people. They have all heard of you."

Myrddyn gave him a wry smile. "I think we can cope."

"If you get the horses, strategos we will meet with you at the main gate."

As soon as we entered our chambers I changed to Saxon. "Arm yourself Lann. I think we need to be careful today." I looked at Myrddyn and saw the same steely expression I knew was on mine. "I want some answers from this slippery Greek."

"And what better place than outside the city walls and well away from prying eyes and ears."

The guards in the corridors were surprised to see two armoured men walking along its mosaic floors but they said nothing. Andronikos was also about to say something when Myrddyn said, "As you were worried about us being mobbed, we thought that we would be prepared for all eventualities."

He was about to say something else but then thought better of it. He leaned down to the captain of the guard. "We will be back before dusk." I recognised the implied message; if we were not back then a search would be started.

There were a number of walls in the city, each one marking the development of the city. The first one was the wall of Constantine. It was impressive but the burgeoning city had spread beyond that and we reached the huge walls of Theodosius. They were a triple wall system and they were as high as twelve men. Even though I had taken us there for ulterior motives I was impressed by the size of these fortifications.

"And these go around the whole city?"

Andronikos beamed with pleasure. "They go from the Golden Horn to the Sea of Marmara. No enemy can take the city without destroying these and it would take the magic of a wizard far more powerful than Myrddyn to achieve that."

Even Myrddyn nodded. "I can see that."

"Let us ride to yonder hill so that we can appreciate them." The hill in question was some half a mile away and we rode with Andronikos explaining how the gates and the walls worked. I could see how we could improve our own walls by adapting some of the ideas we had seen.

When we reached the hill I turned to Andronikos. "Now, strategos, we are away from ears and eyes. " I drew my sword and placed it at his throat. It was done so swiftly that he had no time to react. "I have had enough of your lies and deceptions. I had thought as a warrior like me you had honour and I was wrong. You have no honour. You duped us into coming here and now we are prisoners."

"Please Warlord, I had no choice. The Emperor will not take no for an answer."

"And how much is my son embroiled in this plot? Was he party to my removal from Mona? Is he your man already? Bought and paid for with a few paltry sets of armour."

"I swear, Warlord, that your son is innocent. We merely tempted him with the trappings of war. He would be appalled to hear that you were kept here against your will."

I lowered the sword, suddenly aware that the guards on the walls could see us and might wonder at my actions. "Then speak and tell me the truth. Myrddyn is good at reading minds and seeing lies. He warned me of treachery here and I ignored him because I trusted you. Speak now but my sword still itches for your blood." He dismounted and I joined him with Myrddyn. "Lann, watch the horses and keep an eye out for visitors."

"Even before Hogan was here the Emperor heard about your sword. I had told him of it and he had been hearing rumours of its power. The idea to bring you and use Hogan as your deputy began at that time. Hogan found out much but after he had returned to Mona the scribes gathered all the material about the sword and discovered that it was older than the Empire and had been forged during the years of the Republic. It was said to be a sword which had great power. Then Heraclius began his rebellion in Egypt. This Heraclius is like you, he is a warrior and he leads his men into battle as you do. The Emperor is a leader but not a warrior. He sees you as the natural opponent for Heraclius. He sees you leading his armies and fighting and killing this usurper."

I looked at this huge city before me. The man running it was not fit to do so and I would certainly not fight his enemies for him. "So we cannot leave until I do this?"

"No, I think not."

"Suppose I refuse?"

Andronikos paled. "You would not refuse would you? You could easily defeat this rebel and then return home."

Myrddyn laughed, "You are a fool strategos! Do you think that the Emperor would allow so valuable a weapon as the Warlord here to leave his service? He would either be killed or used to take on the next rebel. It is the way of tyrants and you know this. You are lying again."

His shoulders sagged, "You are right but there is no other way out of this."

It was my turn to laugh. "I have been imprisoned before. Let us worry about that but if we suddenly have extra guards and restrictions on movements then, believe me, you will die. I promise you that. You know that I am a man of my word."

He nodded. "Then I am a dead man for if you escape then the Emperor will have me killed."

"*Wyrd*!"

He gave a rueful smile, "I now know what that word means and you are correct, *wyrd*."

We rode back to the city. I was glad that we had cleared the air and knew where we stood. I would not be staying but we had to find a way out of this spider's web of intrigue. The guards at the gate gave us a curious look as we entered but, as we were smiling, they saw nothing amiss. We reached the palace and it was well before dark. I saw the relief on the face of the captain of the guard. I had no doubt that we had been watched. In fact I was sure that we would be watched every time we left the palace but at least we now had found one place to talk.

As the guards returned the horses to the stables and we were, briefly, alone. Andronikos turned to me. "And what now Warlord?"

I leaned in and said, very quietly, "You let us know of any developments. I will not run like a dog to escape the hounds unless I am forced to do so. I will work on a plan to extricate all of us from this situation and you are lucky, strategos, for Myrddyn has a mind like a steel trap and if anyone can find a way out then it is him."

As we returned to our rooms he shook his head, "You have much confidence in me Warlord."

"I have every confidence in you. Tomorrow you will go to the library and see what you can discover. Lann and I will explore the city and find a noisy place within its walls where we can talk. That should not be difficult."

The Emperor did not eat with us that night. At first I thought that he might be suspicious but Andronikos saw us, briefly, before we went to eat and told us that Heraclius had caused the Egyptian fleet to mutiny and the Emperor was dealing with that problem.

The next day Andronikos sent a servant to escort Myrddyn to the library. I smiled at him. Now that he was a known liar I did not have to treat him as I normally treated men. I smiled and said, graciously, "Lann and I will not need you today, strategos, we will stay within the city walls."

"But the crowds…"

I held up my hand. So far every man I had seen had been shorter than I was and most were considerably skinnier. "I think my nephew and I can handle any crowds we encounter. After all, we are barbarians." The barb struck home. We were being used by these Roman Greeks as expendable barbarians who were fit only to fight their battles for them.

We took our swords but, as it was hot, wore the clothes of the city. My beard and hair had been trimmed and washed and we did look slightly less barbaric than we had but we stood out, quite literally, and we drew stares. None approached us and that suited us. We walked down the hill to the harbour. There was a smaller wall than the one we had crossed the previous day and we used the pass, given to us by Andronikos, to gain access to its ramparts. We saw much activity in the harbour and it was mainly naval vessels. They were obviously reacting to the news of the mutiny. That apart, there were hundreds, if not thousands of ships moored within the harbour. No wonder they were rich; they were trading with every nation in the whole world. We must be a tiny part of that trade and, I suspected, not a particularly valuable one. I felt a fool for having believed the lies of the Emperor and his envoy; he had bribed me with a worthless title, Dux Britannica. It was a joke. I had, however, put my head in the lion's mouth and it would take a miracle to extricate myself from it.

We left the walls and headed along the city, round the ancient acropolis. As we moved away from the place and the harbours of the Emperor we found more markets and people's homes. The spice market was particularly loud and colourful. Hawkers shouted out prices to tempt you. To poor Lann it was just a cacophony as he could not understand a word. When they realised that I was foreign then they changed to Latin. I was assured that the saffron they had had been used by the Emperor himself and that the hot spice had come all the way from far shores of the golden Empires of the east. I waved them all away but their calls continued as we walked down the next street.

I turned to Lann. "This would be a good place to talk. There is so much other noise that we could not be overheard. Let us walk back and we will talk in Saxon."

We turned and retraced our footsteps. "Will we escape, uncle?"

"I will not lie to you. It will be difficult but Myrddyn has not yet seen my death so we will not die here." That was almost a lie for Myrddyn had not yet dreamed of Lann Aelle.

"It is a wondrous city is it not?"

"It is." I peered at him. "Would you like to stay here?"

He shook his head. "Hogan told me before I came that I would like it but it would never be a home. He said that the thought crossed his mind once but he knew that his heart was back in Britannia. I feel the same."

"Good." We had crossed through the market and no one had paid any attention to our words. They still shouted their prices and hawked their wares.

We retraced our steps and reached the city walls again. The city appeared to be made up of groups of peoples who were from the same backgrounds. We heard strange accents and tongues which changed at the end of the block of buildings. I didn't know if that would be useful but I stored it anyway. We found a small beach where fishermen launched small boats. The air was filled with the screams and cries of seabirds and we had to cover our ears to protect them.

Lann laughed and shouted, "No-one could hear us here Warlord."

"No but I have had enough for the day. Let us return to the palace and see what Myrddyn has uncovered."

Myrddyn was not back but Lann and I went to the baths in the palace. This time we did not have it to ourselves. There were others there. I suspected they were officials or soldiers. A stern look to Lann ensured that he was discreet and we just answered questions about our home. I used the opportunity to ask the other bathers about life in the city. I played the innocent barbarian and I think they took me for a fool. When they thought I wasn't looking they mocked me. I just smiled throughout and feigned constant amazement at all things Byzantine. They revealed far more than I think Andronikos would have allowed and I stored it all up to tell Myrddyn when we had the chance.

Myrddyn joined us in the large hot pool just when we were about to leave. We stayed for a short time. We knew that we could not say anything in such a public place and so we spoke in generalities.

"We found interesting markets today. The harbour is enormous and there are many ships there. Different peoples inhabit different sections of the city."

"I too had a good day and I discovered much about the sword you use, Warlord. I look forward to a conversation later."

"We will use the cool room and see you later."

When he returned to the chambers we were dressed and about ready to go for food. The room had a pleasant balcony which looked towards the sea and, while Myrddyn dressed, Lann and I enjoyed a lemon drink watching the ships in the distance. We talked of inconsequential things to confuse any listener there might have been.

After we had eaten, again without the Emperor, we retired to our room. Andronikos was waiting outside the room in which we had eaten. "Did you enjoy your day today?"

"You library is fascinating and full of information."

"And you, Warlord, how were the harbour and the spice market? I suspect you smelled some strange aromas today."

I kept an impassive face. "You are right Andronikos. They seem to travel from all over the world. We walked so far we are exhausted."

"Well the Emperor returns tomorrow, perhaps you will have an answer for him then."

I smiled, "Perhaps. Who can say?"

While we walked to our rooms I was pleased to have my suspicions confirmed. We had been followed and I daresay that all the books and papers used by Myrddyn would have been reported to Andronikos and the Emperor. We would have to tread very carefully if we were to escape.

Once in our room we sat by the open window. The noises from the city would make eavesdropping difficult. Not impossible, but difficult. "We will take you on a tour tomorrow, Myrddyn, we found many interesting sites."

"Good. And I, for my part, can tell you what I discovered about your sword." He looked at me expectantly and I nodded. That would seem innocent and could not jeopardise our position. "They are all correct Warlord. Hogan began their interest in the sword and the scribes researched once he had left. They are desperate to see the weapon for they wish to confirm its identity." He laughed. "For such dry academics they became quite excited about the weapon."

"I think that we can accommodate them. You have intrigued me. How did they manage to trace its lineage?"

"From the description Hogan gave of the blade and the history he knew of it. I added a little but your son was very accurate. The first writing about it came from Claudius the Emperor. He was the one who succeeded Caligula and he invaded Britannia." He took out a scroll from the bag he used. "I copied down this section." Lann get Saxon Slayer so that we may compare for ourselves. The document was written by Claudius himself or at least dictated by him to a scribe. He talks of himself in the third person. It is a fascinating document but I will just read the relevant section." He began to read,

'Its steel blade was so highly polished it was almost silver, with a line of gold trickling sinuously along its length. It was half as long as the tall Queen's body and looked as though it needed two hands to hold it, although the warrior queen held it in one. The handle was adorned with a red jewel, the size of a grape and the Emperor surmised that it must be a ruby, an incredibly rare ruby. There were blue and green jewels decorating the hilt. The black ebony hilt was engraved with what appeared to be pure gold.'

Lann shouted, "It is! It is exactly as described."

"When was this written?"

"When they invaded Britannia. Over five hundred years ago. The Queen who wielded it ruled a land which went from Rheged down to Elmet and beyond."

I whistled, "That is a huge land."

"She was a powerful Queen and," he added significantly, "She lived at Stanwyck. " I felt as though someone had hit me hard. When she died, the sword appears to have been used by a cavalryman from the auxilia. They were based at Eboracum, and also Civitas Carvetiorum as well as in the north to the land beyond the wall."

"Then how…"

Myrddyn became excited. "The family of the warriors who passed it from father to son lived close to Stanwyck. The auxiliary ala ceased to exist over two hundred years ago and after that the sword was lost."

I took the blade from Lann and held it. The blade had fought for Rome and for Britannia. It had come to me, deliberately, and I felt a shiver run down my spine. I had been meant to have it. *Wyrd*!

"And before that?"

"There are legends of a sword which is similar to that one and they appear to be from the mountains north of Italia but nothing was written down. It seems likely that it was taken to Britannia and the Queen's ancestors acquired it."

"It suddenly becomes more valuable doesn't it?"

I suddenly looked to Lann. "Your sword, Lann; when we go to the library, you must take it with us too. They may have the history of yours too."

We left the palace early and went to visit with the scribes. There were genuinely excited to see the blade and they took the original document from its case and read it aloud, as we had done, while they examined the weapon. "So the Divine Claudius saw this weapon. I have never seen a blade as old. And do you still use it Warlord?"

I laughed and it came out a little too loud in the quiet marbled room. "I used it on the voyage over here to kill some pirates."

"Remarkable! And it is cared for?"

Lann stood proudly. "I clean and sharpen it each day for I am the squire of the Warlord."

"Then that makes it even more remarkable."

"Perhaps my squire's sword may be of interest. It was taken from the Saxon king Aella when I slew him in combat. We have heard it is called Bear Killer."

They examined the sword like physicians dissecting a body. They scurried around and then began to measure and make notes. "Of course it will take us some time to complete our investigations but we will let you know." They almost giggled. "This is so exciting compared with our normal studies. We have something which is ancient and still in use."

Lann took the sword back and looked at the six men as though they were touched in the head. "Come, we will walk the walls for some fresh air."

Once we reached the beach with the fishing boats we could talk. "Well Myrddyn, is there an escape plan in your head?"

"I am afraid that the only one I have would need Heraclius to defeat Phocas and allow us to return home. Every ship which leaves the harbour is visited by the customs officials. We would need to join a ship once it had left the harbour. Of course once they knew we had left it would be child's play to send one of their many swift ships after us and capture us."

My shoulders sagged in resignation. "Then it is hopeless."

"I think not. The Emperor is incredibly unpopular. His predecessor, Maurice might have been incompetent but the people liked him. Phocas is hated by all, even some of those in the army who put him where he is. Heraclius will win; it is just a question of time."

"You mean stay here indefinitely? Rely on someone else rescuing me from this cage?"

"If you keep saying no then he may tire of you. He cannot force you to do his bidding."

"Not unless he had Myfanwy and my children here." Even as I voiced the thought my heart sank.

I could see from Myrddyn's face that the thought had crossed his mind too. "Then we must hope that he has not done so or that Heraclius comes sooner rather than later. I fear, Warlord, that we are in the hands of *Wyrd*, once again."

Chapter 5

The next day I was summoned to the Imperial Palace. There were six people there: the Emperor, Andronikos and four soldiers. The Emperor smiled, "Well, Warlord, have you reached a decision? I have heard that you have visited our library and our beautiful city. I am sure that they will have convinced you."

The constant observation and spying was beginning to get me down. I had no freedom here. I was observed and watched at all times. I did not like it. I smiled and gave a slight bow. "I am sorry Emperor but my place is with my people and in my lands. I have discovered that my sword came from the lands of Britannia and has defended that land for five hundred years. I would be doing my ancestors a disservice if I abandoned them to their fate. Besides I know war in my land and not here. The heat and your style of fighting are new to me. I would be a poor leader."

The Emperor's face became angry. "You would not have to be the leader. I would make all those decisions. You would be the figure head. You would be the warrior who killed Heraclius."

"In that case I can say, categorically, that I cannot accept your appointment. When I fight, I lead, it is my way. I am sorry but that is my final decision." I made sure that I held his gaze so that he knew that I spoke the truth.

The anger left him. "I can see that what they say of you is true. You are a man of honour and you speak from the heart. I think that a long spell here in the city might help to change your mind. You are all confined to the palace until you change your mind. You may go."

With that we were dismissed. A wild thought came into my head. If I drew Saxon Slayer I could close with the six men in a heartbeat. They would all die and I would be free. Myrddyn saw me and my face. He grabbed my arm and said, in Saxon, "The guards would kill us all. Lann included. We can still plan!"

I took a deep breath and nodded. The anger went and I knew that he was right again. "Come nephew, we will have to find some way to amuse ourselves eh?"

Once in the chambers again we disrobed. "I was expecting a prison cell or something of that sort. This is, somehow crueler. He is making this a battle of wills."

"He is," said Myrddyn, quite loudly and in Latin, "and he does not know that you and I are harder than iron and we will not break." He winked at Lann. Lann smiled and I was touched in his confidence that we would escape this golden cage.

The next seven days showed us what our punishment would be. We were served food in our chambers. We discovered that we could use the baths, still, but we were escorted at all times. The single guard at the door had been replaced by four and there were others two below our window. Myrddyn was quite amused. "Do they think we can fly out of the window?"

Lann laughed, "Perhaps they heard the story of Din Guardi; you were supposed to have flown from there."

He nodded and smiled at the story. "I do not doubt," he said in Saxon, "that we could easily escape from here. There are only four guards and you two are more than competent at killing but it is how we would escape the city. We have weeks at sea before we can get home."

"We could go across land."

"That would be an interesting prospect; travelling through the barbarians who drove the Saxons from their own lands to invade us. Not to mention the fact that we would have at least a thousand miles of Imperial territory to navigate first. No, we will teach Lann, Latin and you two will practise with your swords and we will escape."

I leaned forward and said quietly, "You have dreamed it?"

"No, but I have been dreaming of Mona and Wyddfa; that means that we will return there. I have just to see the journey and then I can tell you."

Andronikos came to us on the eighth day. He looked tired and drawn. He was not happy. "The Emperor has sent me to you. He hopes you have changed your mind."

"Strategos, you know me. Do you think I will change my mind?"

"No, but I had to ask. I am now charged with staying in the room next to his. There have been threats from the Green Circus Faction." I screwed my face up at the name. "They began as supporters of the Green team at the Hippodrome, but over the years they have become political and some of them who live in Egypt have begun making threats against his life. There are members of the faction here in Constantinopolis." He lowered his voice, "Some of the more vocal members have disappeared. The Emperor prefers his enemies in plain sight." I said nothing but I wondered if this Green Circus Faction would do our job for us and facilitate our escape. "Please, Lord Lann, reconsider, I know that you could beat this Heraclius and once you did you would be free to return home."

I shook my head. "I find I do not like your Emperor Phocas. I will not fight for him."

"Ssh! If he hears that you do not like him…."

I laughed. "Then what? Does he think I like him now? I wish you had never brought us here strategos. For all the wonders we have seen I find it a place full of sickness and corruption. In my land you know your enemies and you fight them, here you look over your shoulder in case another has materialised from your friends."

He shrugged as he left. "It is the price you pay for civilisation."

Nothing changed over the next few days although I did manage to teach Lann Aelle a few more moves and Myrddyn taught him a little more Latin. We noticed that they increased the number of guards and our bathing was restricted to once every other day. Myrddyn found that sad. "It is pathetic and it is petty. I think you are right about the Emperor, and your mother was right to warn us."

"You have not dreamed again?"

He shook his head. "We are far from the power of Wyddfa. I know that there are holy mountains in these lands but I do not think that we are close enough to them for me to use their powers. We are reliant on our own skills."

I looked at the sun setting across the Sea of Marmara. "I hope that something changes soon or we will waste away here and our home may be threatened." I looked over to Lann Aelle, "Make sure you sharpen the blades before you go to bed. They have had a good work out today."

It was a warm night and I slept fitfully. I missed my cold chamber at home with the wind whistling off the sea and thick fur to shelter beneath. I heard a sudden noise outside and I was instantly awake. "Lann! Awake!"

Myrddyn woke and grabbed his short sword when he saw me strapping on Saxon Slayer. I opened the door and saw the four guards dead in ever widening pools of blood. "You two get behind me." I padded down the corridor. I saw a body on the floor and it was not one of the palace guards. I heard noises from ahead and I held Saxon Slayer in both hands. "Lann be ready to defend my right."

"I will Warlord."

As I stepped around the corner I saw Andronikos and the Emperor defending themselves against ten armed men. The bodies of the guards were surrounded by the bodies of more of these intruders. My training and instinct took over and I roared, "Wolf Warrior!" and leapt at them. I swung my sword in an arc at head height. One of them ducked beneath it but two others fell, the sharpened blade ripping open their flesh. I carried on forwards, despite the fact that they had spears and wickedly sharp swords. I swung back hand and felt my blade dig into the side of one killer. Another tried to take advantage of the fact that my blade was embedded in his comrade's body. He lunged at me and would have killed me had not Bear Killer darted out and killed him first. As I retrieved my sword I had time to see, out of the corner of my eye, Myrddyn as he pulled back the head of one of the men on the right and slit his throat.

With my sword withdrawn safely I stabbed forwards, into the back of the giant who was about to spear the Emperor. He roared in anger and swung around to deal with his new attacker. I swung my sword upwards and watched as it ripped open his ribcage and took off half of his jaw. Lann despatched another warrior and the last three tried to run. Myrddyn threw his knife and it struck one in the back. Lann ran down the corridor and, swinging his sword from above his head, the razor sharp sword split the other man's back in two. I threw myself on the back of the last soldier and wrenched his sword from his hand. I picked him up and returned to a wounded Andronikos who was helping Myrddyn to tend to the Emperor.

I turned to Lann. "Hold this one." To the soldier I said, "If you move you die. If you wait then you may live."

Myrddyn looked up. "It is a superficial wound. He will live."

"See to the strategos." I heard more warriors racing to the aid of their Emperor.

"Thank you Warlord. I owe you my life. How can I repay you?"

I turned and saw that the corridor was filled with soldiers and officials all looking in horror at the carnage and blood before them. "That is simple Emperor Phocas. Give me the life of this man and then let us return to Mona." I leaned down so that only he and Andronikos could hear me. "Say it before your courtiers. I would not have you break your word. For just as I saved your life, you know that I could have ended it. And that is why you do not want me as your general. I might get a taste for running the Empire. And I could take it from you for, unlike you, I am a killer."

He bowed his head and nodded, "Lord Lann may have the life of this man and he can leave Constantinopolis whenever he chooses. I give my word."

"Thank you Emperor Phocas." I walked up to the prisoner and said, loudly enough for all to hear. "I give you your life. Go back to Heraclius and tell him that the Warlord of Rheged said that a true warrior does not have others kill for him in the night. If he wants the Empire he fights for it."

The man nodded, "Thank you Warlord. You are what they say of you, a great warrior."

"No, I am just a warrior, for I did no more than any of my shield wall warriors would have done."

Later when we had cleaned up and we were back in our room Lann Aelle asked. "Will he keep his word?"

Myrddyn answered for me. "I saw the fear in his eyes when the Warlord threatened him. He is now more afraid of Lord Lann than Heraclius and he can get rid of us easily. That was a clever ploy with the prisoner. I wish I had thought of that."

"You would have done, Myrddyn, you would have done."

The next morning we discovered how they had almost killed the Emperor. They had infiltrated some of the Green Circus Faction supporters into the kitchens of the palace. They had drugged the food of some of the guards and overpowered the rest. As a result the Emperor began a purge of all those who lived and worked in the Palace. We, as a result, were no longer guarded although I suspect that we were still closely watched. The Emperor and Andronikos were now guarded by two bodyguards at all times. If nothing else the attack proved the loyalty, beyond doubt of Andronikos. I never enjoyed the same closeness with the strategos. I never forget an injury and I bear grudges. If you are my friend then you are my friend for life and if not...

We spent the next ten days preparing for our voyage home. The ship we were to travel on had been involved in a sea battle with the rebels and would need some repairs and so we spent some of our money. To be truthful we spent much less than we should have because when the merchants heard who we were they gave us their goods. The story of the warrior, the boy and the wizard who fought off an army and saved their Emperor was told and retold over and over. I am sure that the goods we had would have been paid for by the stories the merchants would have told. We did not mind their generosity. Myrddyn bought many spices and mysterious chemicals as well as devices to help him build. Lann and I spent a great deal on clothes and weapons for they had a vast range. I made sure that I took plenty of gifts for Myfanwy and my children and ensured that Lann Aelle took something fine back for his mother. Two of the items we did pay for were silk dresses for Myfanwy and Lann's mother. They came from the other side of the world and were the most expensive items in the whole of the city. I knew that Myfanwy would love the smooth material and the fabulous shimmering colours. Finally we took some of the perfumed oils they used in the baths. When we returned home I would have Myrddyn and Oswald complete Hogan's dream and build us our own baths.

The day we left we were summoned to the Emperor. He looked drawn and I noticed that there were two bodyguards close by. Andronikos hovered behind the throne. "I am sorry that you could not aid me as my general but I hope you will continue to serve me as Dux Britannica."

"I will serve the Empire as Dux Britannica and I will endeavour to retake the province of Britannia for Rome."

He smiled, "Good, I did not wish us to part as enemies." He nodded to Andronikos. "My strategos will not be returning with you, I have greater need of him here but I would like you to accept this gift in gratitude for you recent actions on behalf of the Empire." Andronikos handed me a heavy bag filled with freshly minted gold coins. I took one out and saw that they were stamped with the face of Phocas. I had been told this was how Emperors established their credibility; they used coins.

"Thank you Emperor Phocas. I do not believe in murder in the night nor in treachery," I glanced at Andronikos, "and I would do the same again."

"Good. I am not sure that we will ever meet again Warlord. Your home and family seem to be greater ties than the thought of glory but it has been most interesting to meet with you and I have learned much from all of you." He smiled at Lann Aelle, "I was particularly impressed by the courage and loyalty of your squire. I have never seen such bravery against trained killers. You will be a great warrior one day. For you I have this." Andronikos went behind the throne and brought out the small buckler the Cataphractoi used. It was painted blue and there was a bear painted upon it.

"Thank you Emperor." Lann's face lit up with joy and I could see that Phocas was touched.

"Farewell and may you have a less eventful journey home."

Andronikos accompanied us to the harbour. "I am sorry that our friendship ended. I enjoyed having you as my friends."

"We were never friends else you would not have betrayed us. I am sorry too for, until you lied, I liked you and would have fought alongside you in a shield wall. Now we shall part and, like the Emperor, I shall never see you again. Lest you come to my land," I looked him the eye as I clasped his arm, "you are welcome to visit at any time."

"Thank you Warlord. Your chests are aboard." He pointed to the ship which was much smaller than the one we had travelled south in. He looked apologetically at me, "The larger ships are needed for the war against the Egyptian rebels."

"You do not need to apologise. I would take a row boat if it would carry me home."

We went aboard. Here, in Mare Nostrum, ships did not need to wait for the tide and the captain stood by the tiller just waiting patiently. Once we were aboard he shouted, "Cast off forrard. Hoist the mainsail." As he did so the gang plank was drawn back and the bow moved away from the harbour wall. "Cast off aft!" The wind caught us as the rope was thrown and we almost leapt from the mooring. We waved at the strategos and I think he looked sad. The parting was more poignant for him than for us.

As we all thought this would be the last time we would see the great city we stood at the stern and watched it grow smaller as we headed west. It stayed large for some miles and I marvelled again at this wonder of a city. Myrddyn pointed at it when it was ten miles astern. "There it looks as big as Caer Gybi but if it were we would be less than half a mile away."

Lann Aelle looked confused, "What the wizard means is that the city is twenty times bigger and more than where we live. He is putting it in perspective."

"How do you mean perspective?"

"We think we are important but when you see a city like that you know that we are a big fish but only because we live in a small pond. If we lived here we would be a small fish."

I turned to the wizard, "And yet I am happy to be in my pond. At least there the enemies are more obvious than here."

As the city disappeared over the horizon the captain left the steering to his mate and joined us. "Welcome aboard my ship, Lord Lann, I am Basil the master and owner of this vessel. I am pleased to have you on board." He had a glint in his eye as he said, "I hear you are a handy man to have in a fight whether against pirates or assassins. I hope we have neither but I am glad of your company."

"Did the Emperor hire you?"

"You must be the wizard, Myrddyn? Aye we were damaged bringing survivors from the sea battle and this is our reward from the Emperor." He rubbed his hands together, "We are paid to do what I would be doing anyway. We would be travelling to Gwyr and Caer Gybi for trade so my profits are up already. I thank you gentlemen. I cannot promise you a comfortable voyage for we are a small ship but," he patted his ample stomach, "we will eat well and we are a jolly crew and I hope you will enjoy our company."

And enjoy his company we did. It was a small crew with no more than twenty men on board. There were no rowers and the ship was in the hands of the gods and the wind. He was a good sailor and we made good time. He was a good talker and told us of the Empire and the trading routes. Myrddyn and I found it more interesting than Lann Aelle did for we saw a way to improve our prosperity and security by building up trading partners.

Once we passed through the Pillars of Hercules we began to hug the coast. We saw less of our garrulous host for the sea was stormier and wilder as he tacked and turned our tortuous way north. The journey had already taken five more days than the whole journey south had done and we had not even reached the stormy waters off Gaul. The captain was philosophical about that. "The stormy weather keeps the pirates at home," he smiled ruefully, "which means that we just have to watch out for the wreckers."

"Wreckers?"

"Aye Warlord; they are men who prey on ships which are drawn on to their rocks. Until you came to Mona we could not trade there for fear of having our ship wrecked on those treacherous rocks at the western end of the Holy Isle. Even now we have to sail further into the channel to be safe."

"What you need is a light such as the one at Alexandria." Myrddyn had learned much in the Imperial libraries and had been impressed by the Seven Wonders of the World.

"A pharos; aye, that would do the trick wizard."

I looked at Myrddyn and raised an eyebrow. "It is not magic lord. It is a tower with a fire burning at its peak to show ships the safe route. We could build one close to the wall of Castle Cam and we could use it for a lookout as well as a lighthouse. It would benefit sailors and us."

"It would cut half a day at least from our journey." He looked up at the sky. "And I can see a storm brewing here so we will head out to sea and get some sea room away from these rocks."

And so we crabbed our way north until we had passed Gaul and were heading west towards Britannia. As soon as we left the shelter of the land to cross the waters to Britannia it was as though every god of wind and water had conspired to prevent us from reaching our destination. It was so bad that we could make no headway west and had to take shelter in the old Roman port of Dubris. The number of ships seeking refuge was testimony to the storm. After a night in the port Captain Basil decided that the storm had abated enough to continue. He was also concerned that some of the smaller ships in the harbour might be smashed against us and do more damage than the storm itself.

We made good headway until we came to the land of the Southern Saxons. There the winds were tortuous and twisted one way and then another. It was not until we sheltered in the lee of the large island of Vectis that we found some respite from the battering. We edged our way around the coast and then were blown far to the south. Captain Basil resigned himself to the weather. As I helped him to hang on to the tiller he smiled philosophically. "At least this way we avoid the rocks of Scillonia Insula. They are deadly and are said to be where the gods drowned the land of Lyonesse in times past. I am always happy to see those rocky teeth behind us."

I enjoyed our stormy chats for the captain was a well travelled man and knew far more of the world than I did. Like us he was wary of the Saxons. He rated them as pirates. "They are a sea people but not a sea people who traded. They just take and then leave a desert behind. We never go near their ports. They are just as likely to steal your cargo and cut your throats as trade with you. It is stupid really. They would gain more by trading. Your people have learned that and now you are a haven for traders such as me."

The storm abated again although the sail was almost in tatters. I wondered if the captain would anchor to fit a new one but he grinned at me. "The winds blow from the south west and the current runs this way. Even without a sail we will make the coast of Dyfed. I aim to make for Gwyr and repair our ship there. It will only hold us up for one day."

It is strange the way that *wyrd* works. It was almost as though it felt that the captain had challenged it. As we headed along the coast of Belerion another storm erupted and this time it took our sails away completely. They hung in three strips. Captain Basil ordered them torn down. They were a greater danger to the ship and crew as they whipped in the wild wind. He then ordered the oars to be unshipped and every man but the captain was ordered to the oars. We had to keep the bow into the wave to avoid being capsized. I have fought in many battles but the one with the sea that day was my hardest. I pulled on the oar until I thought I would wrench my arms from their sockets. The ship bucked and flew like an untrained colt. The salt spray burned our eyes and made our hands red raw. The blisters we developed burst and the salt savaged them. We did not appear to be making any progress but the captain exhorted us to carry on as we were winning. He kept pointing ahead but I had no idea at what. I felt like a warrior in a shield wall with dead comrades all around who hears his king shouting him to fight harder. All we could do was to continue to fight the elements. Perhaps we would survive. And then suddenly there was a grinding of rocks as we struck something below the water line. Lann Aelle looked ready to jump overboard as the ship rose, shuddered and then dipped, alarmingly, into the grey waters. I put my arm on him to restrain him. The captain ordered us to keep rowing telling us that we were close to shore. I heard him order some of the crew to begin bailing and then Myrddyn stood. "Keep rowing Warlord, I have an idea."

I had no idea what wizardry he was up to but I trusted him. As I glanced out of the port through which the oar protruded I was alarmed at how close the sea appeared to be. It was lapping just below the blade of my oar. I wondered if it would begin to fill the ship and then suddenly we stabilised and the sea stopped rising. As I peered along the oar I saw that it was no longer in danger of flooding us. Myrddyn took his place next to me and began rowing again.

"Well. Don't keep me in suspense. What magic did you use?"

"No magic but we dropped the damaged sail over the side. The sea forced it against the side of the ship and it has blocked the hole. It is soaked already and the water cannot penetrate. Eventually the water will seep through it and cannot last long but there are lights close to the north. I think that we can make port."

The wizard was right but it seemed to take hours to reach it. The captain's voice was welcome as we toiled against the sea. "Just another half a mile and we will be in Gwyr and land!"

The last half mile was the hardest but we made it and we limped into the port with the sea less than a hand span from the rail at the side of the ship. That was how close we had come to being sunk. But for Myrddyn we would have been lost beneath the grey waves. That became obvious when the captain and the crew heaped their praises on the wizard. We tied to the quay and the captain ordered everyone from the ship. He did not trust the ship to remain afloat. We huddled under our cloaks until a thin grey morning awoke us and we could assess the damage.

When Captain Basil returned, his face was grim. "We will have to empty the ship and pull her from the sea. We will have to repair her hull."

"How long will it take?"

"The best part of a month. It is a large hole. I am sorry."

"Is this Gwyr?"

"Yes, why?"

"We trade with them. I may be able to get us passage on one of their ships which travel to Caer Gybi." The captain looked dubious. "I am anxious to return home, Captain Basil. It is nothing to do with your company or your vessel."

The three of us walked to the walled settlement on the hill overlooking the harbour. It was small and made Caer Gybi look impressive. I shook myself. I must stop comparing the size of settlements. There was only one Constantinopolis. The gate was open but there were two guards there. They looked at our weapons and I could see fear on their faces. I smiled. "I am Lord Lann, Warlord of Rheged and our ship has damage. I would speak with the headman."

I think they were both taken aback by the fact that I spoke their language. We must have looked strange with our tanned skin and Saxon weapons. They pointed to a large hall just inside the gate. As we approached four men walked out to greet us." I am Lord Lann, Warlord of Rheged. I need a ship to take me back to my land of Mona."

As I said my name and my destination, their faces broke into smiles. "At last we meet. I am Gruffydd ap Llewellyn, the headman and I am pleased to meet you." His face fell as he pointed to the harbour. "Sadly the storm has damaged all of our boats. Yours is the only one left afloat and I think the gods must favour you."

"I was anxious to return to my home on Mona."

"Can you not wait until your ship is repaired? We could gladly be your host for we have prospered much as a result of our trade with you and your people."

Myrddyn stepped forwards. "Is it not possible to travel over land? How long does it take?"

"By horse it would take seven days, perhaps less if you travelled light but are you not worried about bandits and brigands? Dyfed is safe but Ceredigion less so."

"Do you have horses we could buy?"

"We have but we have few of them and they would be expensive."

The thought of the Emperor's gold in my chests made me smile. "Do not worry about the cost."

"And you would have to ask permission of our king but as his castle is on the way that would not be a problem."

"Good then we will get what we need and bid farewell to our captain."

Captain Basil was appalled. "It is too dangerous, even for a renowned warrior such as you."

"Do not worry about me, Captain Basil. We will be safe enough. My wizard is close to his precious mountain of Wyddfa and he is clever enough to get us out of any danger. Would you take the chests to Caer Gybi when your ship is repaired?"

"Of course but I wish you would heed my advice."

"When you land at Caer Gybi I will hold a feast for you and your crew and I will tell you of the adventures we are bound to have."

He was not convinced but we took our leave anyway. We were armed and armoured and I took the bag of coins the Emperor had give me. It was not that I did not trust the captain but I did not know what expenses we would incur on our journey north. Already I was feeling the cold as the wind howled in from the west. Spring was still some way off and we had become softened by our time in the sun. The headman took us to see the horses which were in a fenced off area at the other side of the town. They were not a good selection but they looked sturdy enough. They were smaller than we were used to and looked as though they were designed for climbing hills. We agreed an inflated price for four of them. I wanted to have a spare in case of unforeseen problems. When I gave them the gold piece they looked as though they had never seen gold before. While my change was counted out they passed the coin around. I smiled as each one bit into it to test its authenticity.

When I had the silver coins in my pouch I asked, "Is there a guide to take us to your king?"

I was about to offer a coin when a youth about Lann's age said, "I will take you Warlord and I will do it for free."

The headman shook his head, "My son is a little eager sometimes and does not know how to behave. Forgive him Warlord."

"No, I have a son and know how they are. You shall have a coin for a good guide is worthy of his hire. What is your name?"

"Daffydd ap Gruffyd."

"Well Daffydd, do you have a horse?"

"No, my lord." He looked crestfallen.

"Do not worry." I took out some more coins. "Another horse for our guide then."

We left as soon as we were mounted for we were told it was a day's ride west to the king's home. I, for one, felt happy that I was back on my island and back on a horse. Life was more predictable on land than on sea.

Chapter 6

Daffydd was a bright and lively youth and he and Lann chattered non stop as we rode along the coast road. Myrddyn spoke quietly to me. "Did Lord Lann notice those two men in the hall? The ones who took such a keen interest in the gold?"

"I did, wizard, although I was sure your sharp eyes would have picked them out. " I looked ahead. The road looked open and clear. It was a Roman Road and ran straight and true. "They will know the land and will find a good ambush site."

Myrddyn pointed to our guide. "They are obviously not friends of his father."

I shrugged, "You know the way it is in these places. Someone always wants what the other man has and they may resent the headman. It makes no difference but we will try to take them alive."

"Are you becoming a Christian then, my lord?"

"No, I just think it is rude to slaughter another man's subjects even if they do deserve it." We did not speak of it again as we tightened our cloaks about our ears. I was glad of the wolf skin. The wind and the rain were driving in from the sea and I felt colder than I had ever felt before. The icy blast helped me to focus and concentrate on watching for ambush sites. I knew that Myrddyn would be doing the same. A huge outcrop of rock had forced the Roman Legionaries, who had built the road, to go around the immovable object. I looked up but I could see no-one hiding close to the top. That is where I would have had someone to observe the travellers I wished to harm.

"Hold there, will you? I think Myrddyn has a stone in his horse's hoof." The two youths stopped and continued chattering.

Myrddyn obliged by dismounting. As he picked up the hoof it gave him the chance to look up at the skyline to see if anyone was at the crest of the rock. He shook his head. As he mounted I said, "We have sheltered behind you long enough. We will ride in the fore for a while. How far to go, young Daffydd?"

He looked puzzled; he obviously had no concept of distances despite the fact that there were mile markers on the Roman Road. "About two hours, my lord."

I suspected his estimation of distances was equally flawed. "Good. I could do with a warm fire."

I slid Saxon Slayer in and out of its scabbard a couple of times to loosen it. I wore, as I always did when riding, my shield slung loosely over my left shoulder. I assumed that, if there was an ambush it would be from our right as we could see the land to our left and it was flat and with few trees. My shield would not afford me much protection. I had no idea what weapons the bandits would have but I hoped that my armour would be their equal. Myrddyn was not just a wizard, he was a fine warrior and had fought in my shield wall. I would not worry about him or Lann but Daffydd appeared unarmed. Lann would have to protect him. As we turned around the rock ten warriors appeared in a semi-circle in front of us. Two were on my left. One smiled as he stepped forwards. I did not give them the chance to speak. I kicked hard at my horse and drew my sword, "Lann! Watch the boy!" I swung at the man who had stepped forwards to speak and took his head off in one blow. Myrddyn had slashed at one with his blade and killed him. I swung my sword at the next warrior who was transfixed by the sight of his leader's head bouncing down the road. I turned my blade and hit him on the side of the head with the flat of it and he went down like a sack of apples.

I put the point of Saxon Slayer to the throat of the next man and roared, "Drop your weapons or you will all die!"

One man at the back, braver than the rest by virtue of his distance from us, shouted, "There are still six of us who can fight."

There was a whistling in the air and then a scream as Lann's arrow thudded into his right hand. "Any more heroes?" They all dropped their weapons. "Myrddyn, collect the weapons. Are you hurt Daffydd?"

I heard his quavering voice, "No, my lord."

"Good. Do you know these men?"

There was a pause and he said, "I know some of them. The one you killed was from my village as were the one Lann hit with an arrow and the one you knocked out."

"Good. " I pointed at the bandit holding his bleeding hand. "You will return to Gwyr and present yourself to the headman. Tell him what you have done. Daffydd here will make sure you have done so. If you do not then you will be outlaw. More than that I will return and hunt you down like the dogs you are and I will not be merciful the next time."

After Myrddyn had collected their weapons we continued our journey. They were laying rocks on the two bodies as we lost sight of them. "Good shot, Lann."

"No my lord it was awful, I was aiming at his head."

Myrddyn laughed, "Well we got the result we wanted. Do you think they will return to the town?"

"I think some of them will but none of them will wish to be outlaws. They hoped to kill us and take the money. They did not give thought to the consequences. Their two dead friends will, perhaps, straighten them out."

King Cloten's castle was a wooden hall surrounded by a timber palisade and a deep ditch. It did stand on the crest of a steep hill and would have been difficult for the local warriors to take. With our bolt throwers it would not last half a day. The guards at the gate recognised both Daffydd and my name and we were admitted. The king, it appeared was still out hunting and his steward invited us into the hall itself. Our arms and armour, even without our names, marked us as warriors of note and we were treated well.

When the king arrived he came directly into the hall. He was a short stocky man. He was all muscle. He had the blackest hair and the blackest eyes I have ever seen but he greeted me like a long lost friend. He threw his arms around me. "Lord Lann, The Warlord of Rheged. This is an honour and a pleasure." He turned to his fellow hunters. "This boys, is the man who defeated that piece of sheep excrement, Iago." He held up two fingers, "Twice! This is a man I have longed to speak with!"

"Thank you for your hospitality King Cloten. Can we stay the night?"

"You can stay as long as you like as my guest!"

"No, one night will be sufficient, I am anxious to get home to my family."

"We shall have a feast tonight. Steward, get the cook to prepare that boar. Come let me take you to your chambers. We are cramped here I am afraid you will all have to share a room."

"Do not worry, we are used to making do."

The meal was a noisy and boisterous affair. They insisted on Myrddyn telling the tales of the deeds we had done. I think he was put out to be considered nothing more than my minstrel but he told them truthfully. I felt uncomfortable when I heard my deeds recounted. It was even worse as they cheered at various points such as when I killed Bladud, or King Aella. They whooped when they were told of Morcant Bulc and his end. I was beginning to tire of it all when King Cloten took me off to one side. He, like me, had watched how much he drank.

"Come, Myrddyn can amuse my men but I could see that you were uncomfortable with the tales of your deeds. It is what I expected of you. Tell me what brings you here."

I told him of my trip to Constantinopolis and what was expected of me and how our ship had nearly sunk and then I finished with the tale of the ambush. "I would have killed them all!"

I shook my head. "We will all need as many men to fight for us as we can if we are to defeat the Saxons."

"They have not come here yet. It is Iago who is our enemy."

"He has merely slowed down their advance. They will come again." I tapped the walls of the hall. "I would build in stone. You live close to mountains where there is a plentiful supply. It is how you will stop them."

"Thank you and for the trade you have brought our way. We are far richer now than we were."

"And it will continue. I have plans to build more ships and stop the Irish slavers while still protecting our trade routes."

"They are a plague on all of us but I had noticed that they have been less active of late." He looked at me, "You?"

"Aye they have tried twice to defeat us and both times they left with their tail between their legs."

"So you would go by land to Mona?"

"Is it difficult?"

"It can be but King Arthlwys and I have an understanding. We are both united against King Iago and I will go with you on the morrow. I would not have you robbed again and it will be good for the three of us to speak. We have much in common."

"You are right. We have much we need to share and I would forge an alliance between us."

"Tell me, why are you not a king? You could have your own kingdom; you have your own kingdom in all but name."

"King Urien made me Warlord and the Emperor of Rome made me Dux Britannica. I am happy with that. It means I protect the whole island and the people who are not Saxons are those I will fight for."

"Including Iago?"

"Including Iago; I fought alongside him once but he then betrayed me. It is the Saxons who are our enemy."

"Then I will be your ally and I suspect that the king of Ceredigion will be a second."

The next day the king and twenty of his bodyguards rode with us along the coast towards the kingdom of Ceredigion. It is a most beautiful land and the coast is the only one to rival my own on Mona. We took Daffydd with us. I did not want him travelling home alone and I thought that Basil could return him, and the horses, back to his father in Gwyr. It was a two day journey along the coast and Myrddyn and I spent most of it in discussion with King Cloten. He reminded me of Rhydderch Hael. He was bluff and he was honest. You knew that if he gave you his word then it meant something.

I worried about his army and his ability to fight off King Iago. His men were unarmoured and most just had a round shield and a spear. In fact the only sword I saw was that of the king himself. They also wore only leather caps. I asked the king about this.

"You have fine iron King Cloten. Why do you not have armour and helmets for your men?"

"We have not the skills to make them." He smiled. Lord Lann you are a Roman. You lived in the land of Rome, behind the wall and you benefited from all that Rome had to offer. Our people were never conquered and we were denied those skills."

"I have fine smiths. We will trade." I pointed to Lann's helmet. "That was made at Castle Cam and we can make many such as those. We can make good swords."

"Swords such as yours, the Saxon Slayer?"

"Sadly not of that quality for, as I have recently discovered the blade is more ancient than the Roman Empire and the skills which forged it are lost. Our swords and axes are fine weapons and, for an ally, we will trade you for the best."

"Thank you Warlord. The ill wind which brought you to our shores was a good wind for us."

The people of Dyfed had been lucky in that their mountains had protected them from the Romans but it had meant that they continued their primitive existence. Unless they became better armed then the Saxons would easily defeat them. I began to formulate some ideas in my head. I would need to refine them with Myrddyn but I saw a light at the end of this tunnel. I saw an alliance of Britons to hold back the tide of the Saxons.

The castle of King Arthlwys was imposing. Although, like Cloten's, built of timber, it stood on a high promontory overlooking the sea. It would be a hard place to attack. That showed him to be a wise king who would defend his land. He was younger than Cloten and far more serious. He had heard of me, which helped.

"You must stay with me in my humble home. I am afraid I only have a warrior hall and not the fine chambers you are used to, Warlord."

I laughed, "It is only recently that I have enjoyed such pleasures. Before then it was a warrior hall and before that a hut on the high mountains. There is nothing wrong with the company of warriors." As he led us to the warrior hall I saw that his men were armed the same as Cloten's. Only the king had armour. I saw that just a few of his guards had helmets and swords. In the warrior hall Lann and I took off our amour. I saw the hesitant and curious looks from the warriors. "Please, touch the armour. It will not bite." I pointed to the helmet. "Try on the helmet."

They were like children. At first Lann was a little unhappy about the warriors holding his precious armour and trying on his helmet. I took him off to one side. "Lann, remember before you were my squire; you wanted to touch the armour and try it on did you not?" He nodded. "Then this is a small price to pay for hospitality and a speedy journey home. If they can break your armour then Ralph needs to improve his skills."

He saw what I meant and smiled. He showed the warriors how the armour fitted together and he showed them his two shields. They were mightily impressed by both. One greybeard came over to touch my wolf skin. "Warlord, is this the famous wolf skin worn by the Wolf Brethren?"

"It is. This is the first that I slew and was the beginning of the Wolf Brethren."

He stroked it as though it was precious. A younger warrior asked, "Warlord, what are the Wolf Brethren?"

The older warrior snorted, "If you listened to the tales told by your elders then you would know. The Wolf Brethren were the finest warriors of Rheged and they fought for King Urien. No one ever defeated them. They are the oathsworn of the Warlord and it is a great honour to be accepted as one." He looked at me, "Is it true that the only warriors who are Wolf Brethren have to kill their own wolf?"

"Aye, they do."

The older warrior looked triumphantly at the youth, "That is a real warrior."

That evening, at the feast, we were bombarded by questions and Myrddyn, once again recounted his stories. King Arthlwys asked me, "Do all your warriors wear such fine armour Warlord?"

The hall became silent and I saw the relief on Myrddyn's face that he would not have to tell more tales and could enjoy the beer. "All of my equites are clad from head to foot in such armour and twenty have their horses in the same armour. My shield wall all wear a coat of mail and have a helmet, shield, sword and spear. My archers and slingers either wear an iron helmet or leather one and they all have leather armour and carry a seax."

There was a collective intake of breath. "Then I can see why you have been so successful."

"It is not just the armour, King Arthlwys; we have stone walls and we keep men training all the time."

The older warrior who had spoken to me before, asked, "Who tends the fields and produces what you need?"

"Because we have peace many people flock to our land as peaceful settlers and we trade with many people. We make goods that they want." I pointed to King Cloten, "On our journey here I arranged to trade weapons with King Cloten. We can do the same for your king and your people."

King Arthlwys looked thoughtful. "What do we have that we could trade with you?"

I smiled and spread my arms, "I do not know but I am sure that you have goods of value."

They began to talk amongst themselves and Myrddyn coughed and said, "What of the gold and copper in your land?"

That caused a sudden silence and the king looked curiously at Myrddyn. "I know you are wizard but how do you know of such things? We have neither."

He laughed, "I am a wizard but I know this by reading. When we were in Constantinopolis and we were finding out about the Warlord's sword I read of the gold mines and copper mines close to the river at Cefn Caer. It was one reason why the Romans came to Cymri. They built mines and took the ore out of the Mawddach."

There was a hubbub of noise and the king turned to the older warrior who had been speaking with me earlier, "Tomas, you are the oldest warrior and my father's closest adviser. What do you know of such things?"

Every eye was on the old man and I saw him rubbing his beard as he trawled through his memory. "Now that I recall there are holes in the ground that people said were Roman mines but they are hundreds of years old and, as far as I know, had neither gold nor copper in them."

Myrddyn smiled enigmatically. "It may be worth sending some men to explore them then. The books I read said that the copper and gold were in rich seams beneath the ground. If you know where the mines are then…"

Tomas smiled, "It is worth the effort my king. I could take some of the younger men and we could visit the mines."

King Arthlwys beamed and looked happy for the first time since we had seen him. "Your coming was propitious and I can see why your wizard is held in such high regard. We have few men in this land but they are brave. If we are to holdback the rapacious King Iago and the Saxons then we need weapons and armour such as yours. I will come with you tomorrow and escort you to your land for I have a mind to visit with you."

I could see the disappointment on King Cloten's face. "I would be delighted but would King Cloten like to accompany us for I have much to discuss with the two of you and I prefer to speak to a man and not an envoy. When I give my word I like to look a man or a king in the eye."

Both kings smiled. King Arthlwys said, "My friend, King Cloten is more than welcome and it will be a pleasant journey through my beautiful land."

We had grown in number since we had left Gwyr. We all travelled on the small horses from the hills but Lann and I were the best armed and Lann preened as he saw the admiring glances from the poorer dressed warriors. Tomas and his miners left us after we had crossed the Mawddach and headed upstream to Cefn Caer. I hoped that Myrddyn was correct and this was not a wild goose chase. I spent each day talking with the two kings about my plans for an alliance of the people of Cymri. The two of them were happy to join with me but felt that they did not have the men that I did and would be the poorer partners.

"It is true that my warriors have experience and skill but that can be passed on to you. I see the alliance as a means to help each other. If King Iago tries to take land from either of you then you will send a message to me and I can bring my army. King Cloten already trades with us and the ships are a speedy way to send messages. As you will see when we reach Wyddfa, we have a bridge to bring men across to aid you."

Once we had crossed the river we were close to the land of Gwynedd. Both kings became wary. "If you wish to return to your kingdoms then please do so. You have been more than kind to escort us thus far."

"No, Warlord, we said we would escort you home and so we shall. This land was mine when Iago's father ruled but we have lost it since." King Arthlwys spread a hand at the twenty warriors who escorted us. "We are poorly equipped to take on Iago's warriors."

"Let me worry about that and your twenty warriors will be worth five times that number of King Iago's, believe me."

The land through which we travelled was much like the land around Wyddfa. The mountains almost touched the sea and there were few people in this harsh land. The few settlements we did pass through welcomed King Arthlwys. I could tell that the land was ripe to return to Ceredigion. We had scouts out before us for this had the potential to be hostile territory. As we were approaching the end of the Llŷn peninsula, we could see Ynys Enlli and the small monastery just off the coast. There was a sudden clatter of hooves as the scouts raced back towards us. "Your majesty there is a fort up ahead and it is occupied. It is the ancient fort of Nefyn."

The two kings exchanged nervous looks. "How big is the fort?" The scout looked at me as though he did not understand the question. "Is it as big as your king's castle?"

"No, it is smaller."

"Does it go from the mountains to the sea?"

"No Warlord. There is a road which passes between them."

I summoned Myrddyn, "I know you do not have our maps with us but you drew them. How far are we from Pasgen's fort?"

"Thirty miles or so. What do you have in mind?"

"I think we can use your magic to get by and if not then my sword will have to suffice." I turned to the two kings. "Will you trust me?"

King Cloten laughed, "I am keen to see Saxon Slayer in action and we have run from Iago long enough. Let us follow you."

We headed along the coastal road. The fort was ancient and was high above the beach. The hill upon which it stood was high but it was no mountain. I could see that it had been built in ancient times as a refuge. The fort was too far away from the road to hinder our progress. King Cloten said, "We could ride swiftly along the road and pass the danger."

"No, King Cloten, we will keep this pace. Do not forget we have a wizard with us and as I can see Wyddfa in the distance I know that his power is growing with each step." Myrddyn rolled his eyes but the warriors all looked in awe at my wizard. "Tell me Myrddyn, will the men of King Iago bother us?" I inclined my head slightly and Myrddyn gave the slightest of nods and closed his eyes.

"No, my lord. They will not stop us!"

"Then let us proceed as though it is not there but ready your arms in case they are foolish enough to attack the Warlord, two anointed kings and the great wizard, Myrddyn."

It was all a matter of confidence, of course, but I was gambling on the fact that the garrison here would not be the best warriors in King Iago's army. I did not ride swiftly along the road but used a gentle gait. I kept glancing casually to my right and the hill fort. We were level with the gate when it opened and thirty warriors poured out. There was a mailed, mounted warrior leading them but the rest were armed much as the men behind me. "Turn and face them but do not dismount yet."

I kept my sword in its scabbard as they tumbled down the hillside. When they were a hundred paces from us, I shouted, "Halt! Who dares to approach the Dux Britannica, the Warlord of Rheged with unsheathed weapons?"

Their leader halted them. "This is not your land, Roman, this is the land of King Iago and he is your sworn enemy. You harbour his treacherous son."

"And what was his treachery? To be the first born? Get back to your hill fort before I lose my temper."

"We outnumber you and there are more men in the fort."

As soon as he spoke I knew that he had few men left in the stronghold and he was not confident of his men. "I drew my sword as I spoke, "Then bring them down and let them meet Saxon Slayer."

I heard a sword being drawn to my right and I heard Lann Aelle say, "And Bear Killer!"

Rather than laughing at my squire some of the warriors behind their leader looked at each other uneasily. Their leader must have sensed it. "Then let you and I fight Roman. I think your reputation is ill deserved and I, Beli ap Llewellyn will fight you and take that sword as my prize."

"So be it!" I dismounted and hefted my shield to my left. He had no confidence in his men and that showed. He was either a brave man or a foolish man to take me on in combat for I had a reputation. I suspect he thought it had been inflated. He would soon learn differently.

He had an open helmet and he was armed with an axe and a shield such as mine. His mail shirt went to just above his knees. It was not well looked after. As he approached me I saw that there was little metal on his shield and it would not take much to destroy it. He also carried a short sword; he was no swordsman. He was eager to get it over with and he launched himself at me, swinging his axe from far behind him to gain as much power as he could. If he had struck me he would have done some damage but it was an easy blow to avoid. I stepped to the right and gave his shield a mighty hit with my sword. Saxon Slayer was sharp and it was powerful. A huge splinter of wood fell from his shield and I saw the look of horror on his face. He stepped back and readied his axe for a second blow. I did not give him the time he desired and I lunged forwards with my own shield while swinging Saxon Slayer in a horizontal arc. Another huge splinter flew off the now battered shield and I could see cracks appearing in the rest of it. He was now moving backwards; I have learned that this is not a good way to fight for you cannot see the ground behind you. He tripped over a rock and fell to the ground. I could have stabbed him there and then but I swung at his shield instead. He held it above his head for protection and the blow shattered it leaving him the metal boss in his hand. He rolled to his feet, terror now on his face. I threw my shield down and took Saxon Slayer in both hands. He swung his axe at my middle and I pivoted round and brought my sword down to sever the hand holding the axe. He fell screaming to the ground.

While everyone stood around watching, some in awe and some in admiration, Myrddyn leapt from his horse and tied a cloth around the warrior's arm to stop him from bleeding to death. He gestured at the nearest warrior from the fort. "Take your leader to the fort and cauterize the stump with fire. He will live."

I picked up my shield and looked down at the white faced warrior. "You are a brave man Beli ap Llewellyn but a foolish one." I turned to the rest of the garrison. "Iago ap Beli is a bad king. His son resides with me. You are brave men. I offer you the chance to join Prince Cadfan, King Cloten or King Arthlwys for these two kings, and Prince Cadfan are worth following."

I walked back to my horse and mounted. As we rode away I saw that ten of the warriors joined us while the rest took their wounded leader back to the hill fort.

"You could have killed him."

"I know, King Cloten, but sometimes mercy is better. Those men may have been his oathsworn and would have felt honour bound to avenge his death. We would have beaten them but some of your men might have died and it was not worth it to gain passage along a road. Choose your battles." I waved at the ten men, now grown to twelve who followed us. "And we have more warriors for our armies."

"How do you know if they will be any good?"

"I don't but I have warriors who can train them."

He and King Arthlwys looked at me in amazement. "You train your warriors?"

I turned to Lann Aelle, "You see this youth behind me." They nodded. "I would bet that he could defeat most of your warriors in single combat. He has been trained by the best. When I go into battle it is Lann Aelle who watches my back and I know that no enemy will get by him. He is trained, as are all my men. I will show you when we reach my fort which should be by sunset."

The last few hours of the journey were quite pleasant. The wind abated for the first time since we had reached Britannia and Wyddfa almost seemed to smile upon us. When we were within two miles of the southern gate I sent

Lann Aelle ahead, "Go and tell Prince Pasgen that he has guests this night." Although the Prince was no Myfanwy I knew that he would appreciate a warning that he had thirty odd visitors arriving.

We halted a mile from the fort, partly to give Prince Pasgen more time to ready himself and partly to allow our new allies to view the fort. "Do you see? We did not make the mistake they made at Nefyn; we have a wall from mountain to the sea. No one gets by without our permission."

"How did you build the walls?"

"With my men and we took the stone from the shore and the lower reaches of Wyddfa. It is not difficult." I looked at Myrddyn, "As my wizard will tell you these are nothing compared with Constantinopolis where the walls are three times as high, twice as thick and there are three times as many; that is a wall!"

We approached slowly so that they could see the power of prince Pasgen's Palace. Cloten pointed to the bolt throwers. "What are they?"

"They hurl a spear up to half a mile and they can go through armour, men and horses as though they were not there."

King Arthlwys looked at the gate as it swung open and then glanced down at the moat. "The weak point of any fort is its gate and yet this one has three ditches and many archers. This could not be taken in a year."

"It could be but only by an army such as mine or that of Rome."

The sentries waved to me as we entered but I was pleased to see that they had arrows notched in their bows in case we were coming in under duress. Prince Pasgen rode up with ten of his equites. Even I was impressed. Their armour glistened and the white plumes made them look like giants. He had them all riding greys and the effect was almost like the sun blinding you. The prince leapt from his horse and gave a slight bow. "This is a welcome surprise, Warlord. Lann has given us the short version of your epic journey but I look forwards to hearing the full story after we have eaten." He bowed to the two kings, "Welcome King Arthlwys and King Cloten. I have quarters for your majesties in my castle and there is plenty of room in the warrior hall." I threw him a questioning glance. "Nothing to fear Warlord but I sent out a large patrol of twenty equites and twenty warriors to see how Bishop Stephen was faring and to ensure that the Clwyd Valley is still free of Iago's men."

I turned to the kings. "Come, I think that you will enjoy your visit."

Chapter 7

We stayed with the two kings for two days at the fort and then I left with my two companions and Daffydd to reach Caer Gybi. I offered the two kings a voyage back on one of my ships but they were determined that they could make their own way home. Both were full of ideas and they had divided the twelve new recruits evenly. I was pleased that the storm had blown up; if it had not then I would not have met my two new allies. *Wyrd*! I think they were secretly hoping that the garrison at Nefyn would try to attack them. They had gained in confidence on our journey north.

Prince Pasgen had sent messengers to Caer Gybi and Hogan, Pol and Prince Cadfan met us along the road to escort us the last few miles. The first thing I noticed was how relaxed and happy Hogan now was. It had done him good to run things in my absence and I now regretted the thoughts I had had when in Constantinopolis.

"Why did you not return by ship?"

Myrddyn answered wryly, "We did but the ship almost sank."

"It is being repaired in Gwyr and will reach us in a few days. I wanted to be home."

There was a glint in Hogan's eye when he said, "Didn't trust me eh? You thought I would make a mess of things."

I laughed, "No, in fact carry on ruling my land for a while and let me become acclimatised to this chill and this cold."

It was his turn to laugh. "We felt the same when we returned but you have not been away as long." There was a pregnant pause. "Was there a problem?"

"Let us just say that I do not think we will be getting any suits of armour any time soon."

He gave a disappointed, "Oh."

"The Emperor wanted your father to lead his armies and to fight the rebel Heraclius. He wanted him to abandon Mona."

"I cannot believe that. He seemed such a reasonable man when we were there."

"That was his plan. He tried to use you to get me to do his bidding. The Byzantines and the Greeks are complicated people. I prefer those who live in this island."

"Even the Saxons?"

"Yes Pol, even the Saxons. You know where you are with them. They will not stab you in the back while pretending to be your friend. And tell me, how are our erstwhile enemies?"

"The Hibernians have made overtures of peace. We have established some limited trade with them but we do not trust them."

"We?"

He grinned in a self-conscious manner. "Brother Oswald, Garth and Pol; they help me to reach decisions that are wiser than they would be."

"Good, I am pleased and now that we are back we can add Myrddyn to that group."

"I was joking before father. You will run things again."

"Eventually, yes, but I want a few days with my younger family. And the other enemies? What of them?"

"The Saxons are up to something. They have been sending ships to watch our coast again but our own ships seem to make them cautious. As for Iago," he glanced at the prince next to him. "He appears to be building up his army. He sent some scouts into the Clwyd Valley but Prince Pasgen sent their heads back to him. I think that something may be building for the summer. Unless things have changed dramatically, I cannot see it being an alliance between the people of Cymri and the Saxons."

I turned to the prince. "What do you think your father intends?"

"I think that he will try to conquer Ceredigion. That will make his southern border secure and allow him to attack Dyfed. He would then control the whole of the coast line except for this part and he would be able to control our, sorry, your trade."

Myrddyn nodded his approval. "Your father's loss is our gain Prince Cadfan. For what it is worth Warlord, I agree. Having just travelled through those two countries and seen their armies I would say that he could defeat them easily if he chose. As for the Saxons; until they retake Chester they will not risk anything. We have shown them that our forts and our ships are more than up to defending against them. Their only chance is to cut us off and make Mona our only source of supplies."

I could see the fort and the bridge in the distance. "Thank you for the advice. Now we have a month or more to plan and I already have some ideas." I turned to Daffydd. "I know that we were talking of your home there as though it was in danger but believe me, it will not come to harm. The Dux Britannica promises you that. Lann, when we reach home let Daffydd share your room with you."

Lann grinned; he could be a big brother to Daffydd now as Pol had been to him, "Of course Warlord!"

The welcome I received from Nanna was worth a thousand storms. She squealed with delight when she saw me and threw herself at me. "I missed you!" She gave me a huge kiss and then added cheekily, "Did you bring me a present?"

"I did and it is so big I couldn't carry it so I sent it by ship." I peered over her shoulder. "Isn't it here yet?"

She glanced around and then said, seriously, "You are teasing me!"

Lann Aelle picked her up, "No, little cousin. I have seen it and it is on a ship and it will be here soon!"

She kissed Lann and said, "I believe you," she wagged a finger at me. "Don't tease!"

Myfanwy shook her head and embraced me. "I don't know what we will do with that one when she gets older." She kissed me. "I have missed you too and you are back sooner than I expected." I moved away from her and affected a hurt look. "I am not complaining but I just wondered."

"Let us just say that the Emperor's motives for the journey were less than honourable but it has all been resolved. I won't be going away again soon!"

"Good. I have organised a feast and invited your brothers for despite your words you will be Warlord again ere long."

"Not for a few days. I have told Hogan that, until the ship arrives with our chests then he can continue to run the land and I can enjoy my wife and children."

The hug I receive told me that I had given the correct answer. In truth, I enjoyed the next six days until I received a message that Captain Basil and his ship had been sighted from Myrddyn's new Pharos. He had enjoyed building it and Brother Oswald, too, had been enervated by the project. For me, it was another sign that we were becoming an important place in the world. I reached Caer Gybi as the ship tacked in to the harbour which now looked tiny to me. Captain Basil was genuinely pleased to see me.

"I worried that you would have been murdered on that treacherous coast my lord."

"It was a good journey and I have more trade for you. King Arthlwys of Ceredigion may well have much more trade for you in the future." I leaned in and whispered in his ear, "Copper!"

His eyes widened, "Truly?"

"My wizard has seen it!"

"Then it will be true! I thank the gods that I took you as a passenger my lord for the people of Gwyr would not take payment for the work on my ship. They said it had carried the Warlord."

I waved away the compliment. "You will get much more trade now and I will see to it that you are afforded special treatment. In return I ask a favour."

"Ask and it is yours."

"Our guide, Daffydd needs to be taken home and I would like the horses returned too."

His face lit up like Myrddyn's new pharos, "I would be delighted for it would help me to repay the people of Gwyr."

That day we began a new trade which made all of us richer and impoverished Iago. I had not thought that trade could be a weapon but the journey from Gwyr to Mona showed me otherwise.

I summoned all my leaders to meet with me in my great hall. Prince Pasgen and Mungo came from the Narrows and they all waited expectantly for me. I had had a table built, since I had returned, which accommodated all of my leaders but was oval so that we could all see each other when we spoke. I took my place next to Hogan and Myrddyn. Everyone looked bemused by the concept. I smiled, "It is good to see everyone's face at last. This will be how we will talk from now on. We are all equal and I value all your ideas equally." I paused and then added, "Of course, as Warlord, I can ignore your ideas but you know that anyway."I put enough levity in my voice so that they all laughed. "Firstly I would like to thank you all for aiding my son, Hogan. He has done a fine job in running my lands with your help. I thank you." Myrddyn nodded and so I knew that I had said the right thing. "I have learned much since I have been away. We cannot rely on free armour and aid from Constantinopolis. We have to be reliant on ourselves. That means that Ralph needs as much iron and metal as he can get his hands on. Brother Oswald, " everyone looked at him, "and Myrddyn will need to be as clever as all of the scribes in Constantinopolis." Brother Oswald blushed but Myrddyn nodded as though it was well within his grasp.

"I have heard that King Iago may be planning an attack on our new allies in the south." I stood and went to the table next to the wall. Myrddyn had placed the map there earlier. I picked it up and dropped it with a flourish on our table. "We will not let him do so. We will attack him and pre-empt his attack."

There was a collective gasp. I was pleased that the look from Hogan was one of admiration. I pointed to the peninsula to the south. "We have travelled this road. It is sparsely populated. There is one poorly defended fort at Nefyn. Garth and Hogan will strike there and work south so that we reach Ceredigion. Prince Pasgen and Mungo will strike along the Clwyd Valley and build a fort at the head of the valley. This will stop Iago from attacking along that route and give us early warning of a Saxon attack. "My brothers," I nodded to Aelle and Raibeart, "Will be responsible for protecting Mona, from the Narrows to Caer Gybi." They both nodded their acceptance. "That is my plan for this year."

I did not know what I expected but it was not universal applause and the banging of hands on the table. Hogan threw his arm around my shoulder and whispered in my ear, "I am in awe of you father. I thought that I was ready to be Warlord but I can see that I have much to learn. It is a brilliant plan."

I looked at him. "Let us just say that a long sea voyage and a ride on a small horse, gives a man time to think. Never underestimate the power of thought my son."

There was a babble of voices and questions which either Myrddyn or I answered. Of course Myrddyn had had a great part in the planning and the idea. We were a good team. I held up my hands and there was silence. "You all have fifteen days to ready your men." I held up my hand. "I know we all trust our men but remember the Saxon spies. Do not reveal your plans in detail until you are on the road. It is not that we do not trust our men but loud voices can travel far."

That night there was an air of excitement and expectancy that I have rarely seen before. I had decided that the Empire was a distraction. I would take whatever they offered but it was not as important as Mona and what we could do. I had decided to see Gwynfor and Gareth and increase the trading links whilst adding ships to our fleet. I was not ignoring the Hibernians. If they thought I was looking east then they would attack and I wanted to be prepared by taking the fight to them. We had four ships now; by the next year we would have six and we would sail as a fleet to stop the Hibernians from slaving. I would take my role as Dux Britannica seriously.

Basil had sailed south and I had sent messages for both kings warning them of Iago's plans. I did not tell them that I would be taking action; it would have done little good anyway. Their armies were too inconsequential at the moment. Once we had traded weapons to them and trained their men then they would be the allies I wanted. As things stood it would be my army who took the risks and fought Iago. I was counting on the fact that he would have no idea of my aggressive intentions.

Brother Oswald's face lit up when I handed him the bag of coins. "This is a wonderful bounty."

He hesitated. I shook my head. "Go on, and speak. If you have a thought then let it have air."

"Do you remember when King Urien, at Brother Osric's behest, minted those coins of Rheged?" I nodded. "We now have enough here to mint a substantial quantity of our own coins; besides these are too large to use."

He was right, of course, they were too large. The headman at Gwyr had struggled to find enough coins to pay me the change. "Can we do that?"

"Ralph can make them and Myrddyn and I can make the moulds. Yes my lord."

"Then let us do it."

And so we began to mint our own coins. At first it was just gold but as we acquired more silver and copper we minted those two. I refused to have my image on them but I allowed them to have Dux Britannica put on them along with a sword, Saxon Slayer. Perhaps I was getting ahead of myself but now that we had allies I saw this as a way of uniting us through currency rather than power and military might. Their use would also spread our name and might increase trade as they would appear all over the world. Gareth was positively overflowing with joy when he told me of the increase in shipping since the pharos had been built. I shook my head when I heard that. It was such a simple thing and we benefited by having early warning of danger. I had

Pasgen and Mungo do the same at their end of the island so that seafarers would be safe, but we would be even safer.

My brothers had been at the meeting with the rest of the leaders but I visited both of them separately to ensure that they understood their role while we were campaigning. I visited Lann Aelle's father first. My brother was impressed by his son's growth both in size and maturity. He now towered over his father. "I will have to watch my son now that he is such a warrior." He was proud of his achievements. I had told him of his bravery in the attack on the Emperor and on the road.

"You will have to spread your men a little more thinly brother. I will leave three ships to patrol and watch for the Irish and I will take 'The Wolf' with me."

"That is a worry Lann; what happens if we succeed in defeating Iago? We do not have enough warriors to hold on to what we have."

"And that is where Hogan, Tuanthal and Pasgen come in. They each have twenty to forty heavily armed equites. I have seen the rest of the land and there is no force which can match them. They can control large areas of land. If we build forts at strategic sites then we can manage any incursions. I am hopeful that my two allies will improve their warriors so that they do not need us. Remember when King Urien took us on. We were untried, untrained and raw but with guidance we became adequate warriors."

Aelle laughed, "Do not do yourself a disservice brother; you became a great warrior."

I ignored the compliment for there was no answer to it. "You will watch Castle Cam will you not? I am leaving Ridwyn to guard it with twenty of my warriors but it is a large castle. We will need the beacons." The beacons were fires manned by farmers and they were across the land. If any invader approached then the whole of the island would know within the hour. Castle Cam could be reached by both of my brothers in less than three hours.

Raibeart was pleased with the responsibility too. "I thought I was tired of war but hearing of your adventures make me regret sheathing my sword and hanging up my bow."

"I find myself yearning for those days; but I fear they are some way off for me and my son."

The army gathered at Prince Pasgen's fort. We were not stripping our defences but I was using my leaders. Prince Pasgen and Mungo would lead forty equites, forty warriors and ten archers to the head of the Clwyd Valley. Theirs was the harder task for we had no idea what they would encounter. If I had been Iago I would have protected my lines of supply to Deva. If the land was free of enemies, Iago's men or Saxons then they would build a fort there. If there were enemies then they would harry them. I wanted Iago's attention to the north of his kingdom so that we had a free hand in the west and south. We watched them go while we waited for the arrival of 'The Wolf'. I had charged the captain with keeping us supplied and watching for good sites for a port. Nefyn was our first target and I had high hopes for that as our southern base. Prince Cadfan was with me and he was vital to our plans. We had just thirty equites; Hogan and Pol with their twenty and Tuanthal with ten of his. The rest we left at Mungo's Burg as a reserve. Miach had twenty archers and Garth had just fifty warriors. As an invasion force it was pathetic but I did not want my allies to feel intimidated by the size of my army. Besides which I was confident that we could manage to defeat whoever we met with the forces at hand.

We headed along the coast; Myrddyn and Hogan were at my side. "We will see it before too long. I do not think they will have reinforced it yet. Inevitably we had Aedh and his very reliable scouts spread out ahead of us. They rode back within two hours of leaving us. "They have men in the fort my lord. They did not see us."

"Good. Ride around the fort and scout out the land to the south. I want to know what lies ahead. The land was empty when I travelled but they may have reinforced the Llŷn. Then return to Nefyn."

It was a cold day but the sky was clear and our archers, although few in number, would not be hampered by inclement weather. I turned to Hogan. "If I am able I intend to take this fort without a fight. I wanted Prince Cadfan with us as he is our secret weapon. I spoke with the men who defected to us here and they told me that there is a great deal of sympathy for the young prince. He fought valiantly for his father and they believe he has been unjustly punished. We can use that disquiet to our advantage."

Myrddyn laughed, "A few weeks in Constantinopolis and you become more cunning and devious." My expression must have surprised him for he held up his hand. "I mean no insult and it is a compliment. You were the complete warrior and now you are becoming a leader as great as King Urien."

"I do not think I am even close to King Urien but I accept your apology. Perhaps I am thinking more like that wise king. It must come with age. These grey flecks in my beard must show that I am becoming wiser." I waved Lann forward, "Unfurl the banner. Let them know we are here."

We rode around the curve of the road. It was not Roman and had many twists and turns in it. When the fort came into view I could see the dragon standard still flying and the walls bristling with warriors. I wondered what they would be feeling when they saw the banner. The last time I had been there I had had but twenty men with me and we had come away victorious. This time our armour sparkled and shone in the sunlight. Hogan and Pol ensured that their men polished their armour every day and it shone like gold in the noon sun.

When my army was arrayed before the gates which rose into the air some fifty paces higher than us I rode forward with Prince Cadfan and Lann. Behind me the two wings of our force were composed of equites. The shield wall was in the middle and the archers were behind them. It must have looked like an army of solid iron which faced the defenders.

"I am Lord Lann, Warlord of Rheged and Dux Britannica. I call upon you to surrender to your rightful ruler, Prince Cadfan ap Iago."

The prince rode forward. "I know that my father has promised you a victory but you will not withstand these warriors." He pointed at my army. "I have fought with them and I know. I do not ask you to surrender. I will not dishonour you. I ask, instead, that you join me and the Warlord to bring peace to our land again."

He rode back to my side and I shouted again, "You have until my shadow reaches yonder rock to decide. If the answer is no then we will destroy you." I turned to Lann. "Leave the banner with me and bring Miach's son; I think we can persuade them to cooperate." I pointed to 'The Wolf' which was now less than forty paces from the shore. "There is one of my ships. There are others."

There appeared to be fewer warriors on the walls and I took that as a sign that there was dissension within the walls. When Miach's son arrived I leaned down to him. "Have an arrow ready. I may ask for a demonstration of your skill." He grinned at me. He had been with Hogan and Pol when they had visited the Emperor and it had increased his confidence immeasurably. He was as good an archer as I had ever met.

When my shadow touched the rock I shouted again. "Well, what is your answer?"

A warrior with a heavily bandaged hand came to the walls. It was Beli ap Llewellyn whom I had fought and defeated. He still ruled. He put his good hand on the wooden wall and shouted. "If that is all you have brought then we have nothing to fear. Do your worst and we will still be here when King Iago arrives next month."

I stored that valuable piece of information in my head and said to Daffydd ap Miach, "I want you to pin that warrior's good hand to the wall. Can you do it?"

"I can try."

"Even if you get close it will have the desired effect. Do it now."

He had the arrow ready and he raised the bow and released the arrow. The men on the walls seemed mesmerised as it rose, reached the top of its arc and then plunged down. It struck the wounded warrior in the middle of his hand and I saw that he was pinned there. "His next arrow can take your head Beli. I spared your life once…"

Suddenly the gate opened. I heard Beli screaming at his men but they had seen enough."Hogan, check to see if there are any other men hiding. I will take the warriors and archers within." I turned to my men. "Forward!"

We marched into the wooden fort. It was in a poor state of repair. I do not think it would have withstood an attack by Cloten's men, poorly armed as they were. Inside the fort, the warriors stood forlornly around their leader who stared belligerently at me. "Drop your weapons." They looked to their leader. "Miach!" The sight and sound of twenty bows being readied had the effect I wished and the weapons were dropped. I turned to Prince Cadfan. "Your highness."

He stepped forwards and his squire, Dai, proudly held his banner above his head. "I am Cadfan ap Iago and the rightful heir of Gwynedd. Which of you here will join me and fight against the Saxons and not our brothers?"

They looked at each other. Then one of the older men said, "I remember your mother, she was a good queen, not like the one we have now. I will join you."

He walked over, knelt before Cadfan and then stepped behind Dai. Soon there was a veritable flood until six men only remained with the wounded Beli. He was helped to his feet by his men and he snarled, "What now whelp? Will we be executed?"

Cadfan showed he was a true prince and he smiled. "No, you are free to go. Return to my father and tell him that I have begun to reclaim my birthright."

They looked at each other. Beli shook his head, "And risk being shot in the back by the wolf's arrows? Do you think we are stupid?"

"Miach!"

The bows were lowered and they all stepped aside. "You have my word, Beli, and unlike your king, I am a man who does not break oaths." Even Beli knew that I would not say such a thing and then dishonour myself. They trudged wearily out of the fort. One or two looked wistfully behind them as though they really wanted to stay.

Once they had gone I turned to the prince. "I will leave you ten of my warriors to help you to organise your men. Will that be enough?"

Cadfan looked at the men who were before him. "I think so. If I am to lead men like this I need to trust them."

"Good. You are right to do so. I would begin to improve the defences. We ought to build a wall from the sea to the fort as we have further up the coast. It will make your land more secure." I swept my hand across me, "Your first land, your highness. I do not think it will be the last. We will call here when we have met with King Arthlwys. I will loan you some of Aedh's scouts and the warrior in charge is Adair. He is a good man. Tuanthal and his men can also stay here. He is an experienced captain."

Hogan and Aedh were waiting for me along with Garth. "There is no one in sight. We saw those seven heading up the valley."

"Garth, leave Adair and ten men to help the prince. Tuanthal, you and your ten equites can stay here. I don't see the point in tiring all of our heavy cavalry out. You can patrol between here and the Narrows. Hogan and Pol should be more than enough with their twenty men. Aedh, leave him a couple of scouts." I pointed up the valley. "I would like to know what lies there." I turned to Lann. "Ride to the beach and tell the captain to find us a campsite close to the shore. It should be ten miles south of here on the other side of the headland."

Hogan looked at me, "Are we not staying here?"

"If it was your first command would you like others watching what you were doing?"

"You are right."

As we rode south Myrddyn nudged his mount close to mine. "I have an ill feeling Warlord."

Warnings from the wizard were not to be taken lightly. "Are we in danger?"

"There is always danger but I fear that there is some malevolent force in the valley to the south." He looked at me apologetically, "This close to Wyddfa I am always more affected by the spirits. It is hard to control. When I sleep tonight I may dream and have a better idea of what the danger is. I am sorry that I cannot be more specific."

"Do not worry, my friend. The fact that you have mentioned it means that we will all be more alert."

We did not follow the coast road but headed for the small settlement of Pwllheli. When we had come north we had avoided passing through it. As we travelled through it a few of the inhabitants nervously peered from behind the doors of their huts. We smiled but said nothing. A few miles further along the road, we saw a fire burning on the beach and the welcome sight of 'The Wolf' lying off shore. The smell of roasting fish made us hurry the last part of the journey and we ate well; secure in the knowledge that none of Iago's men were within sight of us. I went to sleep fearfully for if Myrddyn dreamt then that normally meant that I did too.

When I awoke refreshed I wondered if Myrddyn had been wrong. One look at his face told me that he had dreamed and it was not a happy dream. Hogan stood with me as I asked the wizard of the portents.

He shook his head. "There is danger and evil but, not I think, to us. We need to hurry lord, time is of the essence."

I sent 'The Wolf' to find the estuary called the Mawddach. It had been the largest river we had crossed north of King Arthlwys' kingdom. I guessed that we could camp there. Then I sent Aedh and his scouts out. I gave them Myrddyn's warnings and the serious looks on their faces showed that they trusted my wizard.

"Hogan, you had better keep your men close to us on this part of the journey. We are now between our own settlements and those of King Arthlwys. I do not think there are enemies near but Myrddyn's dreams cannot be ignored."

Chapter 8

We kept the same formation the next day as we followed the coast line around to the Mawddach estuary. Aedh and his scouts hurtled towards us when we were less than five miles from the mouth of the river. Aedh himself reported. "There is a warband of about two hundred warriors. They are up the valley some way. There does not appear to be a settlement now but there are stone buildings close by and it looks like mine workings. They have three men tied to trees and it looks as though they are torturing them."

"Was one of the men a greybeard?"

Aedh looked in amazement at me. "Aye, are you a wizard now too?"

"No but the mine struck a chord. It is Tomas and he is one of King Arthlwys' men."

Myrddyn nodded, "If there are stone buildings then it is likely that it will be Roman."

I looked at my men. We had thirty equites, forty warriors and twenty archers. We would be outnumbered. "What is the ground around their camp like?"

"They have no walls but it is rocky, uneven and they are close to a forest." Aedh had scouted for me long enough to read my mind; he gave the answer to my next question. Our best warriors, our equites would not be of any use. That left me with sixty men to attack two hundred; we had had worse odds.

"Aedh and Hogan, take your men to the east of their camp. When they flee then you can hold them."

Hogan looked at me askance. "You would attack two hundred men with sixty?"

"Sixty of my men? Aye, every day and I would not worry about the outcome. Now go. Aedh send a rider to the ship and tell the captain what we are about. Ask him can he sail as far up the Mawddach as he can without risking the ship; it may help."

As my men left us I turned to Garth and Miach. "They are good men who are being held and I would like to keep them alive. Miach, ensure that no man comes near them."

"Aye my lord, my son and I will deal with them."

"Garth, we will use a wedge. I know we will be outnumbered so let us use the power of our men and the strength of our armour. You will lead and I will be behind you with Lann behind me."

Garth was happy that he was leading. I had not taken the arrow head as I wanted to be able to direct the men once we struck. I knew that Garth would be a rock before me and he would not break. We headed in the direction Aedh had indicated. Miach's archers acted as scouts. The valley sides were steep and rocky. We had to travel along them in a column of four. I was not worried. My men could change formation easily and quickly. My worry was that the men who held Tomas and the others would kill them before we had chance to intervene.

The archer scouts returned. "Captain Miach says that the prisoners are still being held. They have no guards out and no sentries. They feel safe."

"Good. How far ahead are they?"

"Less than half a mile."

"Thank you, rejoin your captain." As the scout returned to Miach, I summoned Garth. "We will move into wedge formation. I know that the men in the rear ranks will need to adjust but I am confident that they can."

Garth grinned, "Aye my lord."

"Come then, let us be about this." I tightened my helmet and hefted my shield on my left arm. With Saxon Slayer in my hand I was ready for combat.

It was not even a trail we followed, it was just a beaten track and we could not move swiftly. As soon as I saw the rear of my archers I knew that we were close. "Ready Garth?"

"Yes Warlord."

"As soon as we hit the clearing then we get into wedge and keep going. Miach will take care of the prisoners; we just kill as many of the enemy as we can." We were only eight ranks deep and the enemy would quickly surround us. We had to strike and strike hard, without mercy.

The enemy had found a clearing which was close to the cliff side where the mine workings were. The old Roman buildings were close to the river and the prisoners were close to the cliff. "Aim at a point between the buildings and the cliff."

"Aye my lord."

My men did not need cheers to fight and we ran silently. Miach needed no orders to loose his arrows; he would judge his moment well. We were less than thirty paces from them when they heard us. The men who turned round looked in horror as the wall of iron clad warriors approached. As Garth killed the first warrior, Miach loosed his first arrows. Every man within ten paces of the prisoners died. The leader, a warrior with a full face helmet, ordered his men into shield wall. It might have been effective had they all had armour and had they been trained but they had not. The shields were not locked and there were gaps when we struck them. Garth killed their leader with his first blow. I sliced down at the man below me who had been knocked to the ground. Saxon Slayer killed him instantly. Miach and his men poured arrow after arrow into their rear ranks. They were brave men but they could not organise. As soon as the first man held up his hands and cried, "Mercy!" I knew that we had won.

Even as Garth killed the next man I shouted. "Surrender or die! I will spare your lives."

One or two of the braver ones continued to fight but the majority dropped their weapons to the ground. "Garth, take some men and secure the prisoners. The rest of you surround them."

I looked behind me and saw that we had lost but one man. That was one loss too many but it was better than we could have expected. Hogan and Pol rode in with their equites and I saw the looks on the faces of the prisoners. They realised they had made the right decision. "Four of them tried to run. They are dead."

I lifted my helmet. "Watch the prisoners, son. I will speak with them shortly." Garth brought over Tomas and his two companions. "How are you my friend?"

He managed a brave smile. "Better for having seen you." He spat at the body of the leader. "That bastard should have suffered. He tortured two of my boys. He wanted us to tell him where the gold and the copper were."

"You found it then?"

"Aye, your wizard was right. They happened upon us while we were working. I think they were heading for the Mawddach to cause mischief."

"Then the king does not know of your find?"

"No. We have not had time to send him a message. They are both rich veins my lord. The ones who were killed were the miners but they told me they had never seen such quantities."

"We will bury them with honour." I looked for Myrddyn. "See to their wounds and then go with Aedh and take them to 'The Wolf'. They can return to their king by boat. It will be more comfortable and quicker."

Myrddyn bowed. "Aye my lord."

I turned to the men who were all on their knees and looking sorry for themselves. I banged my shield with my sword to get their attention. "You know who I am, I am Lord Lann, Warlord of Rheged and you know that I am a man of my word." I glared at them and they bowed their heads. "You have invaded Ceredigion and you have killed brave men who were not warriors. I should kill you all." I allowed that thought to permeate into their minds. "However you have a choice. Prince Cadfan ap Iago is now at Nefyn. He is raising an army to fight his father. You can, if you wish, join him. If you decide not to do that then I will take you to King Arthlwys for punishment. The third way is to stay here but your heads will be separated from your bodies if you choose that." I give you the chance now to make your decision. Stand behind my son and his equites if you would serve your prince. Stand behind my banner if you would be punished by the king and stay where you are if you seek death."

Only two chose death and none chose punishment. I nodded to Garth, "Give them their swords and a warrior's death." We all watched as the men gratefully took their weapons and then held them tightly as their heads were severed.

"Hogan, escort these volunteers to the prince and stay with him until they are ready to join his army."

"Yes Warlord."

"Garth, make camp and we will continue our journey tomorrow."

When Myrddyn returned to us he had the smug self satisfied smile of a wizard who has shown his power once more. I nodded to him. "I am just pleased that your dream did not cost me more warriors,"

The smile left his face. "My power is something that is controlled by the spirits and not by me."

"Good, for I would hate to think that you were playing with men's lives Myrddyn." I looked into his eyes and he gave a slight nod.

"You are right Warlord. Sometimes I forget that the dreams are about men and they can die. I will work on that."

"Good. And 'The Wolf'? She has left?"

"Yes, Warlord. She will drop off the miners and return to try to pick us up."

"It is only another day to his stronghold. I suspect we will meet the ship closer to the king."

And so it proved. With just warriors walking and only two scouts we made remarkably quick time. It helped that we had had an easy victory for men march easier in that frame of mind. The songs they sang were of our victory and they were eager for their next fight. They had never been beaten and yet they were never over confident. I suspect Garth and Ridwyn had much to do with that.

When we reached his stronghold the king was waiting to greet us. He was ecstatic that we had rescued his men. Tomas meant much to him. "Our alliance has proved a success already. Had Tomas died then we would not have known about the copper and the gold. Iago would be richer for it."

"You will need to build a fort to protect the workers. When his warriors fail to return he will investigate. Prince Cadfan has begun to fortify north of the Mawddach but he has a handful of untried warriors only. We need to put some iron along the Mawddach and the Dyfi."

The king had looked worried. "Is Cadfan like his father? I would not like a younger version of Iago close to my new finds."

"He is not like his father but remember I am still Dux Britannica. I will ensure that the lands under my charge are peaceful." I showed him some of the first coins that we had minted. "I have a mind to use these throughout your kingdoms and my land. How do you feel about that?"

He smiled, "I like it and I like that you have not used your own image. I know that you will not try to take power. I think Cloten will go along with it. It means that we can share our coins and no-one is the ruler." He looked at me and nodded. "You are a wise man, Warlord."

Two days later we escorted Tomas, his miners and the forty men who would build and man the new fort on the Mawddach, to the mine. Tomas enjoyed the journey for he was grateful to me for his rescue. His men were also in good humour. As Tomas told me, they no longer felt vulnerable. There was a protector close at hand. The only one who seemed slightly put out was Lann Aelle. "I thought we would have had more battles to fight. This seems…"

"Easy?"

"Aye, my lord."

"This is but the start. Iago will want this gold and he will want to best his son. There will be war but it will not be this year. We have hurt him too much. He has lost two warbands and he will need to regain his strength but he will come again. By then we should have our defences in place and," I nudged him playfully in the ribs, "you will be bigger and stronger. You will be able to protect your old uncle."

We stayed for a few days to enable Myrddyn to advise Tomas on the mine and for Garth and my men to show the men of Ceredigion how to use the resources close to hand to make a stronger fort.

Prince Cadfan and the men I had left at Nefyn had worked hard and there was now a low wall reaching from the side of the fort to the sea. It would not hold an enemy at the moment but, once it was the height of a man it would be an effective barrier. Hogan was stripped to the waist and labouring with his equites. We had learned long ago that physical labour made a warrior stronger. That was obvious from the sweat glistening on toned muscles and bodies.

He paused and wiped his brow. "Welcome Warlord." He pointed to the north. "The prince has decided to build a northern wall too. He lived with Prince Pasgen long enough to see the benefits of such a defence."

"He is wise then." I gestured for Myrddyn to join us. "You know those mountains better than any, could Iago use the high passes to descend on this land?"

Myrddyn shook his head. "Not from the north but from the south? Aye. That is the weak area. Between Cader Idris and Wyddfa there are many passes he could use."

"Then when he gets horsemen the prince will need to patrol them."

"Then there is a problem for we have barely enough horses for our own men. We can ill afford to equip another army."

"We shall have to get them."

Hogan looked at Myrddyn, "How? By magic?"

"No, my lord. We shall steal them!"

Although I was anxious to hear how Prince Pasgen and Mungo had fared in the north I needed to be there to support Prince Cadfan. The next morning I summoned Hogan. "I want you and Tuanthal to take your equites and join

Prince Pasgen. Send Aedh ahead of you to find his whereabouts and then send Aedh to the horse lands to find us some Saxon horses to steal."

Hogan was happy to be doing what he and his horsemen enjoyed the most, fighting our enemies. "If we find Iago's men then what?"

"Defeat them or, if their numbers are too great send for Garth and my shield wall."

Hogan laughed. "Then Garth will have much time to build his little walls."

Garth snorted, "I can remember a time Lord Hogan when you were desperate to stand in my shield wall."

"And if I did not have a fine horse between my legs then I would do so again."

The banter was a good sign. It showed that my warriors were all in high spirits. After they had left I sought out Cadfan. Myrddyn was busily working to improve the defences while Garth and his men toiled with Cadfan's new recruits. We stood on top of the hill and watched as the men worked below us.

"How are the new men Prince Cadfan?"

"They seem willing enough but compared with your men they appear to be almost unarmed."

I nodded. I had seen the envious looks his men had cast at the arms and armour of my men. "You will acquire better arms do not worry. You will need to find either trade or an income." I pointed to 'The Wolf'. "My ships will help you should you need them."

"How did you equip your men so well?"

"We defeated warriors and then used their poorer armour and weapons to make better ones. Ralph can help you there. Miach can advise you on bows for your archers. That would be my first task. Bows can be made easily. We have plenty of yew stored at Caer Gybi but you need the men who are suitable to be archers." I pointed to the short and stocky warriors who happened to be digging the ditch before us. "They would make good archers for they have powerful shoulders. With archers you can keep your enemy at bay. Ceredigion has fine cows. Trade their king for the leather. Leather armour can be useful until you have enough iron. We are planning on stealing some horses for you. These would give you scouts." I pointed to the east. "Myrddyn has told me that there are many passes over which your father can travel and you need to scout them. As soon as this is complete I would appoint a trustworthy deputy to captain the garrison and then explore the area. Find what you have to trade. Get to know your people and convince them that you would make a better king than your father."

He looked crestfallen. "That sounds like a long list of tasks."

"It is. Being a leader is not as easy as it looks. You need a cleric as I have who can manage your lands. Ask Bishop Stephen if there is a suitable monk who would like to do as Brother Oswald does. It will make your life easier. I will see if we have any spare weapons we have taken from the Saxons and others we have defeated and send them to you." I put my arm around his shoulder. "This is just the first step on a long journey. The others will be easier but do not count them for there will be steps beyond number."

"Thank you, Warlord. I know that I sound ungrateful."

"No, you are young and new to this. You will learn. I did."

I took my men and we headed back to the Narrows the next day. The fort was now defensible and the men were being trained already. I left Miach's son to help train his archers while 'The Wolf' returned to Caer Gybi for bows and spare weapons. I hoped that King Iago would take time to seek revenge but there were now over a hundred warriors defending the fort at Nefyn.

When we reached the monastery, we camped. I had not seen Bishop Stephen and I was anxious to find out how the new monastery of St David was faring. As usual he made us welcome but he had some disquieting news for the three of us as we sat with him in the newly built herb garden. "I was pleased when you sent Prince Pasgen for the Saxons have begun raiding south of the Dee. King Iago's men at Deva just hold the bridge and the rest of the river can be used by the raiders. They have taken slaves from north of here." He pointed at the new roundhouses. "Many have taken refuge here."

That was a disturbing thought and reminded me of my own family's fate. "Prince Cadfan is looking for settlers at Nefyn if they wish to journey there. It is a good land and there are few people living there."

"Thank you for that Warlord. Our resources here are stretched a little."

As we spoke I wondered what had happened to Prince Pasgen and my son. I would have expected to hear from them but the lack of news of any sort was disquieting. "Hopefully we will be able to establish a presence at the head of the valley and that should prevent incursions. If you built a beacon then we could reach you sooner. You are a little isolated here."

He spread his arms. "We are in God's hands, Warlord. I will build one at the coast." He smiled, "Otherwise no one could see it."

I would have to see to it that Mungo and his men had a sentry on their tower which faced the monastery.

We left before dawn the next day as I was eager to reach my son and the rest of my warriors. Aedh's scouts found us. "My lord, the Prince has been ambushed. He was saved by the arrival of your son."

"Were many lost?"

He shook his head, "Five equites and three horses but the men of Gwynedd escaped without loss."

I was desperate to find out how the disaster had occurred but I would have to wait. "Take us to them then."

As we rode I turned to Myrddyn and Garth, "What do you think happened?"

Myrddyn closed his eyes and put his arms out before him. "I am sorry Warlord. It is hidden from me." He began laughing and Garth smiled too. "We will have to wait to find out. Speculation will get us nowhere despite your worries for your son who will be safe."

"You are right to mock me. I should be where the fighting is not enjoying the company of monks."

Garth shook his head, "You are wrong to berate yourself so Warlord. You are the leader of our warriors but we have others who can do the fighting. Whatever happened to Prince Pasgen and Mungo will be a lesson to them. They will learn from it."

We reached the scene of the ambush. There was a small valley which led from the Clwyd into the hills. There were many trees, hedges and rocks. It was not the country for equites. That was my fault. I had sent equites because I wanted speed. Hogan and Pol rode up to me.

I dismounted, "Tell me."

"Prince Pasgen has a broken leg." He looked at Myrddyn who nodded and left immediately. "Five equites died and six others suffered wounds. They were led into an ambush by Iago's men feigning a retreat. They had dug pits and the horses fell into them. The warriors who were killed were attacked as they lay on the ground. The warriors of Mungo were too far behind to help. We happened along and I took my men and we scattered the attackers with arrows but this," he pointed to the rock strewn hillside, "is not the country for horses."

Garth smirked, "You mean slow and cumbersome warriors would have been better?"

Hogan had the good grace to smile. "No, archers and lightly armed skirmishers such as they have in the east would have been better."

I waved my arm irritably at the two of them. "This is not the time for bickering or recriminations. We need to salvage something from this. Garth take the warriors up that shallow valley and make sure that there are no others waiting to attack us. Hogan, take your men to the north. Look for Saxons. Bishop Stephen said that there are warbands operating there."

He grinned as he rode off, "That is better Warlord, action at last!"

I found Myrddyn tending to Prince Pasgen. The prince tried to stand. "You have a broken leg. Lie there and let my wizard heal you."

"I am sorry my lord, I have let you down."

"You have learned a lesson Prince Pasgen. The equites are good but they cannot do it all alone." Mungo approached us, "Did you lose any?"

"No, my lord; I am sorry, my men were not quick enough to keep up with the horses."

"It has cost us but not as much as it could have done." I looked around the valley. "Have you found a site for a fort yet?"

He spread his arms. "This looks to be the best place. The valley leading south is shallow. If we dig a ditch and use that to build a mound then we will be higher than the hills and we can control the valley. There is water and there is wood." He pointed ruefully at the rocks, "And as we found out there are plenty of stones."

"Excellent then something good has come from this. We will build a fort here. Mungo make a start." I looked over to Myrddyn. "When can the prince travel?"

The prince tried to raise himself up. "I can travel now Warlord!"

Myrddyn pushed him down, none too gently. "You can travel when I am happy that the leg is mending. A wagon would help."

I smiled, Myrddyn was not one to mince words when it came to healing. I waved Prince Pasgen's lieutenant over.

"Yes my lord?"

"Aidan, take four men and ask the Bishop if he has a wagon you can borrow. Use two of the horses of the men who were wounded. Bring it back here. When Myrddyn gives permission, you can take him back to the fort. Until then you are in command of the equites. The prince can enjoy a rest and run the fort rather than the equites."

I could see that Aidan was happy but Pasgen scowled and glared pure hatred at his broken leg. We all began to help Mungo to build the fort. Time was of the essence. When Garth returned his men joined in too. "We found nothing my lord but they were watching us from the rocks and crags. There was little point in pursuing. Your son was quite right, this is not the country for armoured men."

"I know. We will have to recruit lightly armed men for this fort. I do not intend it to hold large numbers but to deny the enemy the free run of the valley." I shouted over to Mungo. "I want at least one tall tower so that we can signal danger." He nodded and began to give orders.

I mounted my horse, "Come Lann we will ride around and pretend we are an attacker." I knew that whoever would man this fort would be isolated. If I was Iago or Aethelfrith how would I assault it? I was pleased to see there was no steep slope down which an avalanche could be started. Mungo was already cutting back the tree line to provide timber and we could cut it back even further. The stream could be used as a ditch and the natural slope would enable us to make it surround the fort. It would not stop an attacker but it would slow them down. As we rode higher up the slope I could see many rocks which were small enough to be carried by a warrior and used for building. The more stone we used then the more secure it would be. I looked to the north. We could have used the slope there to build the castle but it was a gentler slope. The site I had chosen was steeper and protected the valley from Saxon attacks too. I estimated that we were ten or twelve miles from the monastery which added protection for the monks. It would do. The problem would now be to find warriors to garrison it.

I was pleased, when we returned, to see that the mound was rising as the first of the ditches was being deepened. I waved Myrddyn over, "See if you can divert the stream to give added protection to another wall."

Rather than being daunted by such a task the wizard rubbed his hands together. He gestured to my nephew. "Come Lann Aelle, this is good for you. We will use your mind and see if it matches your arm."

He went with the wizard happily. Myrddyn was a good teacher and knew how to engage young minds. Hogan's intelligence owed much to my wizard.

It was approaching dark when Hogan rode in and I could see from his face that it was not good news. "We have a problem, Warlord. There are Saxon warbands swarming all over the country. King Iago's men are hiding behind their walls at Deva and Wrecsam. We are the only warriors who can do aught about them."

Chapter 9

We ate frugally that night and we kept many guards around the perimeter. I did not worry that we could be beaten by these warbands but we had suffered too many casualties already. I sat with my leaders. I smiled at Pasgen's frustration. Myrddyn had agreed that he could return with the other wounded the next morning. He was annoyed that he would be missing from what was likely to be a campaign against the raiders.

Hogan made his report. "I sent Tuanthal and Pol to the east and the west and I headed north. I counted six warbands. There were no more than fifty in each band. I found houses and farms burning. The men were dead and I think the families had been taken as slaves. We reached Deva. There is a Saxon army there but it is no more than two hundred men. They have ships in the estuary. Tuanthal and Pol reported another eight warbands in the east and the west. They are stripping the land of people and animals. Iago's people are suffering."

I sadly shook my head, "No, my son, it is our people who are suffering. I am Dux Britannica and all the people are my responsibility."

I stared into the fire as I formulated my thoughts. "Warlord?"

"I am thinking, Myrddyn, but I would welcome ideas from any of you."

Myrddyn coughed and began, "When the fort is finished it will need to be manned. That will take away some of our warriors. We only have twenty archers."

"Nineteen."

"You are correct Miach, Daffydd is with Prince Cadfan. When Prince Pasgen returns to his fort we will have sixty equites. We can defeat the individual war bands but should they join together …"

I had come up with a plan even as I was assimilating what Myrddyn was saying. "Hogan, did you see any sign of the families?"

"No Warlord."

"I saw some to the west, close to the river. They looked to be penned and guarded."

"How many were there Pol?"

"I would estimate a hundred or more."

"They obviously have a problem moving them. Deva stops them crossing the river and while they can bring more warriors in by boat, it is difficult to transport families. We start with the families. We must save them. Aedh I want you to send a rider to 'The Wolf'. I want all four ships to be off the coast near to the monastery by the day after tomorrow. Hogan, we will take our equites and begin a sweep from here to Deva and kill or capture as many Saxons as we can. Garth and Mungo we will leave a garrison here but you will take the warriors to the aid of the slaves. Pol will guide you. I want all of us to converge on the Dee in three days time. Our ships can attack at the same time that we do. I want those families saved."

Their faces told me that they approved the idea but Myrddyn came up with the problems. "What about the fort? It will not be finished."

"I know but the men we leave here must finish it."

"You didn't mention my archers Warlord."

"No Miach. Until we have recaptured the slaves I want you in command here. Your archers can help to build the fort and then defend it with the garrison."

He smiled. "A nice rest for me then eh?"

Miach was the most solid and dependable of my captains. He would do whatever I asked and I knew that I could rely on him. "Aedh your scouts will be vital. You have to keep everyone in touch with each other and find the enemy,. You will need to be in two places at once."

He kept a serious face as he said, "So there will be no change for us then?"

Everyone laughed and I knew that, despite the apparent mountain we had to climb, we now, at least had a chance. "And what of Iago?"

"I think Myrddyn that he will be trying to out guess us. By now he will have heard that his son is raising an army. He may think we are stretched. Prince Pasgen, when you return to your fort you will need to warn the prince that he may be in danger and you will need to use your scouts to warn all of us about any danger in the mountains."

The prince was eager to make up for what he saw as his failure. "I will not let you down again, Warlord."

"You did not let me down. The enemy is learning to be cunning. We just have to adapt and become cleverer ourselves."

The next day we sent Pasgen back to his fort with his equites. If Myrddyn was correct then there was greater danger to Cadfan than to us. We would have to make do with thirty equites. Lann and I rode with Hogan, Pol and Tuanthal. Myrddyn stayed at the fort to aid Miach with the defences. This would be the first time I had fought as an equite. I felt inadequate as I rode next to Pol and Hogan on their fully armoured horses, with their long spears in their hands. They had much smaller shields than I did for their armour was more effective than mine. At least my helmet was the same as theirs, having been a gift from Andronikos.

Aedh himself had led the scouts and he galloped towards us. "My lord, there is a warband and they are attacking Yr Wyddgrug." He pointed behind him. It is half a mile ahead and is in a valley close to a river. There is no wall."

"Hogan these are your men, what do you suggest?"

"Thank you, Warlord. Tuanthal and Pol, take half the men and approach from the west along the river. I will lead the rest along the valley from the east. We will catch them between us and use the speed of our attack to make up for smaller numbers."

It was a good plan and I happily rode behind my son. I drew Saxon Slayer and slung my shield from my pommel. "Lann Aelle, the banner." I felt better advancing under my Wolf Banner. It brought us good luck.

The valley had a stream which was not deep but it was lined with bushes and undergrowth and we rode to the side of the undergrowth. I noticed that we rode two abreast which allowed us to travel quite quickly. We saw the flames and heard the screams before we saw the Saxons. I was to Hogan's right. I would be the one protecting my son as Lann Aelle normally protected me. The column went from two abreast to a line of fifteen warriors. They all held their spears in their right hands and extended the heads well in front of their horses. I was interested to see how these worked. We emerged from the bushes and saw the Saxons finishing off the last of the brave defenders. They had no idea what was about to be unleashed. Hogan kicked his horse on and the others did the same. I was not expecting it and felt myself losing ground. Without turning Hogan laughed, "Come along Warlord, keep up!"

The equites used their spears like long swords and jabbed and stabbed with them. They aimed them precisely at those areas without armour and Saxon after Saxon fell to the deadly accurate spears. The Saxons had no answer to the heavily armoured equites. I swung Saxon Slayer and felt it bite into the back of the warrior who was racing to thrust his spear into Hogan's side. Lann Aelle slashed at the face of another who tried to hamstring his horse. The Saxons began to flee, just as Tuanthal and Pol arrived from the opposite direction. Our two lines of armour met in the middle. We had no time for quarter even had they asked for it and soon there were just dead and dying Saxons left.

I dismounted and shouted, "See to the wounded men. Pol, secure the perimeter." As I handed my reins to Lann I noticed that the horses of the equites were breathing heavily. The charge had taken much out of them. I would need to bear that in mind when they were used in the future.

We managed to save four men and boys, but the rest were dead. One of the survivors was the old headman. He had been stabbed in the arm and I could see that he would never use it again. He recognised my shield, "Thank the Allfather you arrived when you did or we would have all been taken. They came from nowhere, Warlord. We had no defences."

My first thought was that they should have had a wall and defended it but this was not the time for such carping. "They will come again you know?"

"Aye, I know but what are we to do?"

"There is a fort being built a few miles back at Ruthin. The Clwyd is a fertile valley and I can protect you there. Here you are too close to the Saxons. If you moved there then there would, at least, be warriors to aid you." I saw the despair in his eyes. "You can start again."

"We have but four men. What of the women who have lost fathers and husbands."

"The men at the fort are good men. They will help you to rebuild and…"

The old man smiled, "And nature will take care of the rest."

I nodded, "If you go there now I will send men to escort you and I will ask Bishop Stephen to send healers for your wounds but Myrddyn is there."

"Myrddyn the wizard?"

I could hear the awe in his voice. "Yes, old man, the wizard is there." I waved Tuanthal over. "Captain, escort these people to Myrddyn and they will build a settlement there. Have one of Aedh's scouts go to the Bishop; he may be able to help. We will camp here. Return tomorrow and we will continue our patrol."

Aedh and his indegeftigable scouts were out before first light. We were ready to ride when Tuanthal and his men returned. "We will wait for Aedh to return. I need to know where the Saxons are and where my ships are."

Hogan examined his horse as we waited. "We cannot keep this up for long, Warlord; the horses cannot cope with the weight."

I had worked that out for myself. "Then perhaps we leave the horse armour. We should not need it."

"I am loath to lose it. Let us see what today brings. Perhaps when Garth and Mungo reach us we can do so."

I said nothing but I had decided that, even if they disagreed, I would rob the equites of their horse armour. What was the good of armour if you could not use the horses because of the weight?

Aedh rode in with all of his scouts. "My lord, I have collected all of my scouts." He pointed to the north. "'The Wolf' and the others ships are anchored at the mouth of the estuary. We have found the slave camp. It is close to Y Fflint. Captains Garth and Mungo are five miles from here and there is a sizeable warband heading from Y Fflint towards Treffynnon. There appear to be sixty men in the band. The village has no walls to protect the people."

"You have done well, Aedh. I want the ships to be as close to Treffynnon as possible. I want the equites to get to the village and dismount. You will defend it on foot until my warriors can reach it."

Hogan looked appalled, "But we are equites!"

"And can your horses charge the Saxons?"

"They could manage one charge." Hogan sounded truculent.

"I need your horses to be fresh for the attack on the slave camp. Obey the Warlord!" I put steel into my voice. Hogan might be my son but I was Warlord.

"Yes Warlord."

"Aedh send one rider to Garth and tell him to hurry to Treffynnon I will join them there and the rest of your scouts can stay with me." As they all left, I suddenly felt naked. I had just eight lightly armed warriors and we had to hold up the enemy until Garth reached us. I grinned at them. "Well boys, it looks like we have the honour of attacking a warband six times our number. Are you game?"

They all roared, "Wolf Warriors!" We were ready.

There was a hollow running alongside the road and we took advantage of it. Aedh and his scouts were masters at estimating distances and the lead scout held up his hand and halted. "They should be half a mile up the road, Warlord."

The scouts all had bows and short swords but they were not armoured. Our only advantage was speed. "I want us to get ahead of them. You will loose arrows from cover and then we will appear before them. I want them to chase us onto my son's spears." I looked at Lann Aelle. "You need to wave the banner as though you are signalling an army to come to our rescue. With luck Garth and Mungo will fall on their unprotected backs." The scouts looked keen to be fighting for a change. "I want no casualties. Five arrows only and then we retreat. They will follow me so I want no heroes. You will get the village and you will help Hogan."

We made swift time down the sunken dell. My horse struggled a little with the weight of my armour but the ponies of the scouts flew over the mossy mud. The lead scout held up his hand and slowed down as we passed the head of the warband. We could hear their noise as we slowly passed them. Two hundred paces further down we halted. I held up my hand and they drew back their bows. As I lowered it they released and reloaded. I did that four times and then we hacked our way through the hedges to emerge on the road. We had caused few casualties but there were bodies lying on the road. "Now Lann!"

As soon as the banner was unfurled the Saxons roared their anger and hurtled towards us. The scouts loosed their last flights as I shouted, "Retreat!" We rode swiftly down the road with the Saxons in close pursuit. Had they had bows they might have tried to hurt us but they had spears, swords and axes only. I kept pace with them so we were always, temptingly, out of reach. I saw the village ahead and hoped that Hogan had laid an ambush. He might still be bridling at losing his horses but he was a warrior through and through and he would know how to lay a good ambush.

As we approached the village I could see nothing and that boded well. I glanced over my shoulder and saw that the Saxons were just forty paces behind me. I heard Hogan's voice as I approached the first round house. "Keep riding! Take them to the end of the village!"

I allowed Lann Aelle to pass me then I wheeled my mount around and shouted in Saxon, "Saxon dogs!" I continued my wheel and galloped through the first of the huts. As I had expected my taunting had allowed them to close with me and they were just twenty paces behind me. I kicked hard and my horse leapt away.

I heard the roar of the Saxons followed by Hogan's voice, "Now!"

The thirty equites stabbed with their long spears as they emerged from the huts. "Scouts, turn and loose!"

I galloped hard and aimed my horse at the warrior with the full face helmet. I extended my arm and sliced down with my blade. It cut the helmet and skull in two. My horse trampled a second warrior and then Lann Aelle was laying about him with Bear Killer. The maces of the equites were doing terrible damage to Saxons who were wearing poor iron helmets. With their leader gone they turned and fled. Lann and I pursued them. It must have looked ridiculous but the Saxons who turned would have only seen a huge warrior on a massive horse. When Garth and Mungo's men charged into them they either surrendered or died. We had won, again.

As our men herded the sullen prisoners together I had Mungo's men collect the weapons to add to those we had gathered from the other warband. None of them were of high quality but Prince Cadfan would be able to use them. "Pol, go and signal 'The Wolf' to close in shore. We can store the weapons on board the ships and our wounded. Although we had not lost men there were many wounds and there was little point in sending a wounded man in to battle.

Hogan approached me, "You were right father. I am sorry for my outburst."

I smiled, "You are a horseman and it is natural that you should wish to ride to war. I am Warlord and for me the burden is the whole army and all of our people. We will have differences of opinion. That is good. It is just important that we fight together. Now make sure you have rested your horses and take off your amour. Tomorrow we fight again and this time you will use your horses."

I waved Garth over. "Warlord, what do we do with these prisoners? There are twenty of them."

"I do not know yet. Just bind them and guard them and we will give it some thought. Did Myrddyn not accompany you?"

"He said that he would join us here later. He was with us until we spied the warband and then he vanished." I cocked an eyebrow and Garth laughed. "What I mean is he was with us one moment and they he had gone. I can understand why people think he can become invisible. He can be as silent as the night when he wishes to be."

"Do not worry Garth; he has a way of reappearing when we need him. How man men have we now?"

"We have fifty warriors."

"Then we will need all of Myrddyn's cunning if we are to rescue the slaves and not lose all of our men in doing so."

The villagers had returned from their places of hiding. They were grateful to us for our help. I summoned the headman and pointed to the stones of the

Roman walls. "Why do you have no defences? These stones could have built a wall. You know that the Saxons are at Deva and that is less than a day from here."

"King Iago told us that the Saxons had been defeated." He looked distraught.

"Then your king was wrong. How many men do you have here?" He looked fearfully at my armed men. I laughed and shook my head. "I am not here to take your men. My warriors have trained for years. How many men do you have who can bear weapons?"

"There are twelve of us."

"And have you weapons?"

"A few my lord."

I turned to Lann Aelle. "Go and bring twelve good weapons and helmets before the ships arrive." He galloped off to fetch the weapons. "You need to use the good Roman stone to build walls around your village. Dig a ditch and build a tower to watch for the Saxons." I pointed to the river a mile or so away. "The Saxons can reach here more easily than many places."

"But my lord, we are farmers..."

"Dead men cannot farm and their families become slaves. That is your choice."

His shoulders sagged in resignation. "Would that you could protect us."

I waved my hand in the direction of Wyddfa. "I have much land to watch and my men will visit as often as we can but you must bear some responsibility. Build a beacon and if they come again then light it. My men are building a fort at Ruthin, just up the Clwyd Valley, and they will come. The bishop has a beacon at the monastery too. Your walls may slow the enemy up enough to allow us to get here." I smiled. "I have been in your position too. It is a short period of work and then your family will be safe. It is worth it is it not?"

"Yes Warlord."

Lann Aelle arrived back with two warriors who were laden with helmets and weapons. They were mainly spears with a couple of axes but they were sound ones. "Distribute these and have your men make shields when they can. If you have archers then so much the better and your boys who cannot fight can throw stones. Give your women knives. You must make it hard for the Saxons and they will go to find easier targets."

The headman was grateful and they shared what little food they had with us. I left them to eat while I went to tell my captains what I intended. By the time I returned I found that Myrddyn had reappeared. "Ah the magician is here again; very good of you to join us."

He swallowed the morsel he had been chewing and grinned at me. "I thought that you would wish to know how many Saxons faced you at Y Fflint."

"You have been there?"

"I played the healer again. There are two hundred men there, or near enough two hundred for some were on board their ships. They have six ships and they are moored in the middle of the river." That fitted in with my calculations. There are a hundred and fifteen slaves. That is their count and not mine. They are guarded by twenty warriors and when the villagers from here are brought then they will be transported across the river."

"Good that fits in with my plan." I gathered my captains around me and explained what we would do. The fact that they all left in such good humour made me think that my mad plan might just succeed.

Myrddyn walked with me by the river. "The plan has all the marks of a wizard, Warlord. You are learning."

"I think it is a mixture of you and my association with Constantinopolis and their convoluted minds. We will see what the morrow brings."

The next day we herded the prisoners together. Those of our warriors who had Saxon helmets and shields led them down the road to Y Fflint. Garth was the captain. It was only five miles. The marched them down the river track. I led Mungo and the remainder of our men down the Roman Road. Hogan and the equites were half a mile behind the prisoners. It was all a matter of timing and what the Saxons saw. We ran down the road to reach our allotted position before the prisoners could be seen from their camp.

It was maddening for me to be reliant on others but Myrddyn had promised me that they would be able to do what I asked of them. Myrddyn was also playing a prisoner and would be a vital part in the rescue of the slaves. When I heard the shout and the roar I had to imagine what was happening. "Now Mungo. Wedge!" We were hidden from the camp by trees and hedges but I could see Hogan charging our men and the prisoners. I hoped that there would be panic amongst the Saxon defenders as they saw the mailed equites charging their own men and the newly acquired slaves. My four ships only had six bolt throwers but I knew that they would be sending bolt after bolt into the Saxon ships. With luck they would try to escape and not notice my wedge approaching.

I saw that the Saxons had formed a shield wall. They had left a gap for what they thought were their own men, returning with newly acquired slaves, to pass through and were preparing to hold off the mailed horsemen. They did not see us approach their unguarded left flank. We did not shout until we were ten paces from the end. The roar made them start and look in horror at the Wolf Banner and Saxon Slayer. Their whole left flank crumbled. Garth and his men left the tied prisoners and followed Myrddyn to the slave compound where they swiftly killed the guards. We were still vastly outnumbered by our enemies but they were disorganised and only saw two walls of iron closing upon them. They broke and ran for their ships.

"Halt!" With so few men it would have been madness to follow them. We turned and headed towards the slave compound. The men we had captured the previous day looked confused as we passed them without harming them. They had bought their lives with the deception. As soon as I saw Garth and Myrddyn leading their charges down the road towards the coast we ran to join them.

"Hogan and I want you and your equites to stop the Saxons pursuing us when we go to the monastery. Avoid contact. Your presence should deter them."

"I will do Warlord."

We had ten miles to go until we reached Bishop Stephen's monastery and with women and children that would take half a day. The scouts led the women and children off and we followed a short way behind. Like Hogan we would stop the women and children being recaptured.

Lann Aelle signalled the ships to withdraw and I breathed a sigh of relief when I saw that they were all undamaged. Looking upstream I saw that the Saxon ships had been damaged but they could be repaired. We had, however, achieved our objective. We had destroyed four warbands and rescued the captured villagers. Once our fort at Ruthin was completed we would be able to control such incursions.

Bishop Stephen had been warned of our impending arrival and all was ready for us when we reached them. The monks were kind and enjoyed looking after children. When we reached the monastery the children were laughing and the tears from the women were with relief that they had survived. I waited anxiously for Hogan to arrive and felt that I could relax when he did.

"They showed no sign of wishing to pursue us." He looked at his horses with concern. "We could not have charged them."

"I know. Take your men and horses back to the island. Leave Tuanthal, Aedh and his scouts with me."

"Why, what have you in mind?"

"We need horses for Prince Cadfan, remember?"

"I will come."

I shook my head. "You have already told me that you and your horses need a rest. We need you in command during my absence. You have already proved to be a worthy leader. I will take Myrddyn and Lann Aelle. Along with Pol and Aedh that should be enough. Stealing horses requires small numbers and stealth. Pol and Aedh have done this before. Your men need you."

I could see that I had convinced him. "And the ones we rescued?"

"I will speak with them. The ships can take the weapons to Cadfan and I will send Mungo and Garth with you to return to their forts. They both need to train more men to garrison our new fort. I think it is safe for a while but once Iago and the Saxons realise we are here to stay then they will try to dislodge us. Pasgen needs to build a line of beacons to link with Ruthin. There are enough farms and settlements to do so."

Hogan put his hand around my shoulder. "And you need to rest too."

I shook my head and laughed. "I have just had a pleasant sea voyage. I am refreshed."

After they had eaten I addressed the former captives. "Your homes have been destroyed and your men folk died protecting you. This is as dark a time as you will have to suffer for there is hope on the horizon." I pointed to the south. "South of us is now free from Saxons. Prince Cadfan is settling the land of the Penrhyn Llŷn. There are warriors there who would be glad of a family to care for. There are many farms on Mona and you are welcome to go there. My son Hogan will be heading south tomorrow with my men and you will be safe in his care. You just need to decide where you want to settle."

I could see smiles on the faces of the people and they went into small groups to talk of their future.

The bishop came to me. "Bishop Asaph said it and he was right, you have a Christian heart. I think what you offer is for the best."

"I have now built a fort at Ruthin. They can see your beacon and there will be another just along the road at Treffynnon. It means that if we all watch then we can see the approach of the Saxons and we should not lose so many fine people."

"And what of King Iago?"

That had worried me too. "I know not. He has been a little quiet since the ambush of my men. I would have expected belligerence from him. He is up to something and that thought is disquieting." Still I can only deal with one problem at a time. I hope that we still have enough time to defend this land of ours.

Chapter 10

I gathered my horse thieves around me. "We will leave our armour at Ruthin along with the Wolf Banner. We will need stealth and not strength if we are to capture some horses."

I could see that Lann was excited beyond belief. Aedh and Pol were legends amongst the young warriors. Both had been involved in some of the most exciting adventures and escapades during my time as Warlord. Lann Aelle was now joining those elite warriors.

"Aedh, you know the Saxon country beyond Gwynedd better than most; where should we seek horses?"

"If you want light horses then it is Gwynedd itself which has the most to offer." He pointed to the mountain of Wyddfa. "There are valleys beyond the mountain which are filled with the herds of King Iago."

A strange smile played upon Myrddyn's lips. "We would also be able to spy upon King Iago. Besides which there is a certain irony in that we will be stealing the horses to give to his son. It has a balance about it."

I shrugged. I did not mind which of our enemies supplied the horses. "Good, then let us leave for Ruthin."

When we reached the fort I was glad that I had left Miach in temporary command. There was a gate and a drawbridge already built and manned. Although the walls were not as high as they would be eventually, it could be defended. "How long to finish it?"

"Twenty days and it will have walls. Another ten and it will be secure."

I took him to one side. "We will need you and your archers on Mona soon. Find a leader amongst the men here."

"I have a couple in mind." He gave me a shrewd look. "So you go into the dragon's den?"

I nodded, "We kill two birds with one stone. We gain horses and we see what the devious king is up to."

We left early in the morning and headed up the shallow valley leading to Iago's heartland. Pol and I wore our wolf cloaks while the scouts, Myrddyn and Lann wore dark cloaks so that we did not stand out. We rode well spread out both to enable us to see further and to avoid ambushes. I allowed Aedh and his scouts to take the lead. They had the ability to sniff out an enemy. I once had that but I had lost it over years. The hills and crags were criss-crossed by paths. Originally they had been made by sheep and goats and then man had made them wider. They were not straight and they provided many opportunities for an ambush. We were lucky, that first day and we made it to the crags overlooking the settlement of Corwen. We were but eleven miles from the fort but we were deep in Iago's land. We halted behind a strand of straggly thin trees which had fought their way up in a harsh environment. We saw our first horses. There was a herd of wild ponies and they had been corralled into a stone wall farm. We peered down looking for signs of warriors but there were none. It looked a peaceful little settlement, much as Stanwyck had been before the Saxons had come.

Aedh led us down as the valley quickly darkened with the approach of dusk. "Pol, take Lann and make sure no one comes from the huts lower down the valley." As the two young warriors trotted off the rest of us went to the corral. We needed the dominant male, the stallion. Aedh knew horses and he quickly found him. He and Myrddyn fitted a halter. The beast began to make noises, alerting those in the farm. "Take him now and the rest will follow."

Aedh led the pony and the rest of us mounted and galloped after them. "Pol, it is time to go!"

A light showed that the door of the house had been opened and I heard voices shouting at us to halt. We ignored them and galloped back to our place of concealment. Pol and Lann galloped up to join us. Although it was dangerous we could not wait this close to Corwen and we rode the twelve miles back towards the Clwyd Valley. The tethered male leader soon succumbed to the apples Aedh gave him and the rest of the herd followed happily. Rather than making for the fort we headed down to the monastery and reached it, tired but relieved that we had succeeded by dawn. Bishop Stephen was surprised to see the scouts and the horses but he took it all in his stride. We took food with them. I did not want to risk leaving the herd this close to their former owners and we continued on to Prince Pasgen's fort. The sentries were amazed to see the Warlord herding horses.

Prince Pasgen had had two crutches made and he beamed with delight when he saw us. "You have done well Warlord. Fifteen ponies!"

"Not good enough for equites but they should serve Cadfan as scout horses. Will you see that he gets them?"

"Aye my lord."

"And beds for me and my men. We need the sleep!"

We spent a whole day with the prince and then headed back to Ruthin. Without the ponies we made better time. As we rode Myrddyn mused. "Those ponies were bigger than the normal Welsh hill ponies."

I had not thought about that until Myrddyn mentioned it but now it was obvious. They had been almost as big as Aedh's pony. "You are right but what does it mean?"

"It means my lord that King Iago is breeding bigger horses so that he has cavalry like we do." He had more to say and I waited patiently. Myrddyn like to reveal his information little by little, as though he was performing a trick. He sighed and continued. "What that means is, he must have bigger horses somewhere that he is using to breed with the hill ponies."

"And that will be down in the flat lands."

"Probably around Wrecsam."

The Mercians had had one success when they had surprised Beli, Iago's father. Since then Iago had beaten them in every battle and had led to his conquest of Chester. Wrecsam would be the perfect place to breed his horses for it was flat fertile land and well protected.

"It would be harder to steal horses from Iago's forts. This would be no isolated farmhouse."

"My lord, we would discover what he was up to and we would not need to steal all of the horses; just some of them." I was not convinced and it showed on my face. "The prince has enough ponies to provide scouts. Information and knowledge is more important, Warlord."

He was right. Infuriatingly he was always right and it was a risk worth taking. "Very well. Aedh lead us to Wrecsam! We will visit with Iago!"

We soon dropped down from the high hills and into the flat lands. We had to be cautious. There would be many of Iago's men using the roads. We did not look like equites; if anything we looked like bandits but that could still get us killed. I divided the ten of us into groups of threes and fours. We could see the walls of Wrecsam in the distance. "Aedh, take your men all the way around the town and meet us here, under this oak. "Pol, take your two men to the north. We will head south. Meet back here."

Myrddyn led Lann with me bringing up the rear. The roads in this part of the land were Roman in places but sometimes the Roman roads disappeared to become tracks. There were clusters of round houses dotted in fertile strips of land but we saw no horses. We spotted the ruins of some Roman villas but they were not the huge ones we had along the wall. The people did not appear to want to inhabit them. When I asked Myrddyn about that he said, "It may well be that they fear the ghosts of the dead. The Romans were not from this land and I think the people fear that their spirits will be restless and walk their old homes."

"And you wizard? Would you fear them?"

"I fear no living man so why should I fear the dead? Besides I have slept in Roman houses as you have my lord and I felt no dead presence."

There were far more settlements in this area and I could see where King Iago made his gold. There were cattle, pigs and even a few sheep in the higher meadows. Frustratingly we only saw a few horses. Lann asked about that. "Why do we only see one or two horses on the farms here?"

"I think that those farms belong to Iago's nobles. They are a mark of their rank."

"Could we steal them?"

"We could, Lann Aelle, but it would not be worth the risk. There are more likely to be armed owners. We would have to spend a long time collecting sufficient horses and they would find us."

When I judged we had travelled far enough we returned to the oak. Aedh was not back but Pol and his two scouts rode in. He seemed quite animated. "We have found something interesting my lord. A few miles north of Wrecsam on the road to Deva they have built a camp and there is a corral with forty horses in it."

"That is more like it."

"However, my lord, Iago has a large number of his army there. We saw the king's banner. He is training his men."

"Then when Aedh returns we shall venture there. The pickings to the south are not worth the risk."

Aedh reached us soon after and we rode, not along the road, for it was a busy one, but along the farm tracks which bordered the road. I was not worried about being seen. We would be taken for Iago's men, especially if there was a training camp north of here. The danger would come from warriors. Pol had found a stand of trees with a small clearing in the middle. It looked to have been used by charcoal burners at some time in the past but it suited us. Aedh left five of his men with the horses while we made our way through the bushes and hedges towards the training camp. Pol had been a scout too and knew how to move without leaving a trail. He held his hand up and we flattened ourselves along the ground. He waved left and right and we wriggled like adders to the line of elders. I was pleased they weren't blackberries or blackthorns. I had no armour to protect me from the thorns. There was enough space at the bottom of the hedges to peer through. The elder bushes were slightly above the enclosure Iago was using to train his men. Our enemy had learned from us. If nothing else our scouting mission had shown me a new danger.

Pol pointed to the right and I could see horsemen and they were trying to form a line. They were men of Iago's shield wall and they were mounted on his horses. The mounts were bigger than ponies but not by much. I smiled as I watched the ragged attempt at forming line and then the movement which I think they intended as a charge. The poor beasts could not move swiftly for they were encumbered by heavy mailed warriors. When they tried to turn it became almost comical. Many of them overbalanced and thundered into the ground. The ponies, suddenly released from their torment, took off in every direction.

Myrddyn grabbed my arm and pointed. There was King Iago with some of his chiefs. He did not look happy. We had learned the lessons he was learning but over a long period of time. We had also had the advantage of warriors who were trained to be riders. Most of Hogan's men had begun as scouts and learned how to ride well before learning how to fight on horseback. We watched as they tried to hurl spears from the backs of their horses. Some managed it successfully but most did not. Even the ones who threw them were not able to send them very far and had little control over the direction. I then looked around the camp to estimate numbers. There appeared to be four or five hundred men. Not all would be warriors but most would. It was coming to harvest time and Iago was making the most of the time he had to train his men. Soon it would be winter and, in the mountains around Wyddfa, no-one went to war.

I signalled that it was time to go and we made our way back to the clearing. The scouts had neither seen nor heard anything. Pol could not believe what he had seen. "We could destroy those with just a handful of lightly armed horsemen my lord."

Aedh nodded, "The horses are too small for armour. They would suit scouts or archers but never warriors."

Myrddyn counselled caution."Remember the larger horses we saw on the farms. They are breeding bigger horses and they will get better. They were climbing back on the horses once they fell off. That is how men learn."

"Myrddyn is right and with only five hundred men in the camp I am not worried but it means we need to spend the winter preparing for a spring assault."

"It will give Cadfan time to prepare too."

"So it will. And now let us head back to Ruthin."

Pol looked disappointed, "But we have no horses."

I swept my arm in the direction of Iago's camp. "We will get none around here. Iago will have every horse in his land gathered."

Aedh brightened, "Then north, towards the Saxon lands. There were always a few there."

"Very well then. It might be a useful exercise for we can see more of the land to the south of Deva."

The land was very flat and fertile as we headed north. We decided to approach as close as we could to Deva and then turn south west to return to Ruthin. We were four miles from the city when we saw the first evidence of the Saxons. Two small settlements were now smoking ruins. We did not approach too closely for the crows were picking over the carcasses. I was beginning to think that we would find nothing when Aedh said. "I believe there is a small settlement called Tatenhale not far from here. We once saw horses close by but it is Saxon not Welsh."

We approached Tatenhale from the north. Any of the villagers would assume we were Saxon. We were lucky and we saw no one. It was mid afternoon and unseasonably warm. That may have helped us for Aedh's sharp nose detected the smell of horse dung. We moved cautiously. We came to a field and there were six horses. They were the kind we used, a throwback to the time of Rome when they were used to pull carts. I could see, in the middle of the round houses, four carts. Whoever owned them moved things around. That meant that there might be armed men but the six horses were like gold. They would be big enough to carry Cataphractoi. I sent Aedh and his scouts to get the horses while we watched the huts. Perhaps they had just returned and were eating I do not know but we captured the horses easily enough.

"Each one of you, tie a halter to a horse and lead him. We can move faster."

With Pol and Lann leading, the six scouts and horses in between, Myrddyn and I brought up the rear. We escaped undetected. Our route took us towards Wrecsam in order to avoid the steep spur of land which jutted south from the Clwyd valley. Once we had passed Wrecsam then we would be at the fort in less than three hours. The sun was setting ahead of us. Things had turned out well. The horses we had stolen had been worked that day and they were happy to follow the scouts. Suddenly an arrow flew passed my head. I turned around and saw twenty of the warriors Iago had been training. "We are being pursued, Aedh, kick on. Pol and Lann join us."

We speeded up but the men of Gwynedd were urging their horses on. When Lann joined us he began to whip at his mount. "No Lann! Keep a steady pace. You will blow your horse otherwise."

Arrows came over our head now and again but a bow is hard to use when riding, especially when riding at the gallop. I kept glancing behind me. One or two of the warriors fell from their mounts as they tried to use their bows, while others were slowing down. The warriors had become a line but they were relentlessly pursuing us. It had been a gloriously hot autumn day and the sunset lasted a long time. The sun was so low in the sky that it was blinding but it was worse for the men pursuing us as they found it hard to see us. If we changed direction they would struggle to see which way we went. The land began to rise as we approached the Clwyd Valley. The warriors behind were spread out over half a mile and there were just six of them close enough to be a danger.

"When I give the word halt and dismount. Myrddyn guard the horses. We will fight them on foot." Pol looked at me in surprise, "They cannot fight on horseback, we have seen that and we know how to fight horsemen. I do not relish the thought of being pursued all the way back to Ruthin. The others may be discouraged if we despatch a couple. Now. Halt!"

We stopped and dismounted in a heartbeat. Myrddyn grabbed the reins and we stood in the middle of the road. Pol was to my right and Lann to my left. The low sun had blinded them and they did not see that we had stopped. The first warrior only saw me when he was ten paces from me. He tried to swing his axe at my head. It is always a difficult thing to do as you are trying to avoid your horse's head. I ducked and the momentum took him from his horse to lie at Pol's feet. Pol stabbed him in the neck. The next two had forewarning and they slowed but they still tried to swing at us. We had no armour but that made us more agile. We easily moved away from their blows. Lann hacked at the leg of one of them as he rode by and Bear Killer bit into flesh to the bone. I stabbed upwards as a warrior's sword went over my head and I found the gap in his mail under his arm. He fell dead at my feet. The other three looked at their dead and dying companions and turned to ride back to the rest of the warriors. They had halted a mile away.

"Lann get the weapons, Pol get the horses." I walked over to the warrior whose leg had almost been severed. I ripped the hem from his tunic and tied it around the knee. It would stop the bleeding but he would lose the leg.

He looked up at me and his hand began to creep towards his dagger. I took it from him and thrust it into my belt. His shoulders sagged in resignation, "You are the Warlord?" I nodded. "Why do you not kill me then? I am one of King Iago's oathsworn."

"You are a brave man to try to fight me from the back of a horse. I will let you live."

"But I will never stand in a shield wall again."

"No my friend, your days of fighting are over." The look on his face was as though I had cursed him with my words.

We mounted and headed west. The warriors rode to their wounded companion but I could see that they were not pursuing us. The three horses Pol led looked to be exhausted. Luckily there were no longer carrying a heavy weight and we could now take it more slowly. Lann and I each took one of the horses from Pol and we joined Aedh who had halted some way ahead. Aedh looked happy. "Nine horses! That is better! He looked towards the darkening road and the men of Gwynedd beyond. "Why did they not fight harder Warlord? Were they afraid?"

"No, they were brave men. They were just lacking in confidence, trying to fight on horseback. If they had dismounted they would have fared better. You know yourself Aedh, fighting from horseback is no easy matter. They will get better and we are now forewarned."

Myrddyn nodded. "And I noticed that they had targets for archers. King Iago has learned his lesson." We continued to Ruthin and safety.

It seemed like we had been away from Castle Cam for months by the time we returned. Myfanwy and Nanna made their usual fuss and Hogan was desperate to find out what we had learned. After I had greeted my young children I retired to my solar with Brother Oswald, Myrddyn and my son.

"We have been lucky this year. We could have suffered far more than we did but both our enemies are building their forces. That much is obvious. King Iago will bring horsemen and archers the next time we fight. The Saxons have spread their net of terror and they are tightening the noose around Cymri. My main hope is that the Saxons and Iago will clash first. King Iago is hanging on to Deva but he is surrounded. When we travelled in that part of the land there were many burnt out settlements. Mercia may be weak but, here, King Aethelfrith is growing in power."

"We have made good our losses in warriors, archers and equites. When Miach returns then he can begin to organise them. How is Prince Cadfan and his new army progressing?"

"I do not know Hogan. I would like you to visit him and take him the three horses we got from the raid. The six bigger horses, I assume would suit you eh?"

His face had lit up when he had seen what we brought. "They are perfect. There is one stallion amongst them. We can begin breeding bigger horses now."

"And the finances, Brother Oswald?"

"Trade is good. People are eager to sell to us for we pay in gold. What happens when that runs out I do not know."

"By then we should have gold from our allies. They are keen to buy weapons from us. I would have the warriors help Ralph to produce weapons from the captured arms. They can fill their time in the winter and it will build up their strength. I fear that the spring will see an offensive on all fronts."

We have to hope that King Iago attacks us and not one of our allies."

I looked at Myrddyn. He had a way of getting to the most important things quickly. He had seen what I knew neither my son nor Brother Oswald had. Our allies would be destroyed if King Iago attacked them. "What we need is to provoke King Iago into attacking us then?"

"To be precise we need him to attack Ruthin. He will see it as a weak and isolated fort. His greatest success was the ambush of Prince Pasgen and that was close to there. We need to make it appear to be unfinished and undermanned."

"But of course it will be neither."

Myrddyn smiled, "Of course. I will spend some time with Brother Oswald coming up with a plan to help us deceive the King of Gwynedd."

Chapter 11

The winter was a cold one, even on Mona which was blessed by constantly warm seas. We had had a good summer and no one starved but the ships which came to trade told us of famine in the Saxons lands, especially in the far north; in the land that had been Rheged. That was good news for it limited the Saxon's ability to go to war. On the mainland the high passes and the low passes were blocked by unusually heavy falls of snow. Prince Cadfan and his warriors were briefly cut off in their exposed fort at Nefyn. Ruthin avoided such deprivations although Aidan, the new commander of my outpost, had to ration food during the coldest spells when there was no hunting. For Myfanwy and my family it was no hardship to be trapped in our castle where we had warm fires and plenty of food. I still had time to plan and meet with my leaders and yet I could see my son and daughter changing, almost day by day.

I waited until we could see that the snow on Wyddfa had begun to melt and then I sailed with Hogan and Myrddyn to meet with Prince Cadfan. We had a built a small port close to the castle. It was really a wooden dock and a few huts but fisher folk settled there now that peace had descended upon the Llŷn Peninsula. We reached the fort in less than a morning and as I looked at the walls I was impressed by Prince Cadfan's endeavours. He strode down from the gate to greet us. He had a beaming smile upon his face. He had grown. His beard was fuller and he looked like a confident warrior and not the diffident youth who had fled to me when his life was threatened.

"Warlord," he waved a proud hand at his walls. "What do you think?"

"I think you have done well. This is now a castle that will withstand attacks." I looked at the men who were busily beavering away. "How many men do you have now?"

"Many joined us over the winter months." He smiled, "We had food and that attracted many. We now have two hundred men. Not all are warriors. Some work in my smithy others work with the boats but they are loyal to me. The horses you sent have been a godsend. They are hardy and we patrolled the coastal ways and the low mountain passes for most of the winter. It was good training. Now that the snow is going we shall try the high passes."

I nodded. "It would be prudent to communicate with your neighbours. We are all allies. We have seen your father's army and you should know that he now has archers and horses. Individually you cannot stand against him but together you can defeat him."

"I know. I am not the innocent I once was. I have learned that being a leader is more than waving a sword and acting bravely."

"Then you are well on the way to becoming a good king." I leaned in and lowered my voice. "Remember last year when the Saxons planted spies amongst my men. You need to be certain of the loyalty of your new recruits."

He smiled, "I learned that lesson when I served with you Warlord."

"I will go to Ruthin but you need to make sure that you control and watch your passes over the mountains. Your father is cunning and we know he has no blood loyalty to you." I pointed to the dock. "Your boats will be beyond his reach. If you are in danger then send to me or Pasgen."

"I will Warlord."

Prince Pasgen had now recovered from his wounds. Myrddyn insisted upon examining the leg to make sure his good work had not been undone. "How is Prince Cadfan? I rarely saw him over the winter."

"I think he was establishing his authority. Not a bad thing in one so young." When he was dressed again we walked down to the beach where I could see Mona and we could talk without being overheard. "Garth and Hogan have successfully built up our numbers again and we will be ready to go to war in summer." I paused. "If we need to. I do not seek war but I feel that King Iago will. The preparations he was making last autumn left me in no doubt that he is intending a war. It may be with the Saxons but I feel it will be with us. Ruthin will be the bait. We need to have the towers and beacons extended from here all the way to the monastery. They should be manned constantly. I need not tell you to rotate your men or they will become bored and disaffected. We need early warning or Aidan and his men will be sacrificed in vain."

"We will do so my lord." Pasgen did not look as happy as he had.

"What is the matter Prince Pasgen? You seem ill at ease with yourself."

"I still feel foolish about falling into that trap last year and I have begun to doubt myself."

"All of us make mistakes."

"It is more than that. I feel... there is something missing."

Myrddyn looked towards Wyddfa and closed his eyes. "It is some years since your family died. I think that perhaps you need a wife." We both looked in some surprise at the wizard. He shrugged. "The Warlord suffered in the same way and then he met Myfanwy. Tell me Warlord, is your life better for having met Myfanwy?"

I grinned foolishly, "He is right."

"Did it mean you loved Aideen and your dead daughter any less?"

"Of course not."

"There were many women who were left without husbands and fathers after the Saxon raids last year. Find a single one."

I could see what was bothering him. "She will not be the daughter of a king or even a noble. She will be something better, a wife. Choose wisely as I did."

There was a pause and Myrddyn chuckled, "As Myfanwy did."

Prince Pasgen laughed with him and it was the old Prince Pasgen. "True. She is a strong minded woman and she is perfect for me."

As we rode towards Ruthin I began to think about Hogan. "Hogan should be wed."

"Why? Do you wish for grandchildren?"

"He needs it for himself. I will speak with him."

"Then pray use different words to those I used on Pasgen for Hogan is different. He has yet to lose a love."

Ruthin was like the outpost of our small Empire. It felt like Castle Perilous had and I envied Aidan. I had enjoyed the isolation and the power that went with it. Aidan was one of Mungo's men who had come from Strathclyde following the Saxon invasions. He was a doughty warrior but he was also clever. He was not inclined to panic and he was popular with the men. He was a perfect choice for our furthest outpost.

We stabled the horses and, leaving Lann to look after them, the three of us walked the fort both inside and out. "Myrddyn's stream works although it freezes over in winter. We have cut back the trees still further; the timber is yonder." I spied the pile of trees which had been felled. The stone walls are half the height of a man and then the ramparts rise twice as high as a man. There is a step along the ramparts and we have holes in the walls through which we can use bows."

We climbed to the tower at the gatehouse. There was just one tower and it served both as a beacon and a place from which to watch. Myrddyn looked around and then said. "Clad the outside of the walls with the trees and cut down some more. Any enemy attacking will not know that there is stone at the base and the upper level is double thickness. You can get you men to dig river sand or get sand from the beach and pour it between the walls. It will make it more fire resistant and add to its strength. The smaller branches can be used to make shelters along the top of the wall. If Iago has archers then they can rain arrows down upon you. You need to cut down the forest all the way to the highest point of the skyline. That is your killing ground. "

I nodded my approval. Myrddyn had thought things out well. "Have you begun work on the bolt throwers? You will need one for each wall."

"No, my lord. None of my men have the skills."

I pointed to Myrddyn. "He has. Give him twenty men and he will build them."

"I will need to get the metal parts from Ralph."

"Then send a rider now. Do it and I will continue to talk with our captain here."

After Myrddyn had left I led Aidan down to his quarters. They were quite basic. "This needs improving. I will have some more comfortable chairs and a better bed sent to you. You need to be able to be happy here."

"It suits me."

"Nevertheless we will improve it. Now, how many men do you have in the warrior hall?"

"We have forty warriors, six scouts and ten archers."

"Any slingers?"

"No Warlord."

"Then I will ask for some volunteers. It is good to have young boys who can later be trained into warriors. How many of your warriors are mailed?"

"Myself and five others but all my men have helmets, shields and a spear. Most have a sword."

"Then we must hope that Iago sends some well dressed warriors and then we can improve your defences." I saw the look on his face; he was not sure if I had made a joke or not. "I will now be honest with you Aidan. I want Iago to attack you and I want him to bleed on your walls. If he attacks here then he will not be attacking Cadfan or the other kings. I intend to have Tuanthal and my son with their equites close by. You will need to signal that you are under attack and then we can catch them between you and the equites. That is why we need the trees clearing. We want open ground for the horsemen. You need to keep supplies of food and water n the fort." I pointed to the snow on nearby Wyddfa. "The snows will be melting soon. You can use the stream to fill barrels with water or perhaps build a pond inside the walls. I have attacked forts before and know that fire is their biggest enemy. With Myrddyn's improvements that will be lessened but we need it eliminating. Have your men make Roman pila. With the advantage of high walls you can rain death on the enemy."

I leaned back in my chair. I had given him much to think about. "If you need to make any other improvements then just do it. You are the captain here and I trust your judgement."

His face brightened. "Thank you Warlord." He hesitated. "Some of the men have found women. They are the refugees who settled close to the monastery. They would like to take wives…"

"That is good. If they stayed here then you would need a separate hall but it would make your men fight all the harder. It seems a good idea to me."

Once I had accepted his first idea then others poured out and I knew that I had made a wise choice for the captain of this fort. By the time I reached Caer Gybi I was feeling almost happy. All of our plans were coming to fruition. However King Iago and *wyrd* intervened to thwart the plan Myrddyn and I had intended.

The new month brought news that showed me I had no right to be complacent. A fishing boat reached me from Nefyn. Dai, Prince Cadfan's squire was on board. "Warlord the prince has sent me with dire news. An army from Gwynedd has crossed the Mawddach and is heading for King Arthlwys."

"How many?"

"It is a large army and King Iago himself is with them. They have horses and archers as well as warriors."

"Return to your prince. I will send orders for Prince Pasgen. Prince Cadfan will need to protect the Llŷn."

His back stiffened, "We will do so my lord."

"Good. I will go to my ally's aid."

I wrote orders for Prince Pasgen to begin south with thirty equites and twenty warriors. I did not wish to strip his fort of all his men. I summoned Garth and Hogan. As I watched the fishing boat leave with my message I began to plan. "Hogan, send your equites to the monastery. I promised Aidan we would be close by in case he needed help. You and Garth will come with me. We will take Miach, his archers and twenty warriors. We will sail to the king's aid. We should be able to reach him before Iago if we sail tonight."

Hogan looked surprised. "Tonight? What about horses and equites?"

"We will not be fighting on horse we will be defending the king's walls until Prince Pasgen can reach him. We will not need scouts just stout hearts."

I summoned the captain of 'The Wolf', Daffydd ap Gwynfor. "We will need both 'The Dragon' and 'The Wolf' to transport the men. I will also need you and your ships to help provide some defence for the king's settlement. The bolt throwers can keep the flanks of the fort clear."

"Yes my lord but it is the season of spring storms…"

"I know you will do your best. Now, when can we sail?"

He grinned, "When can you get aboard Warlord?"

We left after dark. Daffydd and his cousin, the captain of 'The Dragon', knew the waters well. The pharos we had built at various key headlands and rocky shores were invaluable to our sailors and enabled us to sail swiftly along our waters. We reached Ceredigion as dawn was breaking. King Arthlwys' fort was close to the shore on a high and rocky promontory. While Hogan oversaw the disembarkation of our men, Myrddyn and I hurried up to see the king.

The king looked pleased to see us but one look at our faces told him that we were the bearers of ill tidings. "Tell me Warlord, what is the danger?"

"The danger is King Iago who is hurrying towards us even as we speak."

"How do you now this?"

"Prince Cadfan's scouts saw them south of the Mawddach."

"And Tomas and the mines?"

I shrugged. "I do not know. It may well be that he has captured those too but we have not heard."

"If he has hurt my father's friend then I will rip his black heart out myself." He saw Hogan leading the men from the shore. "I see you have brought help?"

"Some archers and warriors; Prince Pasgen is bringing some equites but they are travelling over land and will take some days to get here. We need to hold King Iago until they do."

"You have done this before?"

"Yes your majesty. You need to get all of your people in the area within these walls and as much food and water as you can."

"The water is not a problem as we have a well. As for the food then we are fortunate. We traded some copper with the Empire and have some extra food as well as fine amphora and some armour."

"Good. My ships will remain offshore to help with their bolt throwers." I hesitated, "If you wished your family taken to safety…"

He smiled, "It is a kind thought but if I cannot defend my own family… my wife and daughters will stay by my side." He looked at the armed men tramping into his citadel. "I am afraid we will be a little cramped."

"These are warriors. They have their own bedding and will sort themselves out. I would advise you to send scouts out to locate the enemy. We need to know when they will arrive."

He summoned his lieutenant and a few moments' later ten young scouts on little hill ponies galloped away. I turned to the king. "How many men do you have to defend your walls?"

"There are a hundred warriors."

My heart sank. That was not enough. "Does that include all the men or is that just the warriors with weapons?"

"They are just the warriors with weapons. We have other men in the fort but they have neither shields nor armour."

"And boys?"

"Yes Warlord," he gave me a strange look, "we have boys but what can they do?"

"In my experience if you give a boy a sling or a stone he will do some damage." I turned to find Lann Aelle, "Lann, gather all the boys you can and take them to the beach. Collect as many stones as you can and find or make slingshots!"

Lann grinned and said, "Yes, Warlord." His father had led my slingers for years and Lann Aelle was deadly with the simple weapon.

"We need long poles for your men who have no armour. Iago and his men will try to climb the walls. The poles will push them away. Your ditches should be deeper but we can do little about that. Have your men sharpen stakes and bury them in the ditches with their points uppermost. Collect as many large rocks as you can and carry them to the walls. You need your women to begin boiling water."

"The women?"

"It keeps them occupied and calmer while giving us a weapon to pour upon the enemy as they climb the walls."

Soon the fort was busy with everyone doing something. I found Myrddyn. "You brought the ingredients for Greek Fire?"

"I did but we need a means to throw it and something it can ignite. It is wasted against men."

I shook my head. "It terrifies men and it will break up their shield wall. Find out if there are any men from Strathclyde with us. They can use the hammer."

"The alternative is pots. They have those for they just received a shipment from Constantinopolis. We could hurl them. It would not be as effective as a catapult or a hammer…"

"But we do what we can."

Just then there was a shout from the gate. I ran up the stairs. Three of the scouts were returning and one of them was obviously wounded. The king shouted, "Open the gate!"

"Iago is here! Get your men to the walls. It begins. Hogan, signal the ships to close with the shore."

I ran down the steps to join the king. Myrddyn was there already and he grabbed the wounded boy as soon as he came through the gate. The other two slipped from their horses. "It is King Iago. He is yonder. We were ambushed. He has captured three of the others."

The king patted them both on the head. "You have done well. Find the Warlord's squire and he will give you a sling." He shook his head. "Boys should be playing; not fighting."

"You majesty!"

We ran to join the king's lieutenant. The men of Gwynedd were filling the horizon. Four of the riders around the king detached themselves and galloped up to within a hundred paces of the walls. They hurled four objects towards us and as they rolled I saw that they were the heads of the scouts. "Captain Miach! Kill them!"

All of Miach's archers loosed at the same time and all four warriors fell dead. The men on the walls gave a cheer. The king looked angry. "So now we know who we fight! It is a monster."

They did not attack straight away. We saw their camp fires appear in a semi circle around the fort. He had learned caution. "He will fight us in the morning." We heard the sound of axes in the forest away to the east. "I think he is making a ram." He had used them against Prince Pasgen's fort. He would not know I was within the walls. I decided to keep that a secret from my enemy until I could use it to my advantage.

I hurried to speak with Miach and Myrddyn for I had a plan. We slipped out of the fort when the moon was hidden behind the clouds. There were just five of us. Miach and I watched, with bows at the ready as Myrddyn and the other two archers completed their work. When Myrddyn had finished he opened the small amphora containing the burning coal. He blew on it and his face glowed with the light. We each had five arrows with rags around the end. The rags were impregnated with a Greek Fire mixture. We could not see the Gwynedd camp but we knew it was just two hundred paces away. We were not trying to kill but we were trying to create terror. While Myrddyn scurried back to the fort we each released our fire arrows. They lit up the night sky like shooting stars. We did not wait to see the results but hurried back to the safety of the fort. We heard the screams and the pandemonium as the archers' fire arrows flashed down on the camp.

We had reached the security of the fort and were standing at the gate when Iago's men appeared four hundred paces from the fort. I turned to the king's lieutenant, "I think that your men can just watch now, Afon, they will be wondering if we will attack again. As for me, my bed awaits."

Afon grinned, "Yes my lord."

Despite my statement that I was ready for a good night's sleep, I was still armed and ready for war before dawn. Lann Aelle had sharpened my sword the day before. He had been annoyed that he had not been selected for the raid but he kept that to himself. I knew it from the sour look on his face. He had had the same look in Constantinopolis when he had tasted his first lemon. "Why did you take the risk, Warlord? Sixteen arrows cannot harm them."

I smiled as he fitted my baldric, "True Lann but they were deprived of a good night's sleep and tonight they will have extra guards out in case we try that again. Sixteen arrows is a small price to pay. Now today I want you to direct the slingers. You know how to use them and there is no-one else for me to trust."

He was torn between the honour of being chosen to lead a section of the army and with the displeasure at not being at my side. "But the Wolf Banner my lord…"

"We will not be using it today. I want King Iago to think I am still on my way."

Satisfied that his honour was intact he nodded. "Can we hold out my lord?"

"Today? Yes. The days which follow? That depends upon the resolve of the men of Ceredigion. They have not fought King Iago yet and they do not know what a cunning warrior he is. We shall see."

By the time the dawn broke we were on the walls having eaten and prepared ourselves for combat. Many of the men of Ceredigion were Christians and their priests had made the sign of the cross over them. It seemed to comfort them. A wall of shields slowly appeared from the dell in which Iago's army had sheltered. He had a long shield wall and there were no gaps. They approached slowly, he had learned from his rough handling the last time we had met. I could see two bands of horsemen on each flank. He had anticipated a few horsemen on our side and was ready to negate their effect. From our lofty standpoint I could see the archers behind the shield wall. Had we had all of my archers then we could have slaughtered them. As it was we only had Miach's twenty and a handful belonging to the king.

The enemy halted four hundred paces from the walls. We had placed markers every one hundred paces. They were white rocks we had collected from the beach. They would enable me to decide the best time for my slingers and archers to begin their attacks. Suddenly a group of lightly armoured warriors with shields raced forwards to the ditch. I nodded to Miach. His archers began aiming at the men but they had chosen small men and given them large shields to make it harder for us to hit them. Even so, six fell before they reached the ditch and three as they returned to their lines.

"Why did he waste those men Warlord?"

"He has fought me before and they were looking at the ditch to see how deep it is and if there are traps. He will be satisfied. My ditches are steeper on one side than the other. He knows his men can extricate themselves from these ditches if they fall in."

The approach of the warriors was both slow and measured. I could only see forty horsemen waiting on the wings which meant he had others somewhere else. My guess was that they were guarding the road as scouts watching for me to come down from Nefyn or Mona. It was a sound idea for it would give him ample warning of an attack. When the shield wall was one hundred and fifty paces from the ramparts and the ditch they halted. I saw the archers move closer to the shields to take advantage of their protection.

"Ready Lann? Now!"

Lann's slingers were safely below the ramparts and they could throw blind. They had plenty of stones and all they needed to do was keep up a constant rain of missiles. Lann was next to me so that he could correct their aim.

"Throw!" One hundred keen boys loosed their stones just as the archers were drawing back to loose their arrows. Inevitably some of the stones hit home. Our men and archers were taking refuge behind the ramparts. Our turn would come soon. The boys kept releasing stone after stone. They had that energy which comes from being young. Soon Lann was directing their throws so that the archers and the warriors were taking many hits on their helmets and shields. The arrows they loosed landed in the walls or on the roofs of the buildings. The space behind the boys was littered with spent arrows; arrows which we could re-use. Had Iago been a better archer he could have ordered a steeper trajectory to rain down on my men and boys but he was not an archer.

"It is time. Miach!"

My grizzled captain of archers nodded and roared, "Archers! Rise and loose!" Although the men of Ceredigion just loosed anywhere, Miach's trained archers aimed at the enemy archers. With the advantage of height and their skill, added to the rain of stones, they soon began to whittle down the numbers of archers. It was not long until they withdrew to the safety of their dell. I counted fifteen bodies and I had seen many warriors being carried wounded, from the field.

Micah ordered his men to collect the spent arrows. I turned to the slingers. "Well done boys! You drove them from the walls."

The king shook his head. "I would never have thought to use the boys."

"They are your future your majesty. The skills they are learning can be used to make them archers or warriors when they get older. They learn to obey orders and to help each other."

He nodded. "I can see that now. What will he do next?"

"He still has his ram. He hoped to thin our numbers on the wall for attacking with a ram is expensive in men. He may try something else, let us see."

The morning went by without another attack. As the sun rose in the sky his men appeared again but this time they were spread out and in three groups. He was intending an attack on three sides. This would lessen the effect of both our archers and slingers.

"Every man who has no shield, get himself to the warrior hall." I turned to Lann, "We may have to withdraw the boys. If they are struck then take them to the warrior hall." He started to open his mouth. "That is an order. I want no boy hurt. Clear?"

"Yes Warlord."

"Miach split your men into two groups; one on the north wall and one on the south. Let him think he has weakened this wall."

The slingers threw their stones and they were effective but with arrows coming from three directions it was merely a matter of time before one got hurt. When the first boys screamed in pain I nodded to Lann who raced from the wall. "Slingers! To me!"

Once the rain of stones ceased the shield wall moved forwards. The men of Ceredigion loosed arrow after arrow but they did not strike as many as Miach's smaller numbers did. The men of Gwynedd reached the ditch. "Now Garth!"

Garth and his men had the Roman pila. They hurled them at the shield wall as it began to edge into the ditch which they knew was filled with traps. The spears hit the shields and the soft metal broke. The shields began to droop. I turned to the Ceredigion archers. "Aim at the warriors!"

As their arrows hit unprotected flesh and thundered into shields, warriors fell into the ditch and screamed as they struck the hidden stakes. It was not all going our way as their archers began to pick off our men on the walls. Some of the warriors made it to the wall and I heard their axes as they began hacking at the wooden logs. Unlike our forts the lower levels were not stone but timber.

"Use the rocks!"

The large rocks collected from the beach began to crash down on the warriors who had crossed the ditch. Their helmets could not protect them and they began to die. The survivors could see that they had no chance of completing their task and they gradually withdrew. As the afternoon drifted towards dusk the attack petered out. The men of Ceredigion gave a cheer but I knew that we had not won. The walls had been weakened. When they used the ram it would be destroyed. If they repeated their attack the next day then we would be in trouble.

Chapter 12

As night fell Myrddyn saw to the casualties. We had lost eight men dead and many others wounded. The slinger had an arrow in his leg but Myrddyn's magic saved both his leg and his life. We did, at least, have hot food and that meant much. Men sat with their wives and tried to behave as though this was normal. As soon as it became completely dark I sent Garth's men out to collect the arms and armour of the dead. Miach's men collected arrows and broken pila. We could still use them as javelins.

I ate with the king. "I would that I could fight with Iago man to man and end this. My people should not suffer so."

"Iago will not do that. He has many men and he sees an empire in his future. He would rule the whole of Cymri. He believes that he can beat the Saxons."

"Can he?"

"No. He was lucky when he took Deva the first time for the Saxon army had come to defeat me. Their king will retake Deva when he chooses to. He has had to contend with famine and internal dissension. That will soon end. He will then sweep all before him for he also has ambitions to rule Cymri. His land goes from north of the Roman Wall to the Dee and from this sea to the sea of the Saxons. He has many men he can call upon. He is not a weak king like the king of Mercia; he is the most powerful Saxon king in the land and is not to be underestimated."

"But you have defeated him."

"Yes, your majesty, but the last time he came perilously close to beating us. I will fight him again but when I choose."

As well as retrieving the arms Garth and the men threw the dead to the other side of the ditch. The enemy would either have to remove them or clamber over their decaying corpses. In war you used every strategy you could. Hogan came to me as I stood with Myrddyn on the ramparts. "Warlord, why have you brought me here? I am a horseman. Miach and Myrddyn have their uses but I feel useless."

"I have brought you here so that you can learn how to fight from within a castle. Remember, my son, I am training you to be my successor."

Myrddyn nodded, "Your father learned how to resist at Castle Perilous. You do not have that luxury besides there are others who can lead the equites. You have to ask yourself the question will you be a horseman or a leader. Your father no long fights in the shield wall. He had to make his choice as you will have to do."

Hogan shrugged his shoulders in reluctant acceptance. I sympathised with him. I had wanted to be where the fighting was the hardest but, like me, he had to learn to take the responsibility of leadership.

The next morning saw a repeat of the previous day. From King Iago's perspective he was doing better than he had the last time we had fought. His casualties, although heavier than ours, were far lighter than he could have expected. I watched, with Hogan and the king from the top of the gatehouse. We saw the ram first. Iago had the benefit, this time, of a slope. It meant his men just had to gather momentum and the ram would strike the gate. I summoned Miach. "The north wall will have to do without your archers. Hogan, take command there and take some of these archers with you." He eagerly raced off to do my bidding with the Ceredigion archers behind him. The arrows from the enemy were annoying rather than dangerous. We held our mighty shields at an angle although an occasional arrow got through and pinged off our helmets.

"Miach, get the fire pot here and have your archers target those men pulling the ram."

The king looked at the ram which seemed to be enormous. The men pulling it were below the top of the ram. It must have taken a great deal of effort to get it to the top of the slight rise but now it moved easily. Miach's archers were at maximum range but they still scored hits. Some of them were not mortal but they still slowed it down. My intention was not to stop it but to slow it down and allow us to kill more of his strongest warriors. The enemy archers took the opportunity of loosing without fear of retaliation as our archers tried to whittle down the warriors. We were taking casualties; not amongst my heavier armoured men but the lightly protected men of Ceredigion.

"Myrddyn, this is your idea, you give the orders to Miach and his men."
"I am ready."

The ram reached the point where the weight of the ram allowed it to move much quicker. The men who had reached the ditch had thrown the corpses of their comrades into it. They had no drawbridge and the ram could easily trundle over the wooden bridge which allowed access into the fort.

Myrddyn shouted, "Now, the bridge!"

Miach's flaming arrow hit the pot of Greek Fire concealed beneath the bridge. A wall of flame shot into the air. The bridge was tinder dry and began to burn fiercely. The men on the ram tried to slow down the huge log as it threatened to deviate from its course. I could see their intention. They were gambling on the fact that it would fly across the bridge and strike the gate.

"Now the other pots!"

Miach and his men loosed four arrows in quick succession. The four pots hidden by the side of the track, next to the ram, all ignited at once. It was like an explosion and the men pulling it were either killed or knocked over by the force. The fiendish flames took hold of the ram and it began to burn. It was such a large ram that it would take a day to destroy but it was on fire and, more importantly, it was travelling at a slight angle to the bridge. Myrddyn had placed rocks there to accentuate any deviation and the ram's front wheel tipped off the bridge. It was heavy and the sheer weight of it took it onto its side in the ditch. The bridge and the ram were on fire, effectively preventing anyone from using the front gate.

I heard the sound of voices calling the warriors back to the rise. This attack was over. Just then Lann came running over. "My lord, we need you and Myrddyn, your son has been wounded."

My heart sank but I was Warlord and I was needed here directing the defence. "Myrddyn, see to my son."

I steeled myself to look out on the battlefield. Trying to work out my enemy's next move helped me to take the thought of Hogan dying from my mind. I saw that Iago had formed his shield wall facing us again but it was at the top of the rise. Why was that? He was too far away to launch a quick attack. The inferno in the middle meant he would find it difficult to attack. The only benefit was that it shielded his rear from our eyes.

"Miach put your men on the north and south walls. Lann get the slingers and position them behind the north and south walls. Garth, take charge of the south wall." I turned to the king. I think he is going to send his men and attack where we are weakest, the north and south walls. If you keep a few warriors here in case I am wrong I will take charge of the north wall."

By the time I reached it Hogan had been taken away and Miach rubbed his beard. "It seems you are getting the second sight of Myrddyn my lord. They are here."

I could see that they had attacked strongly before and there were many casualties. Had I not brought reinforcements things might have gone badly for them. The attack was in strength. They still might prevail but, as I drew Saxon Slayer, I was determined they would not. "Slingers on my command loose and keep loosing until you have no ammunition left!" I turned and saw their eager faces and their slings at the ready. "Loose!"

The stones and pebbles crashed down like hail and cracked against the armour and shields. I did not expect many casualties but I wanted their shields up. Out at sea 'The Wolf' was edging closer in and the two bolt throwers at the front were ready. I dropped my sword and there was the sound of rushing wind as two bolts hurtled towards the eager Gwynedd warriors. Their shields might have given them some protection but they were being held aloft protecting their heads and the two bolts took out twenty warriors. In the confusion Miach and his archers chose the leaders and picked them off one by one. The third and fourth bolts caused a panic. Some ran towards the walls and some ran away.

"Ready at the wall!"

There were still more than enough of them to scale the walls and we were perilously short of mailed warriors. I swung Saxon Slayer at the first hands that grasped the top of the walls. I sliced through them both and heard the warrior's screams followed by the thud as he hit the ground. "Don't let them reach the top!"

Miach showed me his empty quiver. "We are out of arrows my lord but look! They fall back."

A messenger came from the king. "His majesty says they have retreated from the front of the fort."

Was he up to something? "Take charge and watch them, Miach. I will investigate."

When I reached the gate I could see that it was true. Iago had gone. He had been so close and yet he had fled. Miach shouted from the north wall. "It is Prince Pasgen, the equites are here!"

So that was it. Iago had been warned by his scouts that relief was at hand. We had survived again. Although many brave men had died for Iago he had not lost and he had more men under his command. He had shown guile and nearly beaten us. King Arthlwys put his hand on my shoulder. "Well done, Warlord. You have prevailed, now go to your son and I will take charge of my own castle eh?"

Lann was at the foot of the stairs with his slingers and he was praising them. He saw me and the question on my face. "Come with me Warlord and I will take your to your son."

Part of the warrior hall had been turned into a safe place for the wounded. Wives were tending their husbands. I saw Myrddyn and two young women and headed for them. He saw me coming and came towards me. "He lives Warlord. He was struck a blow on the head and he is unconscious but he will live. His heart beats strongly and I felt no breaks in his skull. He has broken his left wrist but the Allfather was watching over him and I was able to set it while he was in the dream world. He will still be able to hold a shield." He looked at me. "You need rest too."

"I must go to Hogan."

"No, my lord. He is in safe hands. That is Morag, the king's eldest daughter and her servant. They are better medicine for him believe me. They will stay with him until he wakes and I think he will appreciate their pretty faces rather than yours or mine eh? Come my friend, we need rest too. We are no longer young men."

Myrddyn rarely called me friend and yet that was what he was. When he did so I listened and I did suddenly feel tired. It would take Prince Pasgen some time to make his way into the fort and the rest of the captains had plenty of work to do. I nodded, "Very well, wizard, work your magic."

I went to the rooms I was using and, amazingly, fell asleep as soon as I lay down. Myrddyn woke me and I could see from the candle in his hand that it was night time. "Warlord, Prince Pasgen is here and the king awaits you."

"You should have woken me!"

He smiled, "You were tired and there was nothing to do." He saw the question on my lips and said, "Hogan awoke, took some water, spoke with Morag and then went back to sleep."

The hall seemed bright after the dimly lit chamber. As I walked in they all banged the table and chanted, "Warlord!" over and over. I held up my hand for silence.

Myrddyn whispered, "They see this as a great victory. King Iago fled."

I snorted, "He retreated, and he did not flee."

"Do not disparage their efforts Warlord. They believe they have done well and they have."

I sighed. He was right, as usual. "Very well. I shall smile and pretend that it was a victory."

The king had left a space for me next to him. "Sit here, Warlord, Prince Pasgen can sit on your other side. He has much to say to you."

We sat and a hurriedly prepared feast was brought in. I suspected that they had quickly cooked all the meat and fish which was about to go off but I feigned enjoyment. "So Warlord I know that we have much to learn from you. I would have you advise us so that if King Iago dares to try this again we will not need your help."

Although I knew it would be some time before the men of Ceredigion could take on King Iago I was pleased that the king had seen that all was not well. "You have much stone around the coast. Use it to make your lower levels of stone. Build towers and have at least two ditches with a drawbridge over. The bolt throwers we use would give you an advantage but you would need skilled men to operate them. It is probably better if you provide mail for your warriors and keep your men well trained."

"That is quite a list but you have given my people the appetite for it." He smiled, "I was pestered by the young slingers, all of whom wish to be warriors like your squire. He has made quite an impact."

"He is a good nephew and a better warrior."

"And your son is well looked after." He gave me a thoughtful look, "Morag is quite taken with him. They are both of an age." He added knowingly.

I had not thought of that. Could it be so simple? *Wyrd.*

"Warlord?"

Prince Pasgen had barely touched his food. "Yes Prince Pasgen, forgive my inattention. You did well today."

"No, I did badly! We were spotted by the scouts they had on the road and we wasted time putting on armour. Had we engaged them then Iago would not have been able to flee."

"And you would have had to change into armour to reap any benefit from that." I shook my head. "It is my fault. I knew there was a problem with heavily armoured men. I should have encouraged you all to use more scouts and lightly armoured men to support you. I saw, when I campaigned with Hogan that the equite is a shock weapon but is easily tired. I think we need to keep the numbers of equites to what they are now but add lighter horsemen who can find and engage the enemy until the equites can destroy them."

He looked relieved. "I thought that I had failed you again."

"No Prince Pasgen. We need to evolve. The enemy are learning from us and use horsemen. We need to do the same and adapt. Prince Cadfan is the model we shall use. He has many lightly armed men in the mountains and scouts. They are cheap to arm and cheap to train and maintain. We are moving into a new world Pasgen. The world of Rome is gone and we move into the world of the Saxon. If we want to survive we must be quicker at change than the others."

I was restless that night; part of it was the sleep I had had after the battle and part of it was what I had said to the king and the prince. Could we win? A year ago I had been confident that, with the Emperor's help we could turn back the tide. I now saw that I had been dreaming. Rome was using me and there would be no help coming from that quarter. Whatever we did would be by our own devices. I went to the gatehouse and climbed to the ramparts. The guards nodded and smiled as I climbed and then gave me the space I needed. I looked to the pile of Gwynedd corpses, still burning on the pyre we had built. The pyre for the fallen of Ceredigion would be lit on the morrow when the proper rituals had been observed. I sensed a presence and I looked around; there was Myrddyn.

"Restless, Warlord?"

"I am trying to work out how we can defeat all these enemies. Will we be forever burning our own dead outside our forts?"

Myrddyn closed his eyes, almost as though he was in a trance. He was facing Cader Idris. "I think Warlord," he said after a long silence, "that you have hit upon the strategy almost by accident. Or perhaps it is the Allfather and *wyrd* at work."

"Explain yourself. Perhaps I am still tired but I do not understand."

"Mona has not been touched by an enemy for over a year now. Even Prince Pasgen's fort has been untouched. Your forts at Nefyn and Ruthin are the future. You control the ways into the land and keep the enemy at bay. If we had a fort close to the monastery then the Dee estuary could be controlled. You have come up with a brilliant strategy. Use small groups of warriors in well planned forts and stop the deprivations of our enemies."

"But how do we defeat them?"

"You think that because the field is not littered with Iago's dead we did not win. "I looked at the bodies as they were burned. These were his best warriors. We know that you cannot replace the best quickly. We make our enemies bleed on our defences and then we use our small but deadly army to defeat them on the field of battle and increase our land, little by little."

"So I will not see the victory."

"Oh I am sorry; I did not know that you were doing this for yourself. I thought that you were carrying out an oath made to King Urien to be Warlord."

It hit me then and he was right. This was not about me, this was about my land. My son Hogan, or his son, might be the one to achieve victory. My task was to make his task easier. "Thank you old friend. I can see now. The world is clearer."

"And tomorrow we can see Hogan who will be awake. I have a feeling that his life has changed too."

"Morag?"

"Morag." *Wyrd*!

When we found Hogan he was walking, somewhat gingerly, on the arm of the princess of Ceredigion. It was the first time I had seen her face and she was beautiful. The king was wrong, she was younger than Hogan but that was as it should be. I did not need anyone to tell me that they were both smitten; they only had eyes for each other. I had to cough to get their attention.

"Father, sorry. This is Morag and she has been looking after me."

"Thank you, Morag. You are most kind, I am indebted to you. Myrddyn said the wrist should heal well."

"But he cannot leave yet. He must recover!"

"I think, Princess Morag, that Hogan has a home on Mona where he can be looked after just as well as here."

I could see the distress on their faces. Hogan suddenly blurted, "But I could advise the king on his defences and his army while I recover. That would free you up to return to Mona."

I was impressed by his quick thinking. "Well," I said slowly, "I will have to speak with the king about this. Perhaps he wants the Warlord and not the Warlord's son."

"Oh no, I am sure that my father would rather have Hogan than…" she suddenly realised what she had said and she fled the room.

I could not contain my laughter. Hogan looked cross. "That was cruel father. Can I stay?"

"Just so long as you are honest with me and tell me the real reason."

He looked me straight in the eye. "I intend to marry Morag and I will woo her and ask her father for her hand."

"In which case, you may stay. I prefer honesty, especially from my son. I forgive you for you were in the east longer than I was and it has affected you more. But no more deceptions between us; the truth."

He clasped my arm with his good arm, "The truth!"

"And please consult Myfanwy about the wedding day or I shall never hear the end of it."

He laughed. "You have my word."

Now that I had my plan I needed to have more of my warriors on the frontier. Prince Pasgen, his horses and his armour were sent home first. We would march to the mines and check on the safety of Tomas and his miners. The king had wanted to go but we both knew he needed to bring his defences up to the standard we wanted. As I pointed out to him our ships could pick us up after dropping off Prince Pasgen. It would save time for all concerned.

I summoned Lann Aelle. "Lann I would like you to stay here until Hogan is fit to travel. He will need a squire and there is none better than you."

I could see that he was torn. The praise made him swell with pride but he did not want to be left behind. "Could not someone else do that my lord? He will not need arming while he is here."

"There is another task I would ask you to complete for me. Train up the slingers and find someone amongst them who can lead them."

This time I thought that he would burst from his armour. "Me? You wish me to appoint a leader?"

"The king is happy to go on along with whoever you select. He was impressed with the way you conducted yourself during the siege."

He nodded, "I will do it Warlord and I will make them the best slingers in the land."

"Good."

Saying goodbye to Hogan was easier. He was smitten. "I am leaving Lann Aelle to train the slingers and to assist you." He nodded as though he had not been listening. "Do not overstay your injury." I spoke harshly to jar him from his reverie. He suddenly stared at me. "Ask for Morag's hand by all means. Arrange the marriage but we need you if my plans and those of Myrddyn are to be put into place."

He smiled and grasped my hand. "I understand and as soon as I am able I will return."

"Good. I will send 'The Dragon' back to wait for you. I would be unhappy if she was here for more than a few days."

He grinned. He had understood the implication. "That is all the time that I will need."

As we tramped along the coast to the Mawddach, Myrddyn looked at me ruefully. "We could have retained a couple of Pasgen's horses. It is many years since I walked this far."

"Is this the wizard who walked from Mona to Rheged, alone to be with the Wolf Warrior? You are getting old and soft Myrddyn. It will do you good." Privately I agreed with my wizard. We were getting too old for all this walking but the warriors were listening and I knew that they approved my words. One of Garth's men carried the furled Wolf Banner. We had not needed it at the siege and I still wished it a secret that I was here. I could not give anyone a reason but in my heart I wished it so.

We had scouts out on the flanks just in case Iago had not gone all the way home. It was not a quick journey but it did allow Myrddyn and me to talk with Garth about out plans for the future. By the time we reached the Mawddach I was happier about what we intended. Once we crossed the river I began to see the work that Tomas and his miners had done. They had cut a road up to the mines but they had made it twist and turn. It gave them many opportunities to attack someone coming up the road. I could see a tower quite high up the hillside and there were men on guard. They waved as they recognised us. I left Garth with most of the men and took Myrddyn and eight warriors with me up the steep slope. It was a gruelling walk. I could see that at every turn there was a small wall of rocks. When we reached the mine, which was below the tower it was obvious that Tomas and his men had spent as much time constructing the defences as they had mining. There were walls and gates as well as traps.

Tomas strode out to meet us. He waved an expansive hand at the fort. "Well Warlord, what do you think?"

"I think it is quite impressive. You have done well."

"Coming from you I take that as a compliment. We had finished it none too soon for King Iago sent some scouts along to investigate." He grinned. "One escaped but the rest died."

That explained much. "Did the king not come close then?"

"I do not know. Our tower can see far and we saw you when you crossed the river but upstream is more difficult. We did see warriors but I know not if the king was with them."

Myrddyn and I told him of the battle and how King Iago had retreated. "You had better make sure you keep your defences up. They may come back here for some retribution."

Tomas laughed, "Aye well we have a little surprise for anyone foolish enough to attack us." He led us along a path which descended from the mine. There we saw all the waste from the workings. It was held in place by a log. "When we finish digging we put the spoil here. If anyone comes we release the log and all this lovely rock sweeps them into the Mawddach."

Myrddyn laughed, "Oh how sweet! That is the trick that Iago played on us. "He looked at me and nodded. "It will work Warlord and it is so simple."

"I have to say that I am relieved I did not like the idea of you being so isolated here with the gold and the copper. It is a tempting target for our enemy."

"And not just gold and copper. Come with me." He took us into the stone building they had constructed as a place to sleep and work. He took down a leather bag and removed some blue looking rocks. "We have these too."

"What are they?"

Myrddyn picked one up. "This is an amethyst. It is a precious stone, not as valuable as rubies, emeralds or diamonds but valuable nonetheless. The Romans believed that a ring or bracelet using these would stop a person becoming drunk. Nonsense of course but polished up they would easily decorate a sword hilt or a necklace. Well done Tomas."

He counted out five of them and placed them in my palm. "I would like you to have them Warlord, they are from my share, not the king's and they are a thank you for your aid."

"I cannot accept these Tomas."

"I have no family my lord and I would be honoured if you would take them."

Myrddyn inclined his head. "These are taken from the Mother and, while they might not stop someone becoming drunk, they have an innate power. Five is a mystical number; you must take them my lord. It is *wyrd*."

When Myrddyn spoke like that you had to obey. He understood the earth and the way it worked far better than I did. "Then I thank you for the gift Tomas and I shall cherish them."

We returned down the mountain and I felt strangely at peace. When we reached the river I took out the stones again and rinsed them in the icy waters of the Mawddach. As I did so I could see the blue sparkling beneath the rough stone and I suddenly saw the beauty in them.

"Do we have someone who can make them as beautiful as they should be?"

"Yes Warlord! Me!"

Chapter 13

Myrddyn's new task had to wait until I had met with all of my leaders. We sent 'The Wolf' back to Caer Gybi for Ridwyn and Brother Oswald. The rest of the garrison was experienced enough to manage without them for a day. 'The Dragon' was still waiting for Hogan. If he did not arrive then he would miss out on the planning and the decision making. I sent for Prince Cadfan as he was vital to my plans. I left Aidan at Ruthin. I could not afford for the commander of such a valuable fort to be away for any length of time.

While I waited I listened to the leaders who were there. Mungo appeared to be a little bored with the lack of activity. "You mean you wish for war? I thought you brought your people here for peace?"

He laughed, "Aye Warlord, peace for them but not for me. I was made for war."

"I think I can promise you that. And you Prince Pasgen, what have you to report?"

"I have come to see that we are not as swift as we might be. When we travelled to Ceredigion we spent most of the journey without armour and yet our heavier horses were still not swift enough."

I had thought of that myself. "I think I have a solution to that problem but it will not be cheap."

"I am intrigued. Can you not tell me more?"

"No I will wait until Tuanthal and Pol arrive. I would like Hogan to be here but that depends upon other things."

He gave me a puzzled look. "Warlord?"

I held my hand up. "When he arrives then we can speak. It is nothing of a military nature; I can tell you that."

Myrddyn was by my side the whole time but he kept rolling something around in his hands. "What are you doing wizard?"

"Until we have held the meeting I cannot start work on the stones and so I am rolling them around in my hand and allowing them to rub the rough surfaces away." He smiled, "It is strangely therapeutic. A little like when we were being massaged in the Emperor Phocas' baths. And it makes the stones become jewels." He could be enigmatic when he chose to be.

It was dusk when 'The Wolf' reached us. It arrived shortly after Pol and Tuanthal and their men had finally arrived. Ridwyn looked nonplussed. "Brother Oswald and I wondered why we were deserting your wife and family, Warlord. This seems so unusual."

"It is Ridwyn but I believe that it is necessary and besides are you worried that the men you trained and you lead cannot look after my castle?"

He grinned. "If you put it that way Warlord then they are safe as anywhere."

Pasgen had had a table which was round and enabled us all to speak with each other. It seated twenty one. When I had asked him about that he said that he had consulted Myrddyn about numbers. He had been told that seven and three were magical. By multiplying them together he had arrived at a number which should have been even more powerful. I could not argue with the logic. He said he had the idea from the oval table I used at Castle Cam. Here he had plenty of timber and plenty of room.

I first brought them all up to date with what had happened. Myrddyn said nothing and just rolled his stones together. "This has made me realise a number of things. Mungo's Burg and this fort have too many men. We now have frontiers at Nefyn and Ruthin. We will move some of the excess troops there. They will give us warning of any attack. We can use this fort to act as a garrison. We can train new troops here and have a strike force to get to any part of the frontier where there will be an emergency. We do need, however, another fort. I have spoken with Bishop Stephen and Myrddyn. There is a good site at Rhuddlan. It is a mile from the sea and from the monastery. It is on the Clwyd and there is a hill ready made for a fort. It means that we could control the whole of the Clwyd. As we know from Ruthin, warriors can get over the passes but it is a long and dangerous journey and we would have warning. Prince Cadfan's scouts know the land well and are an excellent early warning for us. With Nefyn controlling the Llŷn and two forts on the Clwyd then the rest of our castles are safe."

I paused, partly to take a drink from my beaker and partly to look at their reactions. So far there appeared to be no negative looks or comments. Myrddyn gave me a subtle nod of approval. He was not divining any negativity either. "Now let us move on to specifics. It has become obvious to me and to Prince Pasgen that the equites are not as effective as they might be. "I saw Pol begin to rise and Tuanthal, smiling, restrained him gently. "Even my son Hogan has seen weakness. We cannot use them as cavalry. They are too heavy we need them as a shock force and for that we have enough of them. We will never have more than sixty from now on." That was a shock for them and there was much restless movement. "Allow me to elaborate and then criticise, you know I welcome open discussions." They relaxed and sat back. "Every equite is to be given another, lighter horse and a squire who will be mounted too. This effectively doubles our horsemen. The lighter horse would enable them to travel much faster than on the heavier mounts and Cataphractoi mounts would last longer in battle. The squires would be as Lann Aelle is and Pol was. Not boys but young men who wish to be equites. The equite will train them and the scout will aid them. When we fight the squires will be armed with a spear and a shield. They will wear a helmet but that is all. We have seen the enemy's attempts at horsemen and they are poor. They will improve. I believe that our new system will be more effective."

I paused again and this time Pol asked, "Could the squires be given bows? It would make them even more effective."

"You think the idea would work then?"

"I think the idea is genius." He nodded towards Myrddyn.

Myrddyn smiled, "Thank you for the compliment Pol but the idea was the Warlord's."

"It means that if we keep the idea of three columns we would have forty in each rather than twenty and we could cover a greater range."

"Yes, Tuanthal, and they would be based here. This would be where we house all of our horsemen. Garth, you will command here with my fifty best warriors. You would train new warriors and decide where the warriors and the equites needed to be sent. I envisage that two of the three columns will patrol for seven days at a time. One would leave and travel north to Rhuddlan and then Ruthin. After three days the second one would travel south to Nefyn and the Mawddach. When the first patrol returned the second would patrol Rhuddlan and Ruthin when the second returned… well you get the idea."

"I like that. It would stop the equites becoming bored with the same patrol and we would all have one week rest."

"Yes Tuanthal but I foresee a problem. What happens if they do find trouble? One patrol will be too far away to help and the second will have just returned from a patrol and be tired."

"That Prince Pasgen is a problem that you, Tuanthal, Pol and my son will need to work out. I am no equite. If this was Garth who was talking I would tell him that his warriors would have to suffer and get on with it. I realise that equites and their horses are different from my warriors." There was sarcasm and a rebuke in my tone and it had the desired effect.

Pasgen blushed, "Sorry, Warlord, you are quite right, we will solve the problem."

"Now as to Rhuddlan; we will take every warrior we have available there in the next couple of days and begin the building. It will take that long to reorganise the garrisons. Mungo you will command there."

"What of Mungo Burg and Castle Cam, Warlord? Will we strip them of all warriors?"

"No, we will only be taking the best fifty warriors. I want a garrison of forty warriors and ten archers in each of the three forts we have. With the fifty warriors of my oathsworn here it gives us a total of one hundred and fiftyy men who can go to Ruthin, or Nefyn or Rhuddlan if needs be."

"I wondered when you would get around to the archers."

"Yes Miach, I want your son to command the archers at Rhuddlan and you will be here with Garth training the new archers and slingers. Once we have moved the excess warriors from the forts then we will know how many can man Rhuddlan and Ruthin. If a man has a family I would prefer he stay at

Mungo Burg or castle Cam. A man fights harder for his family. Use the single men for the frontier forts."

There was silence as they took it all in. We all became aware of the rocks rolling in Myrddyn's hand. "What in the name of the Allfather are you doing wizard?"

He smiled enigmatically, "I am making precious stones for the Warlord."

I almost laughed as they all nodded. It was as though the wizard could do anything that he desired.

Aedh asked, "And my scouts? What of them?"

"You have twenty now?" He nodded, "You need forty. Ten will operate from the three frontier forts and you will have ten here for you to use as you see fit. We will call each ten a contubernium; the Romans used that as an idea and I like it. We read about it when we were at Constantinopolis. Promote your best scouts to lead each contubernium for they will be the eyes and the ears of the army."

"And my army Warlord? You have barely mentioned my men."

"That is, because, Prince Cadfan, I do not command your men. When you become king you will be an ally but I can only advise."

He smiled, "Then what would you advise?"

"I think you concentrate on training men who can fight in the mountains. You will need some mailed warriors like my oathsworn but few as yet. It will be through others that you gain the throne unless we have many desertions from the enemy. I would urge all of you to take prisoners from the men of Gwynedd. They can be offered service with the prince or slavery. You will also need archers but they can be trained here. Any of your warriors can be trained here."

"Are you bearing the expense?"

"Are we Brother Oswald?"

The cleric had listened carefully. "The treasury is healthy my lord and if all works as you describe it then we will become richer."

"I want our smiths to produce weapons for us to sell to our allies. At the moment Prince Cadfan, you have no revenue," I grinned, "when you do then we will ask you to pay for your weapons."

Just then the doors burst open and Hogan stood there with Lann Aelle behind him. "I came as soon as I could. What have I missed?"

Pol laughed and said wryly, "Everything!"

Hogan looked perplexed. "Come and join us, son." Lann Aelle stood looking uncomfortable. "You too, nephew. You are my squire and we have no secrets." I looked at my leaders. "Let me see how well you were listening young Pol. Tell Hogan what our plans are and we will tell you if you are right."

The smile was wiped from his face but he took his medicine, stood and began to tell Hogan of the plans. They were reasonably accurate although Tuanthal had to correct him twice.

"Well done Pol. Now son, is there anything in those plans that you object to? Now is the time to speak."

We all looked at him as he rose and looked at us with a serious expression on his face. "No, I am quite happy to be based here but I am afraid that the accommodation will not do. I am not going to share a chamber with Pol or Tuanthal. I want somewhere building for me."

The looks of happiness on the faces of his friends were wiped off in an instant and the others stared at Hogan. His rudeness was out of character.

"How have we offended you, Lord Hogan?"

Hogan smiled, with a twinkle in his eye, "Oh you haven't but I don't think my new bride to be, the Princess Morag would be happy to share a room with both of us!"

Although it was not the way I would have broken the news it was an effective way of ending the meeting with a celebration. Prince Pasgen sent for some of the good wine and we all toasted my son. "And now," I added, "I would like an oath." They all looked shocked. "No-one mentions this until Hogan has told my wife. If she finds out we all knew first then my life will be a misery!"

We left Myrddyn, Garth and Oswald to oversee the new fort while we returned to Castle Cam to break the news. Once on board I asked Hogan about the king's reaction to his proposal.

"He was overjoyed father. I think he likes me." He shrugged, almost apologetically, and I think he likes being related to you. He feels safer somehow."

"I am happy too, for whatever that is worth. When will the wedding take place?"

"Morag's mother is a Christian and she would like it at Yule. It is a holy time."

I was relieved. That suited me. It was some months away and I would not be distracted from my major reorganisation of the army. "I take it the wedding will be in Ceredigion?"

"Yes. Is that a problem?"

"I don't think so. We will ask Myfanwy."

Myfanwy, of course was delighted. Women like weddings. Nanna, who was becoming more of a young girl than a child, was also delighted that there would be a wedding. Hogan was subjected to a torrent of questions. When he finally escaped I sat with Myfanwy in my arms and told her of my plans for the land.

Unlike my leaders she had concerns. "Will we be safe here? What if the Hibernians come again?"

"We will strengthen the defences and I have a mind to train the men of Caer Gybi and the farms to fight. I will see Gwynfor and Gareth. I think if we ask them to train one day a month we should have a reliable force who can protect the fort if attacked. Don't forget, my sweet, that there will be warriors at Aelle's and Raibeart's forts. I intend to ask them to take on the responsibility of patrolling the island with scouts. I am sure they will agree."

"But you will be on the mainland!"

I shook my head. "No. I have leaders there who can make every day decisions. Hogan and Morag will be there. I will only visit the mainland to see how the defences are progressing. If we go to war then I will be there, of course, but my place will be here. So you see you needn't worry about being attacked, the Warlord and Saxon Slayer will be here."

She cuddled in to me. "Then I am happy."

My promise meant that I was able to spend the next few months overseeing, with Myrddyn, the building of the fort. It was an excellent site. The river wrapped itself around the hill giving deep water for over half of the walls. We put our usual three ditches on the other side. We built a series of outer walls, as at Castle Cam and then a traditional Roman fort in the middle. We were preparing for large numbers of refugees who might need to take shelter. We built a quay on the river so that 'The Wolf' and 'The Dragon' could supply the fort if besieged. Satisfied that all was going well we visited Ruthin and Aidan. There, too, they had deepened ditches and clad the walls as suggested by Myrddyn. Aidan was delighted with the new arrangements and the ten scouts he would soon have at his disposal. There had been small scale attacks at the fort but they had been Iago's men testing the defences.

"My worry, my lord, is that they come in winter."

"It is fifteen miles from the new fort. The beacons will alert Mungo and that means he can have men to your aid in half a day. Can you hold out for a day?"

"Easily."

"Then there will not be a problem. Our defence is based on small forts, well protected by reserves. At the moment we do not have the reserves but next year, or the year after will see us fully prepared."

The autumn storms meant that our ships were less useful and the journey back to Mona took a long six days. I had become used to travelling by water. The ride did afford me the opportunity of talking with Hogan and Myrddyn. "Although Garth commands the main castle you do know that you are the strategos for the mainland?"

"I didn't. Does Garth?"

"Of course. Garth can command a shield wall but he has little knowledge of horses and only a rudimentary knowledge of archers. You have studied and understand strategy. You have an able deputy in Pol. I am happy."

"Are you Myrddyn?"

"Your son is wise, Warlord. He asks the one who he knows understands. Yes I am happy Hogan. You have learned well. Morag will be good for you and give you the stability your father had at Castle Perilous."

"Then I am happy." He suddenly saw that Myrddyn was polishing a stone. "What is that?"

"Your father was given five raw gems and I have been polishing them. This is the last one."

"May I see?"

"Of course not! Your father has yet to decide what to do with them. They are polished but they are not finished. That is true is it not, Warlord?"

"It is and do not mention them to Myfanwy either. Myrddyn and I are still debating on how they should be used."

I could see the look of disappointment on Hogan's face. He was being excluded and we had never done that to him. "You have much to plan Hogan. Do not let these stones distract you. All will become plain in the fullness of time."

I was not looking forward to the journey. The month before Yule was always a stormy one although Daffydd, my captain, seemed confident. The night before we left we had a feast with my brothers, their families and mine. The next time they saw Hogan he would be married and heir to the Ceredigion throne. It was a pleasant time. Lann Aelle had a fine voice and he sang songs written about our battles against the Saxons. It was stirring stuff.

After we had cleared the platters, I stood. "Some beautiful amethyst stones have come into my possession. Myrddyn has been working on them for some time and now Ralph has finished his work I would like to give one of them to my wife Myfanwy. Although she will never have the title of Queen, to me she is a queen and will always be so." I held out my hand and Myrddyn handed me a copper and silver crown set in the middle with the amethyst. It was beautiful. Even I, who have no eye for beauty, saw it. I place it on her head. It was cunningly made so that it could be adjusted. The copper and silver were delicately interwoven so that they sparkled in the candlelight but the gem held pride of place. It was the biggest of the five and the most magnificent.

Myfanwy was not given to shows of emotion but she burst into tears and threw her arms around me. "Thank you…" she sat beside me too overcome to speak.

"My son is getting married and I have a present for him. What he does with it is his concern." I could see the worried look on his face. I handed him a single amethyst set into a silver and copper pendant.

When he took it he grinned with relief. "It will make a lovely wedding gift for my bride."

Everyone applauded and then suddenly they all stopped as Nanna stood on her chair and stamped her foot. "Where is my present? Mother has one and Hogan has one. Don't you love me father?"

The tears were welling up in her eyes. I wagged an admonishing finger at her. "You need to learn patience my girl. Of course I have one for you." Nanna's was a smaller version of the one I had given Hogan. She squealed with delight.

"Now say thank you to your father and then say sorry for being so rude!" Myfanwy had recovered her composure.

"Thank you and I'm sorry!" She threw her arms around me and kissed me.

In the end the voyage was not as hard as I had anticipated. The seas were calm and the sky was blue. It was cold but that was why we had brought furs. We even managed the voyage in half a day thanks to a following wind. Morag and Myfanwy liked each other immediately which was a relief to both Hogan and me. A priest of the White Christ officiated and the service seemed to go on interminably. I could see Myrddyn fuming with impatience. He would conduct a second ceremony when the couple were in the shadow of Wyddfa. The wizard was sure that it would bring untold benefits to the couple.

The day following the wedding saw the king and I walking his new defences. The king proudly told me of all the changes that he had wrought. I was worried that he would get carried away with what he had seen as a victory. "You must exercise caution your majesty. We need to weaken Iago much more before we try to rid the land of him."

The king smiled, "I am not deluding myself, Lord Lann. Had you not been here we would have lost. If he returned again in the next months I would have to send for you or lose. But we now have hope and I will not beard the dragon until we have made both our armies much stronger."

"And King Cloten?"

"He is just relieved it was we who had to fight Iago. He has copied my forts and my changes. He too will be ready. And the prince?"

I knew that both kings had never met the prince and were suspicious of any son of Iago. "Like you he is cautious, but he is building, steadily. When the time comes he will be a good king and we will win."

He smiled, "I am pleased that you have used our gift of amethysts well."

"You knew?"

"When Tomas found them and told me of them he spoke of his idea of making a gift of them. It shows your nature that one is returned to me and my daughter. I take it as a symbol of the union of Ceredigion with your people. I know you will use the other two wisely."

And as I sailed home the next day, I wondered how I would use them. I saw that Myrddyn was right and there was a power in them; a power which came from the earth itself and the mountains that were the backbone of our land.

Chapter 14

Perhaps the amethysts did bring us good fortune. We had two years free from war. There were small scouting raids by both the Saxons and the men of Gwynedd but they were easily repulsed. The three frontier forts were improved and enlarged. I deemed that it would take a well-equipped army to storm them. The new squires proved a great hit and enabled our patrols to be particularly effective. My leaders felt that our peace was due to their long and arduous patrols. They were able to snuff out any problems long before they reached our forts and settlements.

Sadly the lands around us, the areas beyond our frontier forts became stripped of people. We had an influx of refugees. That proved to be a benefit for they brought skills we needed. Many of our warriors took wives from the refugees and there were many new children born.

I became a grandfather; Artorius and Aideen were both born in quick succession. The event was the cause for great celebration both in our land and Ceredigion. Poor Myfanwy fretted that she was too far from the babies to be able to spoil them as much as she wished. Prince Pasgen followed Hogan and married. He soon became a doting father and husband and the haunted warrior who had fled from Rheged was a memory only. Lann Aelle became a man. His role changed from that of a squire to that of a bodyguard. I found his presence comforting when we rode with Myrddyn to inspect the frontier. My body told me that it needed to slow down from war. I knew that I had been lucky to avoid any serious wounds thus far and I wanted my grandchildren to play with a grandfather who was whole.

Back at Castle Cam, Brother Oswald and Myrddyn had finally finished our bath house. I suppose in terms of Byzantine baths it was quite primitive but it suited us. They had worked out how to make a hypocaust to keep the house warm in winter. Until she had used it Myfanwy had complained that the hall needed heating more urgently. There was a hot pool, a warm pool and a cool pool. It was a pleasant place to relax. Myfanwy was sceptical until I took her to share the experience with me. She was hooked immediately. The children, Nanna and Gawan, enjoyed the water and it became a daily pleasure for each of us.

Myrddyn and I were enjoying its warmth one spring morning. As we lay in the warm bath I reflected that we had both become older without looking older. It was strange. Myrddyn took out the amethyst I had left with him. It was the smallest. I had kept one; I suppose it was a good luck charm. Certainly, since I had carried it with me, we had had peace. Myrddyn turned it around in his hand. "Do you remember in Rheged, a few miles from Glanibanta there was a lake half way up the mountain?"

"Yes. There is a long narrow lake like Wide Water and then, as you climb you suddenly come upon the small lake. Why?"

"This amethyst is the same colour as the water." He paused and I remained silent. I knew he had not finished yet. "When I was last in the cave at Wyddfa I wandered towards the back and found a small pond there. In the torchlight I saw that it was the same colour as the stone."

"I take it there is an inference from this?"

"You are allowing your mind to stagnate because we have no wars, Warlord. The stone links Rheged and here. The stones did not come to us by accident. There were five of them and we were meant to have them."

I took the stone from him, mine was in my chambers. "Do you think there is a purpose for them? I mean we have used three; what of these last two?"

"I cannot see it yet but I know that there will be a purpose and we should keep them about us at all times."

I sensed criticism in his voice. "Even in a bath house?"

"Even in a bath house." It is strange but as things turned out he was proved correct.

Myfanwy decided that we would visit Hogan and his family for the midsummer solstice. Myrddyn always liked to be close to Wyddfa at that time. Miach was also anxious to see his son who had now become a father himself. We were still getting recruits and it seemed a good idea to take the ten new ones along with some new weapons and armour made by Ralph and his smiths. Taking my young family was not easy and I admired the calm of Daffydd, the captain of 'The Wolf'. He seemed not to mind all the chests and boxes dragged aboard by my wife and her servants. We also had to bring Wolf with us. In the last three years he and Gawan had become inseparable. Although the sheepdog was now old, he was highly protective of my family and Gawan would not leave without him.

Eventually we set sail. It would be less than half a day for the voyage although Daffydd was a little concerned about the lack of wind. It was a balmy day. I did not mind the slow pace. It was pleasant to watch Mona slip by to our south. We had to head north first to avoid the shoals which lay just north of Mona but once we turned east we found a little more wind. Myrddyn sniffed impatiently. "Had we gone by horse we would have been halfway there by now."

"With all the boxes and the children asking, '*Are we there yet*?'. No Myrddyn, this is better and easier. I, for one, like it."

It was then that *wyrd* took a hand. The lookout at the bow shouted, "Ship to the east!"

That in itself was not threatening but when the helmsman shouted, "Ships coming up on our stern," then it did.

Daffydd shouted, "Are they Irish?"

A moment later the bad news we feared was confirmed, "Aye my lord!"

We had a bolt thrower at the bow and one at the stern but there were three Irish ships. I left the command of the ship to the expert, but the defence was up to me. "Lann Aelle, get the recruits armed. Bring our bows up. Miach, if you get the chance, take out the helmsman on one of the ships."

The men assigned to the bolt throwers were already loading them. "Myfanwy, take the children below deck."

She shook her head, "If we are to die today then let us do so in sunlight not hiding in the dark!" There was no arguing with a strong minded woman. Myrddyn had joined the bolt thrower crew at the stern.

I wandered over to Daffydd. He had every sail catching as much of the wind as we could. "They were waiting for us my lord. They have oars and can easily catch us."

"I assume we cannot return to Cybi?"

"They would catch us quicker that way. They have planned this well. If there had been a breeze then we would have had a chance but this way…"

"We could head for Aelle's burg."

"Not yet my lord for there is a ship between us and its protection."

"You are the sailor, what do you suggest?"

"Take out the ship coming towards us and head for your brother."

"Good! Then we will do it." Half of the problem we faced was not knowing what to do. At least we had a plan now. "Myrddyn, can you hit the ship before us?"

"Yes my lord." He hurried forward as Lann Aelle distributed the weapons and brought me my bow.

"Miach, discourage the ones pursuing us."

I went with Myrddyn to inspect the target. The Hibernian ships were smaller than we were but they would each have up to forty men on board. They would have eighteen oars on each side and a sail when they needed it. We had twenty men on board who could fight. We needed to lower the odds against us.

The ship before us was closing rapidly which made Myrddyn's task more difficult. The Irish boat was coming at us head on and was a small target. Myrddyn's first shot went a little too high and cracked through the mast. Had they had a sail hoisted then we would have damaged them; as it was the broken spar fell to the deck where it was thrown over. I daresay we injured some of the warriors who were rowing but it did not slow it down. The second shot was either better aimed or luckier. It struck the boat just above the waterline. It would make the boat gradually fill with water. I heard the bolt thrower at the stern crack into action. They had two targets and would have to choose one target or the other. I hoped that Miach chose wisely.

Myrddyn hit the ship again and he must have hit some rowers for the boat slewed dangerously towards the coast. The crew of the bolt thrower desperately reloaded as the target briefly wallowed before them. By the time they had reloaded the Irishman was beginning to turn to sail parallel with us. They were now between us and safety. Myrddyn managed to hit it again close to the waterline and I could see that it was moving more sluggishly. I went to the stern. One of the pursuing ships had been hit a couple of times and I could she was moving more slowly. Both ships were now in bow range. The three of us with bows took them out.

"Aim for the ship which is already damaged, if we can disable her then the odds are down to two to one."

As Miach pulled back his bow he grumbled, "Oh good, just eighty warriors to fight then!"

The three of us were good archers and we all aimed at the stern. We didn't just loose one and see the effect we released five in quick succession. One or more must have struck the helmsman for the boat suddenly swung towards the shore. The crew of the bolt thrower took advantage of the ship being beam on to us and loosed one which struck her below the waterline. The ship was already damaged and we could see that she was sinking. The crew began to row for the safety of the shore and I hoped that there were men at the watchtowers at Aelle's Burg to see them.

The undamaged ship had taken advantage of her consort's demise and had closed so that the bolt thrower could not strike them. I looked to the right and saw that the first ship we had damaged was sailing two hundred paces from our right hand side. I could see, in the distance, Aelle's Burg. "Captain, edge the ship towards the shore."

"But there are rocks there."

"I know and hopefully we can sink a second ship. Besides my brother's men have bolt throwers too."

I hoped that the rowers were tiring but they still appeared to be closing from both sides now. By edging south, 'The Wolf' was drawing away from the more dangerous undamaged ship but it meant that the first ship we had struck could board us. "I want every armed man on this side of the ship. Myfanwy, arm yourself!"

The three of us with bows began to loose arrow after arrow towards the ship to the south of us. I kept one eye on Aelle's fort which was now less than half a mile away. I could see warriors on the ramparts and knew that we had been seen. The Irish captain was a brave man and he edged his ship closer to us. Even while I was releasing my arrows I gave commands. "When they try to board us stop them! If they board us we are lost. I know you men are new but you will be fighting for your lives."

Suddenly I heard a crack as one of Aelle's bolt throwers struck the damaged ship. It was a mortal blow. The ship suddenly sank lower into the water. In a last desperate attempt to close with us the captain put the tiller hard over and she turned to within forty paces of us. The wind, the tide and the last efforts edged her closer to us and we now had the problem. If we turned away from her we would be turning towards the last ship and she was undamaged.

"Miach, you watch this ship. Myrddyn get the bolt crews to help Miach stop any of that ship boarding us. The rest of you to me! We are going to have to repel boarders."

By the time we reached the other side I could see that the Hibernian ship was thirty paces away. I had an idea. "Captain, steer hard left! Now!"

I thanked the Allfather that my men all trusted me and Daffydd did as I had asked. The Irish captain was not expecting that and we suddenly loomed up on his right side. We cracked through his oars. I could only pray that we had hurt some of his warriors. "Hard right!" The hull of 'The Wolf' ground along the flank of the pirate, gouging planks, and allowing water to flood in. Unfortunately it meant we were next to them and ten ropes with hooks at the end snaked over the water. I hacked at one and then another. More were thrown and then we were fast together. I hefted my shield around. "Lann Aelle, on my right. The rest of you get behind me."

I hoped that the crew would cut the ropes holding us or the sinking pirate might drag us down with her. The first Irishman who stepped aboard was a half naked giant with a body covered in tattoos. He roared at me and Saxon Slayer struck him in his vast belly and he fell on the men clambering behind him. There were however, just too many of them. The twelve of us could not keep them at bay and they swarmed over the side. Lann Aelle fought like a hero and the deck where we stood remained free of the Hibernians as we killed them before they could clamber aboard. The recruits were struggling and gradually being forced back so that we ended up in a circle. I found myself fighting a warrior with an axe and a sword. I had slipped my shield dagger into my left hand so that I had an extra weapon. Two warriors attacked Lann. One had a war hammer. He struck Lann's shield and Lann cleverly deflected it. Unfortunately for me it smashed into my hand and Saxon Slayer. The sword was dashed from my numbed hand. My opponent saw his chance and swung his axe over his head. With nothing left to deflect the blow I did the only thing I could, I put my head down and charged. I hit his chin with my helmet. He fell to the deck and I ripped my dagger across his stomach. I stood and left him dying.

Pausing only to grab Saxon Slayer and hoping that I could still wield it, I stabbed the hammer man in the side with Saxon Slayer. The blade went right through him and into Lann Aelle's other opponent. Now that we had breathing space we turned, back to back to face the pirates who remained. The better armed ones, it seemed, had attacked Lann and me. The ones left had a sword or an axe. With my family on board I was in no mood for mercy. The young warrior who advanced towards me looked terrified. I took his sword on my shield and slid my blade through to his backbone. I withdrew it with a backhand motion and Saxon Slayer sliced open the next warrior's side.

Suddenly I heard a scream and saw three warriors moving towards Myfanwy. She had the children behind her and Wolf was growling next to her. Suddenly Miach leapt forwards to stab one in the side. His companion brought his axe down and it split open the old archer's head. Wolf suddenly leapt at the warrior and fastened his teeth around the Hibernian's neck. He had his throat cut by a third warrior.

I roared with anger and brought Saxon Slayer down to split him from the head to the crotch. As the second warrior looked in horror I punched him with my shield and swept his head from his body as he tried to stagger to his feet. I spun around filled with hate and anger. I just wanted to kill! Myrddyn's voice came to me, "My lord, they are all dead."

I stood panting; my children were whimpering and Myfanwy was trying to comfort them. I could hear the slop of the water on the hull and the groans of the dying. I was still angry. I found the warrior whose stomach had been sliced open. He still lived but he was coughing up blood.

"Who is your chief?"

He laughed and spat a gobbet of blood at me. Lann Aelle went to despatch him but I restrained him. "Well you will die warrior and soon your King Felan will join you."

"He is too clever for you."

I turned to Lann, "And that is their chief. Throw this piece of meat overboard. Let the fishes feast on him."

"No! Kill me; give me the warrior's death!"

As Lann and one of the surviving recruits threw the man over I shouted, "Warriors do not attack women and children!" He screamed as he struck the water.

I went to my wife and put my arms around her and my children. There were no words to say but I saw her eyes fixed on Miach. He had been with me since Rheged and I valued him as a friend as well as a captain. My band of brothers was getting smaller.

We pulled in close to the shore and my brother's stronghold. He and his warriors came to the beach. "Are you safe brother?"

"I am but Miach and Wolf both died bravely." I pointed to the sea. "There will be bodies and wreckage washed up. You may be able to save one of the Hibernian ships. I would be grateful if you could. I have a debt to pay."

Aelle nodded, "May the Allfather be with you. I will send Gawan a pup when my dog has whelped."

Gawan's face brightened a little as he heard that. Wolf was descended from a dog we three brothers had had as children. Aelle still bred from her original line. There would be another Wolf.

We sailed in silence along the coast. I smiled at Lann Aelle. "You did well nephew."

He shook his head. "No my lord I nearly got you killed. You had better give me the sword so that I can see if it is damaged."

I laughed, "This is Saxon Slayer. This can not be harmed." *Wyrd*! As I slid it from its scabbard I saw the pommel had been damaged and one of the jewels which had been there was shattered and in pieces. I looked at Myrddyn in horror. "This is an evil sign, surely."

Myrddyn picked up the sword and closed his eyes. He shook his head. "It does not feel that way." He looked at me with a curious expression on his face. "Which would you rather have lost: a jewel from the sword or one of your children?"

I looked over at them still huddled and shaking. He was right. I had sacrificed part of the sword. "But the sword is ancient. Is its power now lost?"

"Until it is whole again it has no power. We need to heal the sword."

Lann Aelle looked at the wizard curiously. "How?"

"It has lost a stone. We replace it."

My squire still did not understand, even though I did. He shook his head. "It would have to be a special stone!"

I reached into my pouch and took out the amethyst. "Like this one perhaps?"

It was only when I held the stone next to the sword that I saw it was the same size, exactly, as the one which had been destroyed. The colour matched perfectly with the two adjacent stones; in fact it was a better match than the damaged one had been.

Myrddyn gathered all the shards of the jewel and put them in a small leather pouch. "And we will need to use these." He pointed at Wyddfa, now even closer. "We must visit the cave and the home of the mountain. There we will heal the blade and make it stronger. This is a sign from the mountain; this sword will save this land!"

When we landed Hogan could see the distress on Myfanwy's face. She looked up at me and said, "Next time we come by wagon!"

Hogan shook his head. "Next time we visit with you."

That shook Myfanwy from her self pity. "Come, where are my grandchildren. Nanna and Gawan have made them presents."

"I will take you. We have built a room just for the children." He lowered his voice, "I get more sleep this way."

"I remember."

Lann Aelle still held on to Saxon Slayer. He was gripping tightly to prevent any more damage. I looked at Myrddyn. "What do we need to do?"

"Tomorrow is the summer solstice. The three of us are inextricably tied to this blade and we will all need to be there for the ceremony. Until then the blade should not be touched. Give it to me, Lann Aelle, and I will put it somewhere safe."

My nephew looked distraught still. "I am so sorry, Warlord. I should have just taken the blow."

I shook my head. "It was meant to be. I understand that now: the finding of the jewels, the sea voyage; all were put into place. I am content."

"Then you will not seek revenge on Felan?"

"Oh no Lann; Felan will die and I will put his ships and his village to the sword so that he bothers no-one again." As I said it I made a silent oath to myself. I never broke an oath and I would not break one to myself.

It was a subdued celebration. I still had Daffydd ap Miach's face in my head and could not celebrate as I should have done. He had lost a father and his son had lost a grandfather he had never seen. The loss to me of a captain was great but it could not compare to the loss of the family. After I had told him his face had become like steel. "You are going after this Felan?"

"I am. I will destroy this nest of vipers once and for all."

"Then I will lead the archers." It was a command and not a request. I could see it in the resolve on his face.

"You will and you will lead all of our archers for your father thought you the finest archer we have."

"I will never be the man my father was."

Myfanwy, of course, along with Myrddyn managed to lighten the mood. Myrddyn entertained with some tricks. He normally disliked the conjuring lesser wizards used but he knew this was the time. Myfanwy sang silly songs. Morag had never heard them and laughed until the tears flowed from her eyes. By the time we retired we had a semblance of the joy we should have had earlier.

No one said a word as the three of us left on foot to climb Wyddfa. Myrddyn carried the tools he would need and I carried the sword. Lann Aelle was our grim-faced protector. The last time we had come we had ridden but it had been winter. It was a totally different prospect in high summer. The woods at the base of the mighty mountain teemed with life. Had we been in a mood for hunting we could have fed an army for a month. The steady and breath sucking climb allowed me time to think for speech was out of the question. I had never questioned the sword before. Until I had visited Constantinopolis I had just thought I had found a good sword. Now I could see that it was more complicated than that. The lives of all those who had wielded the blade for hundreds of years were inextricably entwined in its blade and its life. I was under no illusions; the blade lived. Past battles came to mind and I knew that it had saved me for I had fought, many times, beyond my skill. Those victories had been Saxon Slayer's. What we were now doing was a dark and important ritual. Bishop Stephen and the followers of the White Christ would not understand but to my men it was as normal as breathing or eating. The blade needed renewal and so we were in the most holy of mountains with the most powerful of wizards with a jewel hewn from another holy mountain. I felt the hairs on the back of my neck prickle with excitement.

We had brought flint and some kindling but we quickly found more for we would need to heat the metal of the mount to hold the stone in place. It would be more than unlucky to loose the amethyst; it would be a disaster. We walked deep into the cave with the torches burning brightly and throwing strange shadows on the roof of the cave. I suspect Lann Aelle was terrified but he never showed any hesitation at all. I know that he would have been afraid for I was the first time I had come with Myrddyn to his lair.

We had to duck our heads in some of the passages but Myrddyn seemed to know his way. We had just ducked beneath a large rock when we suddenly emerged into a huge cavern and there was the most beautiful blue lake in the middle. I think I stopped breathing briefly for the lake was the exact same colour as the amethysts. The lake almost filled the cavern and the cavern would have taken the whole of Castle Perilous within it. We were in a special place, a place made by the gods.

Myrddyn began the fire while I took out the sword and the stone. There was a large slab of rock close to the water. It looked like a table. It could have been made to lay the sword upon. I put them both down and noticed how the torchlight sparkled on the water, Saxon Slayer and the amethyst.

I noticed that Lann was shivering. "Cold?"

"No my lord." He tried to shrug. "I don't know why I feel this way, it is strange."

Myrddyn didn't look up from his fire making. "It is the power of the mountain you are feeling. It is not just rock; there is a spirit within. You feel the spirit of Wyddfa. Close your eyes Lann and let it speak with you."

"I am afraid."

"It will not harm you. It only fights our enemies."

I watched as Lann closed his eyes and he remained silent for some time. When he opened them there was a look of awe upon his face. "I saw a woman and she spoke with me." I looked over to Myrddyn and shared a smile. "I did not understand her words but she smiled and I felt at peace."

"That is the spirit of the mountain. Come, the fire is lit and we must prepare." The flames from the fire danced upon the roof and then reflected back into the water. The water was no longer just blue but had crimson and gold flickering and skimming across its still surface.

Myrddyn had a small crucible and he placed it on the tripod he placed over the flames. He took out some copper. "This is copper from the same mine which yielded the stones. It will bind the stone tightly to the sword. The sword and the stone will become as one. The stone will be in the sword and the sword bound to the stone. It will become as the mountains. We must wait. Warlord, hold the amethyst. You must be the one to place it into the sword. Lann Aelle, you must hold the sword steady."

I took out the stone and found that my hand was shaking. Lann gave me a wan, nervous smile. Myrddyn stared intently at the crucible. As soon as it bubbled he took the long metal hand and lifted it off. "Ready!"

He poured the molten liquid into the socket. "Now Warlord, and I will say the words." As I placed the amethyst into the molten metal I heard it softly hiss and then Myrddyn began to chant,

"Spirit of Wyddfa, protect this sword.
Spirit of the stone, protect this sword.
Spirit of Wyddfa, enter the sword.
Spirit of the stone, enter the sword.
Stone and sword, become one.
Sword and stone protect the land.
I name you Saxon Slayer.
Now you will be reborn."

There was a sudden hiss and then silence. Myrddyn said, "Give me the sword Lann Aelle."

Holding the weapon by the blade, as carefully as a father with his new child, he walked into the icy lake and reverently laid it down in the water. There were a few bubbles and a soft sigh and then Myrddyn left the water. "Warlord you may retrieve your sword. It now knows its name and it awaits your touch."

I was feeling nervous myself as I stepped into the blue water. I closed my eyes with the cold and I heard my mother's voice.

"Now is the sword come home.
Take the sword from the water."

I reached down and grasped the hilt. I felt a surge rush through me as though I had a sudden power. I felt as though I had been struck by lightning. I turned and Myrddyn and Lann were both on their knees. I raised the sword and cried, "Saxon Slayer!" I do not know if it was one of Myrddyn's tricks, a trick of the lights or something more mystical but the blade of Saxon Slayer suddenly flamed bright red and seemed to flash like lightning all around the chamber.

Myrddyn stood and smiled and said, "Now is the sword healed and with it, we can heal the land."

Chapter 15

I felt different as I descended the mountain the next morning. I dreamt, as I had done the last time I had slept in the cave but this time there were no words, there were just pictures of my mother playing with Hogan's children. It did not worry me that there had been no message. My mother or the spirit of the mountain only ever warned me of imminent danger. I took the dream to be a sign of stability.

There was relief when we returned. The mountain was a brooding and constant presence. It must have seemed either foolish or brave for anyone to willingly enter its bowels. The one thing everyone wanted to do was to see and touch the sword. Although it did not look as powerful in daylight as it had in the cave the addition of the stone of blue had made the weapon even more beautiful. The new copper moulding shone like new gold and made the blue of the stone even more intense.

We stayed seven more days. I took the opportunity to visit with Mungo and Aidan at their outposts. Their regular patrols and those of the equites kept the frontier free from both Saxon and the men of Gwynedd. Settlers, however could only be guaranteed safety if they lived with a couple of miles of the fort. One disturbing report came from Mungo. The Saxons were increasing the numbers of ships in the estuary and along the coast. Mungo's bolt throwers had taught them discretion and they kept out of range. I decided to use one of our smaller ships to sail along the coast and keep an eye on things.

Aedh was at Ruthin and I sought him out. "Have you a good deputy you could leave with your men for a while? I have need of you and eight of your scouts."

Intrigued Aedh nodded eagerly. "I have and we have just trained some new scouts, former slingers. This will be a good chance to blood them; while the frontier is quiet."

"Good. Bring your men to Pasgen's tomorrow."

Daffydd had already selected the archers he wished to come with us for he knew of my plan. "You have a week to ensure that the frontier defences will not be compromised. Make your way to Castle Cam and our plans should be in place by then."

All of this activity made Hogan suspicious. "You are going to go to Felan are you not? I will come with you."

I was calmer now that the sword had been healed. I had, even before the sword was damaged, been irritable and short. The healing of the sword had been the healing of me too. "No Hogan. It is not that I do not need you but this work is of a different type. I will take Pol with me for he has done this before. I do not intend to risk an army. For one thing we do not have enough ships. I am going to hurt them so that they never again despoil our land. This is your domain. You are vital to the safety of all of us. The peace we have had is to your credit. And there are your children and your wife. There is always a risk in these missions. I will not risk my heir and the father of my grandchildren."

"But you will risk yourself."

"When you are Warlord and you take those decisions you can decide if the risk is worth it. For me, I see no risk. I dreamt no dream last night. I will be safe."

My family was nervous about boarding 'The Wolf' but the captain made a great fuss of them. The ship had been totally cleaned and repaired. There was no sign of the battle. Even so I was glad when we docked. The children would travel easier the next time we sailed. As we had passed Aelle's settlement I saw that they had dragged the remains of the Irish ships ashore and were repairing one of them. It would give us another ship to use, eventually.

Aedh and his chosen men arrived a day early. They were all young and they were all keen. Scouts are thrill seekers by nature and the thought of a secret task for the Warlord was just too tempting to refuse. I gathered Aedh along with Myrddyn, Garth, Daffydd ap Miach and Ridwyn in my hall. Pol would join us when he could but these five were vital to the planning.

"Firstly let me thank you for coming here. The fact that you are happy to sail to Hibernia to punish Felan for his many offences is gratifying." I had already been finding out as much as I could about these Irishmen and I displayed the map which Brother Oswald had drawn based upon the information we had received. "It seems that this Felan lives on the coast in the south east of the island. There is a large river there. It appears to have many names. The important fact is that it is wide and it is sheltered. They can moor many ships and they are protected from storms. Felan has a small fort and hall on the south of the river. It is not a fort like those we build. It is made of wood and has no ditch.

We could just sail over and attack it but I want someone to go and look at the place. That will be you, Aedh and your volunteers. You need to find a place we can land unseen. My plan is to land fifty warriors led by Ridwyn. Myrddyn and the archers will stay on board their ship. When we have killed their king I want the fleet destroying and, as we all know, fire is the best method." I smiled. "Myrddyn is an expert. I want the archers on the ship as we may be pursued. The archers can protect us. There are too many unknowns at the moment, and we will only finalise these plans once Aedh has returned." I peered around the faces. "Do not tell anyone what we are about. It takes only one careless word and Felan will be waiting for us. He feels secure on his island; I want that delusion to continue."

Aedh and his scouts left after dark. The captain was going to land them on the other side of the headland from Felan's fort. We both thought this would be the best place to land our attacking force but Aedh would confirm that. As we watched it sailing west Myrddyn said, "There is much responsibility on that young man's shoulders."

"There was as much on ours when we were both younger than he is now. He will cope. He has been doing this for a long time."

Myfanwy was not certain that my decision was a sound one. "If we had not been in danger would you be doing this?"

"He has attacked us three times now, my love. One of these days he will get lucky and he will hurt my family. I cannot risk that. With the bulk of our army on the mainland we need to know that the Hibernians will not be a threat. I am sending a message to the whole of the island; if you come to my land then I will punish you. They only understand force. We will be fighting our neighbours ere long. I would like to do so without looking over my shoulder."

She nodded. Myfanwy was clever and I had learned to explain things truthfully to her. "Just make sure you come back safe."

"Myrddyn says that the blue stones will protect the wearer and I believe it too. Keep the stone safe and it will keep us all safe."

She took her crown and looked at the jewel. "It does comfort me when I wear it. I just feel overdressed."

I laughed, "You can wear it around your neck if you wish like a torc. I am sure that Myrddyn or Ralph could adapt it."

She brightened. "I wanted to do that but I didn't want to offend you. You seemed so proud of the crown."

I shook my head. "The pride was in you not the crown. It is yours to do with as you choose."

"Then I will see Ralph tomorrow."

I spent the next day at Caer Gybi, anxiously awaiting the arrival of 'The Wolf' and my scouts. Despite my words to Myrddyn I was not certain that they would return safely. If I had been with them then I would have been confident. Many things could go wrong as I had found out when I had been ambushed by Iago's men all those years ago. It does not do to be overconfident. The sun was beginning to set in the west. I wondered if they might return after dark. As soon as I saw the prow of my ship I felt relief. Aedh's wave made me relax just a little.

I forced myself to wait in Gareth's office but I was desperate to hear their news. They filled the tiny office when they arrived. "And?"

"And we have found a place to land. It is close to where the captain dropped us. There is a gentle rise and a walk of less than a mile before you reach the fort. The ships are moored in a line across the river, it makes a sort of bridge and there is a warrior hall on the northern bank. I think they use it to protect the harbour. Felan's fort has one building for the warriors and one for Felan. We did not go inside but we could see all of this through the gate. He had many visitors this morning. I was not noticed. There is a settlement on the river half a mile away and the people there appear to be fishermen. He has no more than forty men in the fort. We counted twenty but they were the guards on the walls and gates."

"How many north of the river?"

"A couple of hundred but that is an estimate. We counted as best we could but we were across the river."

"How many ships?"

"There are ten. They were the size of the ones which attacked you Warlord."

"You have done well. We will return to the castle and we will tell the others your news. We will be crossing the water soon. I do not want to waste another day waiting for him to act."

We worked out the rest of the plan that night. Pol had arrived and was keen to get on with it. "We will not take spears, sword and axes only. There will be no banners." I saw the look of disappointment briefly flick across Lann Aelle's face. "I want the men who go to be volunteers. If we have to leave in a hurry we cannot wait for those who are wounded or late." I glared around the room, "That includes me."

We left during the afternoon when the volunteers had been chosen. Every warrior wished to come. We had thirty archers aboard 'The Dragon with Myrddyn and the rest of the men were with me on 'The Wolf'. The wind was favourable but we still took some hours to cross. I could see no towers in the headland above the beach but we disembarked quickly. The two ships put about as soon as they could. By the time we were half way up the slope they were tacking towards the north. Aedh led the way with three of his scouts. The others spread out in a thin screen to warn us of anyone approaching.

As we had expected the gates were closed and there were guards on the walls. We had expected nothing less. There were just ten sentries, four on the main gate and the other six spread around the walls. We used our shields to lift ten warriors up to the walls. Four warriors raised each of the men selected to climb over the walls. They had no helmets upon their heads and they carried only daggers. Lann, Pol and I stood watching with bows at the ready in case they could not silence all of the sentries. We watched as, one by one the guards were killed and their bodies lowered to the walk way. Each of my Wolf Warriors could move silently, like a shadow, and the sentries were all despatched without a sound being heard by the warriors sleeping in the warrior hall. I gave my bow to one of the scouts as did Pol and Lann. It would only get in the way now. We swung our shields around to our front and drew our swords. This was now warrior work.

We ran around to the front gate and the men who had killed the sentries descended and opened it. Ridwyn took most of the men towards the warrior hall. We left two on guard at the gate. I took Pol, Aedh and Lann Aelle towards the hut we assumed was Felan's. There was a guard dozing at the door. I nodded to my nephew. He moved to the side and approached the guard from behind. He stepped behind him and drew his blade across his throat. There was a slight gurgle and the dead sentry was lowered silently to the ground. We stepped inside and we saw Felan with three young women and a boy draped around his bed. There was the heavy, sickly smell of drink. They were all half asleep but the appearance of three heavily armed warriors woke them immediately. The four young people tried to hide behind Felan. The years since I had last seen him had not been kind to him. He was now bloated and overweight. His face had the red blotchy look of someone who drinks too much. There would be no honour in killing this treacherous chief but that would not stop me. He would die as quickly as I could manage it. This was for the sake and safety of my people.

"Felan, tonight you are going to die. You are a worthless warrior who is as deceitful as a snake. Three times have you tried to hurt me; the last time you made the mistake of attacking my family and that I never forgive." I pointed Saxon Slayer at the others on the bed, "You four are only guilty of poor judgement and I will let you live but spread the word. If any one tries to hurt me or my family then this is the justice they will receive. Now go but go silently or my men will kill you!" I could hear the sounds of combat as my men slaughtered the men in the warrior hall. The four grabbed furs to cover their naked bodies and they raced from the hut, terrified looks on their young faces.

When they had left I pointed at the sword above the bed. "Felan, take your sword so that, even though you do not deserve it, you can join your oathsworn."

He looked terrified and he cowered against the wall of his hut. "Let me live. I promise that I will never attack you again!"

"You have made that promise already! Take your sword or you will die where you lie." He could see that I would do as I had promised. He grabbed his sword and his shield and faced me. He was not a good warrior and he weakly hacked at my shield. Even though I could see that his sword was a good one I barely felt the blow. I brought my sword over my head and split his skull and his body down to his chest. I saw his heart briefly beating before he slumped to his death. He died quickly. "Pol, take his sword!"

Pol grabbed his sword and we ran outside. I saw Ridwyn who was gathering the men together and tending to the minor wounds. "Fire the fort." We went to the main gate to look at the harbour. I could see our two ships. They were close to the line of moored vessels. The fort being fired would be their signal to destroy the ships. I felt the wall of heat as Ridwyn's men set fire to the huts and the walls. "Ridwyn, form a wedge and lead the men down to the ships."

The four of us tucked in behind the wedge as we ran down the gentle slope to the harbour. I trusted Aedh's information and did not think there would be any more men on this side of the river but I was taking no chances. We reached the harbour as the first ship was fired. Daffydd greeted me. "My archers killed the sentries silently."

"Good, rejoin 'The Dragon'. Ridwyn take the men and board 'The Wolf'."

The flames from the fort had awoken the warriors on the southern shore. They raced down the hill towards their ships. Already half of the ships were on fire. Suddenly a rain of arrows from my archers fell on the Hibernians, many of whom were half dressed. Some of them made the first ships. I could now see that there were gangplanks between the ships. It was both a crude bridge and a barrier to the inner harbour. Myrddyn had timed it well and the bolts, covered in Greek Fire hurtled, like flaming comets, towards the last ships. As the men took shelter on the boats they were engulfed in flames. The deadly fire took hold quickly and could not be extinguished with water. The ones who threw themselves in the water to douse the flames continued to burn and Daffydd's archers loosed more arrows to slaughter the warriors who raced down the hill. Felan's fort was like a beacon for them and they were running to the aid of a king they did not know was already dead. The whole of the river was lit by the flames from the inferno and I could see, on the lower slopes of the riverbanks, the bodies of the warriors slaughtered by my men. Discretion led the rest of the Hibernian warriors to scurry back to their hall. Too many of their braver comrades lay dead and their cries and screams could be heard above the crackling of the flames.

As we tacked around to head back to sea I shouted, "So dies any Hibernian who dares to attack the Warlord of Rheged!" The words echoed in the night. I did not know if they had heard but, standing at the stern and lit by the flames, I could be seen.

There was an eerie series of sounds as we sailed east across the brightly lit waters. We could hear the screams of the dying and the gurgle of ships as they sank. It felt like a people dying. Felan and his line ended that day. His brothers were killed by Ridwyn's warriors in the warrior hall. With his oathsworn slain there were was no one left to lead his decimated people. Other leaders took advantage of his death and moved in with their own warriors. Felan's lair had been an attractive one. The rest of the island took my message to heart and we were never again bothered by Hibernians. They raided further south, in Cymri and they raided the Saxons but my taste of terror left them in no doubt about their destiny if they tried to cross swords with me.

As we headed through the dark I wished that I had done this before and then Miach would still be alive. I resolved then to be more ruthless and decisive. My mistakes cost others their lives. Pol came over with Felan's blade. "My lord, here is the king's sword."

"It is yours Pol."

He looked at me in disbelief. "But Warlord, it is the sword of a king!"

I pointed to Lann. "He has the sword of a king and I do too. Why would I need another? You have earned the sword for the service you have done me and my son. Take it and give it the honour it deserves."

None of us felt any exultation. We had rid the world of a rat. We did feel safer and it was a statement for the rest of our neighbours. We began to hear the stories from the sea captains who visited our port after travelling around the rest of Britannia. Kings were openly fearful of the wrath of the Warlord. The Dux Britannica was seen as an instrument of the Empire. I supposed Phocas took some credit for that but he deserved none. It also heralded a period of peace for our people. The Saxons and King Iago appeared to have taken heed of our actions. They knew that to take us on they would need to be far stronger than they were. The Saxons withdrew to north of the Dee and King Iago to the land to the east of that river. They began to build defences against us. Our scouts and spies told us that they feared that we would invade them. We had no such intentions but it allowed our three allies to build their armies and to recruit from the disaffected men of Gwynedd. As the year drew to a close we were as secure as we had ever been.

We also received embassies from other nations. The kin of the men of Strathclyde sent envoys seeking an alliance with us. Although we could not see how that would benefit us soon we went along with it as it sent a further message to the Saxons that we were far from finished. Our trading partners also increased as other nations, too far away to be allies, saw us as a viable port with which to trade. Soon we were taking more in revenue than we were spending and even Brother Oswald was happy. As I looked at Saxon Slayer I wondered about that night in the cave and the changes it had wrought. Our star was rising and we had the support of the spirits. It was a good time for us all.

Chapter 16

The peace last until the year that the Emperor Phocas died and Emperor Heraclius took control of the Byzantine Empire. We heard of the war and the end of Phocas from traders. We had it confirmed when an Imperial ship arrived with a message for me from the new Emperor. There was no envoy. I read the letter which addressed me still as Dux Britannica. Myrddyn stood watching me as I read the document. Brother Oswald looked quite concerned.

I handed it to him when I had read it. It was not something I would keep from my most private advisers. "Well?" asked Myrddyn.

"It seems he is a warrior like me. He took no offence at our saving Phocas and he appreciated my gesture. He wishes me to continue to be Dux Britannica and he will continue to support us."

"Yes Warlord but he makes no mention of any finances to accompany it. It is an honorary title and costs him nothing."

I smiled at the priest. He sounded almost petulant. "I know Oswald. Let us just say that Phocas' gold was a gift from the gods."

I saw Myrddyn's smirk. Brother Oswald could not say that it has come from his White Christ and he had to choke in the thought that it had come from some pagan deity. "Besides it does not change us or what we do. Since Felan was killed we have had peace for these last years."

Myrddyn wagged an admonishing finger towards the east. "Iago is planning something. Aedh's scouts have told us that there are new warrior halls being built close to the frontier and Aethelfrith and his people should now have recovered from the disease which killed so many. I believe that war is coming and coming soon."

Now that Nanna and Gawan were so much older we could travel to visit Hogan and his three children on the mainland more frequently. Myfanwy always preferred younger children and the fact that Hogan had such a young family drew her to them like a moth to a flame. Myrddyn never minded the trips either as he spent increasingly long hours in the cave beneath Wyddfa. His power seemed to be growing and his warnings of war were a sign that we ought to visit Hogan once more.

I never thought of myself as getting older but Myfanwy noticed the grey in my beard and my hair. Myrddyn never seemed to age which was a constant source of annoyance to my wife. There was no getting away from it though; all of us were getting older. In the case of Hogan, Pol, Lann Aelle and Daffydd they were just coming into their prime. Our prime was long ago. Mungo, Garth, Prince Pasgen and Ridwyn were like the strategoi of Constantinopolis, they would be great leaders in war but not in battle. I knew that they would be resentful when I told them that they could no longer fight in the shield wall or in the fore of a charge but I needed them to use their minds. We had plenty of brave and resourceful young men who could take risks.

Hogan had had quarters built for us at his castle. As it was only now used to train recruits then there was plenty of room. Our finances were so stable that we could afford to pay our warriors and we had many recruits. Some still came from north of the wall while others came from the far south west of the land. Many were young warriors desperate to fight alongside the legends of Britannia. I knew that we were the legends. The tales of our swords and our deeds were told and retold over and over again. The killing of Morcant Bulc and the death of Felan, both in their own castles were both popular sagas. There were many embellishments; Myrddyn had flown us into Din Guardi. He had summoned a dragon to burn the fleet of the Hibernians. The ten ships became a hundred. The handful of warriors we killed became an army four of us slaughtered.

The legend of the sword drew them in too. The young men who joined us all asked, without exception, if they could swear their oath on the blade of Saxon Slayer. This was another reason for our visit, there was another batch of recruits who were ready to take the oath. I did not mind for I knew that they would never break that oath. Since the spies had infiltrated our army and nearly caused a disaster not a man had run nor had anyone spied for an enemy. That was largely down to the power of Saxon Slayer.

Prince Cadfan joined us for the ceremony. We trained his recruits although they did not swear on Saxon Slayer. The night before the ceremony we had a small celebration of our own. My army was now the largest it had ever been and was ever likely to be. We had our equites and squires who were a potent mobile force. We now had over one hundred well trained archers and fifty slingers. There were three hundred warriors in my shield wall and another three hundred manning the forts and castles. Finally we had Aedh and his fifty scouts. They were now acknowledged as the masters of their trade. They could hide within ten paces of a warrior and he would not know. They could traverse mountain passes that would trouble a goat and they could pass for Saxon or warrior of Gwynedd with ease. It was their reports which had worried Myrddyn. Added to which I think he had divined a threat.

Prince Cadfan had grown into a fine warrior. He had his fanatically loyal troops had fought off many smaller attacks from his father's forces. He had three hundred warriors under his command. They were mainly men of the shield wall and scouts but as Hogan pointed out that was all that they needed so long as we had the equites. The two were not merely neighbours, they were good friends and, as I knew, that could sometimes make the difference in a battle.

He sat next to me as we ate. "I envy you your sword Warlord. My men will swear loyalty to me tomorrow but they will covet Saxon Slayer, as I do."

I put down the bone I had been gnawing and leaned back in my seat. "You have a sword do you not?"

"Aye my lord but it is no Saxon Slayer."

I laughed, "Do you know who named it Saxon Slayer?"

He looked at me in surprise. "Is that not its name?"

"It was not until I slew some Saxons and called it thus."

"But I know that it is a sword older than the Roman Empire."

"True but they did not call it Saxon Slayer. The Romans did not name swords. It is our people, the Celtic peoples and the Saxons who do that. I did not know it was a famous sword but I knew that it was a good one. Does your sword have a name?"

"Why no; it is just an ordinary sword."

"And it will remain one until you decide otherwise."

"What should I name it?"

"The sword will tell you. The next time you use it and it performs a great deed then that will be its name. Lann Aelle's sword is Bear Killer. He has never killed a bear with it but the name suits. There will be a name and your blade will let you know." I paused, "Now that you know that you need a deed."

Understanding filled his face. He looked at his sword anew. "It is not as well decorated as Saxon Slayer."

"Then decorate it yourself. Ralph and his smiths can engrave on the blade. You can use precious stones if you wish although they do take a lot of looking after. Better to have a well decorated scabbard and keep the blade functional. Men will see the scabbard and remember that."

"Thank you, Warlord. You have been better than a father to me and I am grateful. You have told me things a father should have done. You have never lied to me and every piece of advice you have given me has been as precious as gold. I will not forget." His shoulders sagged. "Although it is unlikely that I will ever be able to repay you for my father seems to grow stronger."

"Does he Prince Cadfan?" The question in Myrddyn's voice made us all suddenly think about the prince's statement.

"He has more troops and more castles. Does that not make him stronger?"

"He has more men than the Warlord but if he brought his whole army to battle and fought the Warlord, without any allies, who would win?"

"The Warlord of course!"

"And why?"

"He has better soldiers who are better armed and better trained. The Warlord is a better leader."

"The Warlord is ill. Would the army still win?"

"Yes for Hogan would lead or Prince Pasgen…" He smiled as he listened to his own words. "It is not the number but the quality."

"And you have the quality. You have many of your father's best troops for they deserted to you. Now if you cannot train good leaders in case you are ill too... well..."

"Point taken! There is hope then Myrddyn?"

"There is always hope and, generally, good wins out over evil."

My two allies had also built up their forces. While they were still not strong enough to take on Iago alone he dare not attack both of them. The marriage had cemented the alliance creating a country unified in some ways and it ran from the Dee in the north to the south of the land. It was like Rheged had been in the past; our backs to the sea and our enemies before us. The difference was that we had a better alliance. There was no weak link like Morcant Bulc and no dissension in our ranks.

With our five ships patrolling the waters off our coast we had early warning of danger. It was while we were on the mainland that they brought us news of a Saxon fleet. Daffydd had grown into a great leader. His cousins were the other four captains and he ruled them with an iron fist. His father the great Gwynfor had passed away peacefully the previous year and Daffydd was now the head of the family. He ruled the family the same way he ruled his fleet.

"There are fifty ships my lord."

"Do you think they are heading here?"

He shook his head. They appear to be gathering at the Maeresea and the Dee. If I was Iago I would worry. Even if there were but forty warriors on each ship then they could easily assemble two thousand warriors. Deva could fall to those sorts of numbers."

"Keep a watch on them. If they attack Deva then Iago might be driven away but I do not think it would bode well for us."

Myrddyn and I walked along the beach that night discussing the news. "We have information from Aedh and his scouts about Iago but we do not know what the Saxons are up to."

"Then we should spy on the Saxons."

"That is a little risky. They have no one south of the Dee. They would be suspicious of a newcomer would they not?"

"Perhaps, although if the newcomer came from, say Mercia or the East Angles, then they would be less suspicious as they would appear to be from their own people."

"It would take some time."

"It would but if we found out what they were up to then it would be time well spent."

"And you have someone in mind I take it?"

"Yes, me and Lann Aelle."

I was shocked, "My nephew? Why?"

"He is resourceful. He looks like a Saxon and can speak it like a native. He has all the skills needed as well as the courage which others might lack."

"Would he be safe?"

"As safe as you were when you travelled with me."

I knew that Lann Aelle would be safe but I still fretted about him. He was like Hogan and Gawan, he was another son and I could not bear the thought of his life being thrown away. "How would you reach them?"

"We would leave from Ruthin and head east until we were beyond Iago's lands then travel towards the Roman fort and approach Caedwalestate from the east. There was a Saxon settlement there before Aethelfrith; perhaps there still is. We will say we are seeking service with a Saxon lord to find glory fighting the Welsh."

"That might work but Lann Aelle has to agree."

Myrddyn laughed. "And you think he will not jump at the chance! He will be serving you and the boy idolises you. He will do it and I will keep him safe. I promise."

Of course Lann Aelle agreed and they left the next day. To help them sneak through the enemy lines I went with Tuanthal, Pol and a patrol of equites. We would make a raid on one of Iago's settlements. It would make Iago look inwards and it might give us an insight into his plans. We escorted the two, now dressed as Saxons, as far as Yr Wyddgrug. They headed east and we headed towards Gwersyllt which lay to the north of Wrecsam. Aedh and his scouts had told us that there was now a warrior hall there and they had begun to dig a ditch. It was not far from Wrecsam and might just be part of the defence of Wrecsam. If I had been Iago then that is what I would have done. It was, however, less than fifteen miles from Ruthin and could be reached over the Clwyd Hills. I had wanted to see for a while what sort of force he had there and this was the perfect opportunity.

It was also the first chance I had had to see the squires and equites operating together. The equites were not wearing their armour. They would don that once the squires had located the camp. The squires were half a mile ahead of us and were just as effective as Aedh's scouts. We were less than two miles from our goal when they returned. "The camp is ahead. We have left two men watching."

The squires then helped the equites to dress in their armour and mount their heavier horses. Leaving two squires behind to watch the mounts we moved towards the warrior hall. The horses moved much better than the last time I had seen them. Half of the equites had a long spear and small shield while the rest had a larger shield and javelins. As we had ridden Tuanthal and Pol had assured me that the combination worked well. Each warrior also had a sword and a mace. I just relied on Saxon Slayer.

We reached the two scouts and saw, below us, the warrior hall. The ditch did not look deep but that could be deceptive. The warriors were not in the hall but were in front of the ditch, practising. I could see that they were a mixture of traditionally armed warriors and warriors armed with javelins and little armour. They would find no difficulty infiltrating through the passes in the hills. Now I knew what they were about I could plan.

"Tuanthal, how do we disrupt them?"

"Send the squires to attack the flanks while we charge the middle. They will run but the ditch will slow them down and we can use the javelins."

"I am here to watch. You command!"

"Thank you Warlord." Pol commanded the spear armed warriors and I rode with them. Tuanthal led the javelin armed men. We emerged from the woods and trotted down the gentle slope. The squires had galloped off and I saw them charging into lines. The warriors saw them and they turned to face this small annoyance. Suddenly they saw us as the horses hooves thundered across the ground. Some tried to stand and some fled. The ones who stood were the warriors in mail. The long spears allowed Pol and his men to strike the shield wall above the shield in the unprotected throat. I had no such luxury but I sliced down on bare and vulnerable heads as I galloped through.

We reached the ditch and I heard Pol shout. "Halt!"

They took out their maces and began to strike at the lightly armed warriors who tried to get close. Their weapons could not pierce the armour either of the horses or the equites and they fled. The javelins from the squires were hurled to strike them down.

"Fall back!"

We retreated in good order and reached the woods quite quickly. We had not killed many but we had frightened them. My intention had been to make Iago look to his defence rather than to attack and I hoped I had done that.

As we rode back, the equites now without armour Pol asked me, "How was that Warlord?"

"Interesting but without the squires you would not have achieved your objective. Once there is a barrier your spears are useless. If they had had men with axes then you would have suffered a defeat."

"Which is why we need the squires and when they become equites they appreciate the efforts of their brothers far more."

I had learned much and had valuable information for Aidan. "When we reach Ruthin then you may continue on. I will stay for a few days."

Pol looked appalled. "But how will you return to Lord Hogan?"

"I believe there are scouts who do the journey. If you are worried about me then I will travel with them but I feel quite safe in my own land."

I told Aidan of my fears. "The enemy can slip lightly armed men over. I know too well how easy it is for them to slip over a wall and catch sentries unawares. We need to make it almost impossible for them to sneak soundlessly close to the wall."

"And how do we do that Warlord?" The question came from curiosity rather than insolence.

"There are many pines cones close to here and pebbles. Lay a circle of them around the ditch. Plant blackberries, hawthorns and roses. They will tear at them."

They will take some time to grow."

"But when they do they will act as early warning. Put game birds, geese and chickens close to the ditch. They will alarm you."

I stayed a couple of days with Aidan we continued to come up with improvements for this vital bastion. I enjoyed the challenge of devising defences hitherto not used. I went with the scouts to the east and south and approached the defences I knew were there. It was then we had an idea. We were approaching through the bushes which were four hundred paces from the walls. We had cleared a large area to enable our bolt throwers and archers to have a clear field of fire. One of the archers cursed as yet another blackberry grabbed at him. One of the others said, "My lord, if we wove some of the bramble shoots together they would form a barrier. They are still a defence even in winter."

It was an excellent idea and we spent the rest of the morning making nature our defender. Out mailed gloves protected our hands but we all had scars and cuts on our faces. We next stood close to the hedges and looked at the fort. We could see the ditches quite clearly and the trail the scouts used to return to the fort. "Do you always use these paths? Even at night?"

"Yes Warlord."

"Then let us dig some pits. You scouts go to the ridge and make sure that no one observes us."

I had every warrior not on sentry duty digging pits. We carefully stripped away the turf and dug holes about the depth of a man's leg. We embedded a stake in the bottom of each one and then covered the top with thin branches. We put a layer of the soil we had removed and then the turf. The spare soil was deposited in front of the walls as extra protection to the stone base.

"Captain Aidan, make sure that your men only use the track and then aim your bolt throwers to cover it. If you are attacked at night then you should be able to ensure that any warriors cannot get close without being noticed."

"Will you return to the valley today Warlord?"

"No it is getting late and I am of an age now where I need my rest."

The scouts had gone hunting once they had ceased watching for observers and we ate a fine wild pig. They were a fine set of warriors in this last outpost of my land. I loved being with them for it reminded me of my home in

Rheged. To our front were only enemies and to our rear the friends we protected. It was a black and white existence.

I had worked hard and fell immediately to sleep. I was awoken by one of the scouts. "Warlord, Captain Aidan sent me for you. There are warriors outside the walls."

I grabbed Saxon Slayer and followed him. Aidan was on the walls. "The sentries heard men coming through the blackberries. There was too much noise to be animals."

I looked up and saw that there was no moon. They had picked a perfect night for an attack. "We wait now for them to spring the traps. Have your archers ready to loose as many arrows up into the air as they can and have your bolt throwers clear the trails."

It was nerve wracking; waiting in the dark for an enemy you knew was creeping up to the walls. Suddenly there was a scream followed by another. "Now captain!"

The bolt thrower cracked and the arrows soared into the night. There was a roar as the enemy realised that they had been seen. "Loose a fire arrow!"

As the fire arrow rose into the black sky it illuminated the land before the fort. There were hundreds of warriors, most of them lightly armed. I could see in the brief moment of light that many were in the traps and others had been struck by arrows but there were many of them. They raced to the walls. Every warrior and scout stood alongside me at the top of the ramparts. The men of Gwynedd screamed their charge and hurled themselves at the walls. The javelins and arrows thinned them out and the few who reached the walls were slain easily. Dawn was but an hour away when the attack faltered and we waited for dawn to see what remained.

Over forty warriors had died. Others were so badly wounded that they had their throats, mercifully cut by our men as they cleared the field. We had the weapons collected and the bodies piled on to a pyre. When we lit and sent them to the Otherworld it was a message for King Iago. We were ready and we were waiting.

The scouts escorted me and the spare weapons and armour. Hogan had the worried look of a mother rather than a son. Myfanwy, too, was pleased to see me. "We were worried when the others returned without you."

"I will not worry until Myrddyn dreams my death. Besides it was most productive."

I sat with Garth, Hogan and Myrddyn to discuss my findings. "Iago is training lighter armed warriors who can use the high passes. We need a message sending to Prince Cadfan. His father will try there next. We bloodied his nose at Ruthin but he will learn from the experience. All of our frontier forts need to be more creative in their defences. We were able to take Felan's stronghold far too easily. If our enemies learn from us they will begin to use the night as we do to make their strikes."

Myrddyn ruminated and then said, "Fire."

We looked at him. Garth smiled and said, "A little elaboration would throw light on your idea."

"Precisely! Each night the fort lights four braziers two hundred paces from the fort on each of the four sides. They will throw enough light off to show anyone who is approaching. It is a cheap way of defending the forts. The warriors collect dead wood anyway. It would be a way of clearing the forests back further to copse the smaller branches and use them as firewood."

Hogan nodded, "That would work. Cadfan might find a problem at Nefyn."

I shook my head, "Nefyn has much driftwood. His men could collect it from the beach. But he needs to increase his patrols into the mountains." I pointed at Wyddfa. We are lucky here. The mountain is so steep on this side, especially since the rock fall, that Iago cannot approach closely but Nefyn and the Mawddach are a different matter. Perhaps you could send a message to Morag's father advising him of Iago's plans."

"I will. The men are wondering when you will gather our allies and destroy King Iago. If Cadfan were king then all of our resources could be used against the Saxons."

"It will be soon. We are ready but our allies are not. They have much catching up to do. The worst decision would be to attack early and be defeated. When we attack I want us to win and win decisively. As soon as Iago is defeated then the Saxons will expand; at the moment he is a buffer between us and them. If they took Deva then we would have to fight for our lives. Next year. Tell your men to be patient."

When Myrddyn and Lann Aelle returned it was with the news that the Saxons were planning to assault Deva. They were building camps all around the isolated fort to stop the trickle of supplies that King Iago was sending them. There would be no more reinforcements for Deva for a while. The good news was that King Aethelfrith's attention was not on us.

Chapter 17

When we were ready we had to move in secret. The two kings left their borders and mines well defended but brought the rest of their warriors; the best armed and the best trained to Nefyn. Garth assembled our army at Rhuddlan. Myrddyn and I journeyed to Nefyn to discuss our strategy. There were just five of us in the room Prince Cadfan had chosen. We overlooked Wyddfa which was a constant reminder to all of us of the power of the mountain and the link between all of us and the land.

Prince Cadfan was crucial to my plans. He had spent many hours with Hogan and Pol. The three of them had exchanged ideas on ways of attacking an enemy. Their schooling in Constantinopolis came to their aid. He was ready to lead. I hoped that my other two allies would not feel the need to flex their military muscles. I used Myrddyn as the teacher. He was well respected by all of my allies.

Brother Oswald had drawn a detailed map of the land. I am not sure if the two kings had ever seen such a detailed map but they peered at it as though it was part of Myrddyn's magic. "Your army will have the longer journey but you will not be encumbered by heavy horses. It is seventy miles to Wrecsam. You will travel to the lake at Bala. You will need to use your scouts to cut off any garrison which is there as we do not want King Iago warned of an attack from that direction. It may be that Prince Cadfan can persuade those who fight for his father to come over to our side. That would be preferable than spilling the blood of those we wish to fight for us eventually. Bala is half way. If you do not have to fight them then you can rest there for a day. You have three days to reach Wrecsam. Your scouts must let us know when you are close for we will be the bait."

King Cloten asked, "How will you achieve that?"

"We will leave a day earlier than you and we will approach Wrecsam slowly. We want King Iago to think that he outnumbers us, which he will. We will fix his attention to his front which will allow you to attack his flank. With three armies, even though each one is smaller than his, attacking his left flank we should achieve victory. We have to stop him retreating to Wrecsam. We do not want a siege. We want to destroy their will to win." He smiled. "I want them to think that we have used magic to surprise them."

Myrddyn sat and I stood. "You have five hundred warriors between you and this is your chance to defeat King Iago once and for all. With Cadfan on the throne we will have peace between brother kings and we can then defeat the Saxons. This will be the golden age for the land of Wyddfa and Cader Idris."

The prince accompanied us to our horses. "I want to thank you Warlord. I told you once before that you have been more of a father to me than my own ever was and I will not let you down. I will lead our armies to victory. We will be there when you expect us. I promise you."

"And I told you Prince Cadfan that you are truly noble and I know that you will be a man of your word."

We only had to ride as far the docks for 'The Wolf' was waiting. Our mounts were used to being transported by sea and happily walked aboard. The journey gave Myrddyn and me the time to finalise our own assault. We were leaving skeleton garrisons to protect our forts. Every warrior who could fight in a shield wall was with us. Every archer would be there under Daffydd's command. We had a little over six hundred men. The scouts had estimated that King Iago had almost fifteen hundred warriors. Some of these were in garrisons but over twelve hundred were at Wrecsam. We would be outnumbered two to one when we began our attack.

This was the first time we had gathered our whole army together. It was quite a proud moment for me. Young Gawan had begged to join me but he was too young. I did not want to worry about my young son when the whole of our future was at stake. Lann Aelle carried my Wolf Banner proudly as we rode with the sixty equites, then came my warriors followed by Daffydd and his archers, finally came the squires with the spare horses and armour of the equites. We could have brought another five hundred men but that would have stripped Mona and my forts of their best warriors. I remembered that there were ten Saxon ships not far away and they could easily land a force to take advantage of our absence. I was happy that I had the best warriors in Britannia at my back. If we lost it would be because of my incompetence and not the quality of the warriors under my command.

We halted just south of Ruthin and made camp. Here some of Aidan's warriors and scouts joined us. With an attack on Wrecsam the frontier fort should be safe. Aidan had confided in me, when I had stayed with him, that his men yearned to prove themselves in battle rather than fending off attacks of a few lightly armed warriors. I was more than happy with their contribution thus far. Without their efforts we could not have made the rest so prosperous. Aidan himself led his contingent and he was confident that his deputy, Tadgh, could defend the fort as well as he could.

Prince Pasgen and Hogan had not camped for some time and they found the Spartan camp a little hard to bear. They were used to soft beds and baths. Garth and Mungo found it quite amusing. They were hard men who frequently went out on long patrols with their men and they had slept rough before. No matter what the outcome of the battle I was pleased that we had the opportunity of fighting together. Myrddyn and I spent the last few hours before sleep going over the fine details of the plan. Much depended upon the two of us. I was confident that my men would not let me down; I did not want the two men who had conceived the plan to be found to be wanting.

The next morning brought with it an icy wind blowing from the east. I hoped that this was not an evil portent. The scouts were well to the fore and were vital to the plan. I had told Aedh that his normal strategy of staying hidden was to be abandoned. I wanted them seen. I wanted the new horsemen of King Iago to come chasing after them. Although I did not know for certain I was convinced that King Iago did not have enough food in Wrecsam for a siege. Our spies had told us that they had had a poor harvest. The fact that he had been keeping Deva supplied had eaten into his reserves. He could not stay cooped up in his stronghold for long. He would want to fight us, in the open but with the walls of Wrecsam at his back. I needed him fixed in place to allow my allies to strike him at his vulnerable left side.

When we were four miles from Wrecsam we halted and the equites were equipped and mounted on their war horses. They looked magnificent and seemed to sparkle in the icy sunlight. The ten squires who were left behind to watch the mounts had been drawn by lots and none of them looked happy. The equites took their place on the left flank while the squires were on the right. My shield wall marched in column but we would fight in a wedge formation. The archers marched behind the warriors. I led the whole, magnificent army with Myrddyn at my side and Lann Aelle behind me with the banner.

One of Aedh's scouts galloped up. "Warlord, King Iago's horsemen are pursing Captain Aedh."

Good. Ride to the squires and prepare them to attack."

"Yes Warlord."

It was flat and open fields before us and we saw the scouts hurtling towards us. They were feigning fear and the men of Gwynedd had bought the deception. They were whooping and cheering as they raced after the thin line of scouts. They saw us just as I ordered Lann to lower the banner. They halted in a ragged line, unable to believe what they saw. Their delay cost many their lives as the squires, eager to prove themselves with the Warlord watching, tore into them. The horsemen at the rear, some twenty of them, turned tail and raced back to Wrecsam. The well trained squires halted and chased the riderless ponies back to our lines. Five of the squires took the mounts to the other squires at the rear and the scouts formed a line of mounted skirmishers half a mile ahead of us.

We marched forwards. There was no hurry in our gait. We wanted King Iago to have time to react. The last thing we needed was to try to take a fort. I wanted him to attempt to defeat me in battle. I had judged that he thought he could defeat me and would then prove to the other kings that he was the better general.

The two lines of equites were to the left of our line and I knew that they would intimidate not only King Iago but all of his warriors. So it proved when King Iago marched his army out from the walls of Wrecsam. He placed his strongest warriors on his right. He personally led out his oathsworn whom he placed behind him in a shield wall. Garth had already ordered our men into a wedge formation of three arrow heads. He led the middle one.

I rode forwards with Myrddyn and Lann. I halted out of bowshot of the enemy. I did not trust King Iago to follow the conventions of war. "King Iago ap Beli I am here to avoid war and unnecessary bloodshed. Your son Prince Cadfan," I waved, vaguely at the lines of men behind me, "has been abused by you. He is the rightful king of Gwynedd. With him ruling this land there will be peace for all. Leave now, with your oathsworn and surrender the field to us and you can live. Stay and fight and you shall die."

The field became quiet and then King Iago began to laugh. "You are a fool! The whelp who ran to you is not my son. This is my son." It was then I noticed the boy on the pony next to him. "Cadfan's mother deceived me and he will never be king of this land." He glared at my serried ranks. "Wherever you are cowering boy, hear those words. You will never be king. As for you Lann of Rheged, you too are a fool. You bring this handful of men against me. I have two thousand men here. We did what you could not. We defeated the Saxons. Do your worst and at the end of the day I will wear the sword you call Saxon Slayer. It will truly belong to a mighty slayer of Saxons."

His oathsworn and the shield wall all banged their shields and cheered. I noticed that the others did not. Perhaps they did not believe that I was a fool.

"This is your last chance Iago before I unleash my men upon you."

"You do not frighten me with your words or with your so-called wizard, the trickster, Myrddyn!"

Myrddyn answered. His voice was far more powerful than one would think and his words boomed out across the field. "And I warn you King Iago. Today I will bring forth an army from the heart of Wyddfa and it will be the spirit of our holy mountain which defeats you. It is Cymri herself who will beat you."

This time his oathsworn and shield wall remained silent. I could see King Iago's face suffuse with anger. He shouted, "I will kill you both myself!"

His banner lowered and his men marched forwards. "Now Lann!"

Lann Aelle waved the banner once and then we withdrew to the rear of the wedges. A shield wall does not move swiftly and King Iago had made the classic mistake of not changing formation. If they tried to move swiftly then they would lose cohesion. Hogan led the equites in a charge towards their strongest warriors. Daffydd began loosing arrows in flight after flight to soar above our wedges. King Iago and his advisers had learned the value of shields and armour. His men protected themselves and suffered fewer casualties. Garth and his men were in wedge formation and could move quickly. The shield wall they struck was not solid; men had been killed by arrows while others had slowed down to protect themselves. The line bowed inwards as the three wedges hacked, slashed and slaughtered the Gwynedd shield wall.

I peered nervously over to the right where Hogan's sixty warriors had charged over four hundred men. I need not have fretted. The first line had broken the wall with their spears and the second line had thundered in with maces, axes and swords. The enemy right flank began to curve back towards the walls of Wrecsam. Garth and his men had penetrated deeply into the Gwynedd shield wall and were now in danger of being surrounded.

"The second signal Lann." Lann dipped the standard twice and the squires, all fifty of them, charged and threw three flights of javelins at the Gwynedd left flank. The pressure on Garth decreased and Daffydd's archers score more hits. I saw Iago shouting orders and his oathsworn began to move further left to protect the flank from the horsemen. I nodded to Lann and he waved the standard three times. The squires withdrew and the oathsworn cheered at their apparent victory.

"The horn, Lann." Lann took the Roman Buccina and gave three blasts on it. My well trained wedges began to subtly change direction. The left wedge held while the middle one moved slightly left and the right one moved almost in echelon. We now had a line which was facing south west. The horn should have signalled Prince Cadfan but of him there was no sign. So far our whole pan had worked perfectly but the flaw was that if our allies did not arrive then it would break down completely and we would lose.

I summoned Aedh. "Send scouts and see if you can find Prince Cadfan."
"Aye my lord."

The sheer weight of the number of the enemy was now forcing my wedges into one round shield wall and we no longer had the momentum which gave us the edge. I was just about to dismount when I heard a groan from the shield wall and a strangled cry from Lann Aelle.

"What is it nephew?"
"Garth has fallen, King Iago has slain him."
That decided me. "Myrddyn, direct the battle. Lann Aelle, bring the banner."

I drew Saxon Slayer and began to work my way through the warriors. There was a mumbling which grew slowly into a shout which became a roar as we approached the front of the wall. "Wolf Warrior! Wolf Warrior!" The warriors at the rear began to bang their shield in time to the shout and I could feel the fluttering of the banner above Lann's head. I sensed, rather than saw, the line stiffen as my oathsworn heard my arrival.

Iago could see my banner and I saw him furiously fighting one of my warriors. His fury gave him added strength and his sword sliced through the helmet of the warrior who fell dead at his feet. I stepped into the gap and promptly punched the warrior to the right of Iago and then sliced Saxon Slayer across his open throat. With room to my left I turned to face Iago. He tried to swing the sword at my head but there was no room for the movement and he merely caught me a blow from his hilt on my helmet. I head butted him when he tried to withdraw his sword for another blow. My helmet had been given to me by Andronikos and was stronger than any helmet I had ever seen. The strengthened nasal was as hard as a sword and I heard his nose break. Blood splattered all those in the Gwynedd front rank and King Iago recoiled from the strength of the blow. I took the opportunity of slipping a dagger into my left hand and then punched again with my shield. The warrior who had stepped in to protect King Iago's right was not ready and the blow knocked him to the ground. Lann Aelle slew him. I stepped forwards again suddenly aware that we were all moving forwards.

Saxon Slayer was impotent in a tight shield wall. None of us could swing our weapons and it became a battle of strength as to who could force the other one back. My men had trained for years and we all practised this push. Punching with shield and sword hilt we knocked the men of Gwynedd backwards. King Iago had a face filled with fury. The blood from his broken nose gave him a terrible aspect. "You can still surrender, King Iago!"

"Surrender? We still outnumber you. You are going to die."

"Outnumbered? What of the army of Wyddfa that Myrddyn promised?"

He tried a punch with his hilt which I countered with my shield. "They are another of the magician's lies."

Suddenly there was a wail from the rear of Iago's line and, above the heads of his men I could see the banners of Cadfan and the two kings. They had arrived. "Then who is slaughtering your men?"

The Gwynedd line slackened and Lann Aelle stepped beside me and chopped down on the neck of the warrior before him. It allowed me the chance to swing Saxon Slayer across my body to slice into the top of King Iago's armour. It tore though some of the links. Mail armour is only good when it is whole. I could see his leather vest below the armour. Fear replaced the fury on his face. He had more room now and he swung his sword overhand at me. I countered with Saxon Slayer. I saw pieces of metal flayed from his sword and he stepped backwards. I gave him no chance to recover and swung my sword at his leg. The mail protected it but I saw that it had suffered another rip. I punched with my shield and he was forced to step backwards.

I saw that Cadfan and his allies were now less than fifty paces from me. The men of Gwynedd were fighting back to back. They were no longer fighting to win they were fighting to survive. I had to end the battle soon or there would be no army left for Prince Cadfan to lead.

I feinted at Iago's shield and he turned it to face the blow which never came. I turned the blade and sliced across his middle. A large rent appeared in his mail shirt. He tried to chop at my head but I took the blow on my shield and then punched with the crosspiece of my sword. His shield was too low and the end went into his eye. He screamed in agony and I punched with my shield again. The blows to my shield had made some of the metal stick out and one of the pieces caught on the ripped mail of the king's mail shirt. As he tried to step back he found that he could not. He began to overbalance and I pulled Saxon Slayer back. I aimed for the gap in his mail and my blade skewered him to the ground. I twisted as I withdrew the bloody weapon and saw that it was a mortal wound. He tried to raise himself and speak but he collapsed backwards, his life blood flooding from him.

I shouted, "King Iago is dead! Long live King Cadfan!"

I saw the warriors of Gwynedd look at each other. The oathsworn were almost all dead and they could see their king dying. They began to throw down their weapons. We had won but at what cost?

I looked around and there was Lann Aelle. He was grinning at me. I grasped him about the shoulders and held him to me. "Well done Lann!"

"No, Warlord, any praise should go to you. You held the line when we were about to be defeated. The victory is all yours."

I looked around the battlefield. We had lost far fewer than the men of Gwynedd but they had not suffered as many deaths as I had expected. The king's oathsworn had taken the brunt of our attack. To my horror I saw, behind the king, the body of his dead son. I do not think anyone would have deliberately killed the boy but in the heat of a battle then there are tragic deaths. I saw Prince Cadfan approaching. I began to kneel. He shook his head and raised me up. "No Warlord, you kneel to no man." He embraced me and both armies cheered. "I am sorry that we were late. Our allies are not as used to fighting and campaigning as we are." He shrugged. "They will get better after all we have our first real victory."

I looked at the knot of my warriors fifty paces away. "But at a cost, Garth, my oldest captain has died. He was the last of the Rheged shield wall. This day marks the end of an era."

The prince looked distraught. Garth had taught him much when he had first come to live with us. We both went to the warriors who were crowded around his body. Eoin who had guarded his right looked at me with tears in his eyes. "He is smiling my lord. He will be waiting for us in the Otherworld."

"He was a brave and doughty warrior Eoin. He had fought with me when I had but twenty men. I will miss him."

I looked beyond the shield wall and saw, to my great relief, that Hogan too had survived along with Tuanthal and Prince Pasgen. They were even more precious to me now that we had won than they had been before. Myrddyn dismounted and looked down at Garth. "I will miss him and his pointed comments about magic. He will be a hard man to replace."

"He will be an impossible man to replace." I began to weary of the day. It was not a good taste in my mouth but a bitter one. I know that we had not lost as many men as we had expected but Garth was too great a loss and I cursed Iago for his greed and his treachery.

Myrddyn spent most of the rest of the afternoon healing. King Cadfan entered Wrecsam and accepted the oaths of his new subjects. None of King Iago's oathsworn had survived but the rest of the army appeared happy to offer their allegiance to the young king. King Cloten and King Arthlwys came to me as I stood by Garth's body.

"We now know what you have done for us, Warlord. For us war was a raid by a neighbour." King Cloten spread an arm around the battlefield. "This is war and we are novices. We would like you to continue to lead us into battle. We have spoken with King Cadfan and he is in agreement. We will fight as Cymri under the Wolf Banner. If we disagree about sheep thefts and cannot agree we will let you decide."

"But I am no king."

King Arthlwys smiled, "And that gives you more power than you can imagine. You have shown that you can see beyond boundaries and you can see the way ahead. I have heard of this Great King Urien and for us his greatest success was in making you the warrior you have become. We will follow you."

I sighed. The weight was back on my shoulders and I could not rid myself of it. "Then there is one more thing we must do. We need to go to Deva. There are brave warriors there who defend against the Saxons. We should either raise the siege or rescue them. On the morrow we will meet and decide."

"As you wish, Warlord."

Hogan and Myrddyn knew how distraught I was and they visited me in the house I had been allocated. Lann Aelle sharpened my sword and I stared into the fire. "He is happy you know."

"Who is happy?"

"Why Garth of course. He once told me that had you not chosen him as the leader of your oathsworn then he would have died in Rheged with the rest of King Urien's warriors. You gave him a station he could never have hoped for. He had no family but that is because your family was his. He was as proud of Hogan as you were, probably more because he had a hand in his training."

Hogan shook his head, "More than a hand. He made me the warrior I am today. I received no special treatment because I was the son of the Warlord. He worked me harder than the other recruits and I loved him for it. "

"Garth was the essence of what makes you a great leader. He had limited ability but you made him better than the raw material and he did the same with those he trained. It was the same with Miach and Riderch. They stayed with you because they believed in you and what you stood for. You have never broken your word and that is a rare thing. You never asked any man to do something you would not do. The men are still in awe of the fact that you went into Din Guardi and into Felan's lair. They know of no other leader, King Urien included, who would do that."

I had not heard that before and it both gratified and worried me. Would my labours never end? I had hoped that with a united Cymri I could retire to Castle Cam and watch my grandchildren growing up. Now I felt obliged to carry on. "Thank you for that. I needed someone to speak to me and make me see sense. This is when I miss Myfanwy. She knows me better than any. Tomorrow we hold council. I want all of my leaders there for we have decisions to make."

King Iago had had a large hall built for what he thought would be embassies from other kings. We met there. "The three kings have asked me to continue as Warlord." I paused and looked for the nods from each of the three of them. "I accept." Everyone banged on the table. I held up my hand for silence. "Before we can do that we need to do something about Deva. There is a garrison of warriors there and they have been besieged for some time. We either need to raise the siege or to rescue them."

A murmur of small conversations rippled around the room. King Cadfan stood. "I would not expect my brother kings to travel that far from their kingdoms. They have already gained my throne for me and they need to return home to defend their borders."

"Surely that can wait?"

"No King Cloten." It was Myrddyn who spoke. "We may not have liked King Iago but the Mercians feared him. they do not fear King Cadfan, yet. You need to fortify your borders and prevent incursions from our enemies."

Coming from Myrddyn the kings accepted the advice and they nodded. I sensed relief on their part. Neither of them was a warrior king and they would go back to trading and making their people rich. There was nothing wrong with that. I stood. "Then King Cadfan and I will leave a garrison here under the command of Dai ap Gruffydd for we do not want to lose to the Mercians such a key town. We will travel to Deva in the morning. We know what we must do."

Chapter 18

We were a small but well trained army which headed the short journey to Deva. None of us were under any illusions. The Saxons would be there in force and they would be fresh. We had fought a long hard battle and we would be outnumbered. Aedh and his scouts rode in and their faces told us the story. "They have many camps, my lord, and Deva is ringed by Saxons. We estimated at least a thousand on this side and there are ships in the Dee and they are filled with warriors, or at least, there are warrior camps by their boats."

We had halted five miles from Deva and we could now plan. We had less than eight hundred men. We had to make a decision. I drew Myrddyn, Hogan and the king to one side. "We will be making the decision. I can see that Aedh thinks that it is fruitless to attempt anything."

Cadfan sighed, "You are probably right. There are three hundred men at most in the fort. We could lose more than that in attempting to relieve it."

"So we let them die?"

Myrddyn had this way of cutting to the key question. I could see the look of horror on Cadfan's face. "The decision to leave them there was your father's and not yours."

"And yet they are the brave men of Gwynedd. How could I look at my other warriors knowing that I had let them die."

"I ask you again, King Cadfan, what do you wish?"

"I wish to rescue them but I will do it with my own men."

I clapped him about the shoulders, "Well done! You are twice the man your father was."

Then Hogan smiled and said, "Of course we will not let you do it alone, we will help you."

The look of relief on his face was worth a ship load of gold from Constantinopolis. "Well Myrddyn? You have a plan?"

"It is one which has stood us in good stead before now my lord. " I nodded. "A few of us sneak into the fort and help the men inside escape when an attack is launched on those besieging."

Hogan and I nodded but Cadfan looked appalled. "How do you get inside? No forget that, how do you get by the Saxons?"

"That is simple. We use Saxon speakers, me, Lann Aelle and Aedh."

"And me, of course."

Hogan's face froze. "No father, you are Warlord and we cannot risk you."

"But you will not be risking me, I will. And it is decided. You, Hogan, will command the army. I would suggest an attack on the two camps by the bridge. Use the archers to keep the others at bay. Give us one night to contact them and then attack."

"How will we know you have succeeded?"

"We will launch three flaming arrows the morning after we arrive. We will break out when we see King Cadfan's standard at the bridge. We then retreat to Ruthin. They will not expect that."

They tried to dissuade me but I was set on this course of action. Had Myrddyn joined in their remonstrations then things might have been different but he seemed happy about it.

"My mind is set but who else is there? King Cadfan cannot go for we need him to lead the rest of the people. Would you go Hogan? Can you pass for a Saxon? All four of us have been chosen for our skill in deception. All of us, Myrddyn and me especially, have done this before."

We spent some time finalising how we would defeat the Saxons. Hogan and Cadfan were left in charge of our warriors. While we were spies they would have much to do. Myrddyn's plans were never simple affairs.

We donned Saxon war gear; we had plenty. I gave Saxon Slayer to Hogan for safe keeping. The blade, like my wolf skin marked me out as Lord Lann. We had our story. We were warriors of King Cearl of Mercia. We had heard that there was plunder to be had and we wished to join with the men of Northumbria. Once we had passed through their first camps we would adapt our story.

We left towards sunset. To arrive after dark would arouse suspicion. The scouts escorted us as far as the first Saxon camp at the eastern end of their perimeter. They had scouted it out and told us that there were only twenty warriors and they were watching the river crossing as it could be forded by brave men on horses. We left the safety and security of the woods and joined the road which led from the east. We did not try to be furtive but we talked of battles and wars we had fought in; all in Saxon of course.

Two Saxon warriors stepped out from the hedgerow with spears levelled at us. "Halt. State who you are."

As they spoke others appeared from the riverbank.

Myrddyn spread his arms and said, "Thank the Allfather that we have found fellow Saxons." He pointed vaguely to the south. We were chased by the horsemen of Gwynedd a little way down the road. We barely escaped with our lives."

Although they were still suspicious I could see that they were intrigued and they lowered their spears slightly. A warrior with many battle rings on his arms and a scar on his face stepped forwards. "How did you know they were the men of Gwynedd?"

Myrddyn shrugged. "We had had to cross into their land to reach here. Who else could they have been? They did not speak our language."

The spears lowered a little more. "Did they wear armour?"

"Horsemen with armour? Whoever heard of such a thing? No, they were on ponies with spears. There were more than ten of them. Had there been less we would have fought them for we are seasoned warriors."

"And why are you here?"

"We have journeyed from across the seas. We landed in the land of the East Angles. Some of our brethren were slain and we moved towards Mercia. We fought for King Cearl and helped him to settle the west of his kingdom. But we are not his oathsworn and seek employment."

The warrior turned to one of his men, "Scanlon, light a torch, I would look at these warriors."

I surreptitiously loosened my sword in its scabbard. It was a good sword and had been taken from one of the oathsworn of King Iago. I hoped I would not have to use it yet. Scanlon returned with the burning torch and the leader held it to Myrddyn. He moved on to Aedh. I could see that he wondered about those two for neither was a well built man. Our story of being warriors, hung by a thin thread. He examined Lann Aelle and seemed happy enough. He saw the battle rings on the hilt of Bear Killer. I hoped he would not ask to see the blade as he might recognise it as Aella's. I put that thought from my head for that had been many years ago. When he came to me he saw my scarred face and my battered armour. He looked at my sword. "Let me see your sword."

I drew it out but held on to it. "That is not a Saxon blade."

"No, it belonged to a warrior of Gwynedd. I slew him and took this. It is a better weapon than mine was."

He seemed satisfied. He pointed to Lann and me. "You two will be welcomed by Eorl Aethelward. I can see that you have fought in the shield wall. As for your two…" He shrugged. "You have come at a good time. We begin our final assault in the next few days. Just as soon as the rest of the ships arrive we will rid the fort of the men of Gwynedd. You had better stay with us here tonight. We are all wary of warriors who suddenly appear at night." He pointed to Deva, a mile away across the river, "We are close to King Iago's men."

"It is not quite dark; could we not visit with this Aethelward? We are anxious to begin work."

"Aethelward is north of the river. It is Ardal who is in command and he is by the bridge." He smirked. "He has a bad temper and he would not be happy to be disturbed. We captured some female slaves today and he will be enjoying them." I could see that he wanted rid of us and did not want to share his food with us as hospitality dictated. "But if you wish to incur his wrath…" He gestured with his hand for us to pass.

"Thank you er…?"

"Carl and these are my men."

"Thank you for your kindness Carl and do not judge a warrior by his build." Myrddyn grinned, "Sometimes smaller warriors can do great deeds."

They all laughed, "We have yet to see a small man beat a big man but I admire your courage. If you survive your meeting with Ardal I shall share a mug of ale with you. Keep on the track next to the river." He laughed, "And don't fall in!"

I noticed, as we made our way down the overgrown track, that the night was cool and a fog was already rising from the waters. It might be prove a useful weapon. When we were a little way from their camp we halted. We huddled together. "That was useful information about the slaves. It means they might well be occupied."

"Yes Warlord but we still need to get over the river."

"Aedh, find the next group of Saxons. We might as well wait a little while; they will be drunk and more occupied the later we leave it."

"And the fog might be thicker." I could see Myrddyn's mind working on how he could use the weather to our advantage.

Soon the fog was so thick that we could not see the other bank. When Aedh appeared, silently from its grey gloom Lann Aelle almost cried out. "There is no one until you reach the bridge. You can just make out the glow from their fires. There are many armed men but they are pleasuring themselves."

"All of them?"

"No Myrddyn, they have sentries who are watching; six of them. I could not see the far end of the bridge."

"So wizard, how do we cross this river? Do we walk?" I pointed at our armour. "We cannot swim."

"No but we can float." He crawled across the reedy undergrowth and grasped a dead tree which had floated down and become snared in the grass and weeds of the bank. He pointed to another further along the bank. "These will support our weight. We lean on them and push them out into the stream. The current should move us towards the bridge. When we are close we gently direct the logs, by kicking until we are close to the northern bank of the river."

I could see that the other two were worried but I was not. Myrddyn was a clever man. If he said the logs would bear our weight then they would. "Aedh, you and Lann Aelle take the other log. Myrddyn and I will take this one. Follow us but make no noise."

As I stepped into the river it felt icy although I knew it was not. Alarmingly the fog was above our heads but Myrddyn smiled. He was happy and he knew where we were going. I just hoped that the other two would be able to see us. We pushed away from the bank. The log dipped a little but took our weight. There were branches we could use to get a better grip. I glanced behind me and saw, to my great relief, that I could see Aedh. The current was slow but powerful and we only needed an occasional flick of our legs to correct our direction. The lights from the fires at the southern end of the bridge were a great help as they illuminated the Roman arches. Had there been sentries on the bridge then we would have been spotted but the fog made us invisible. I could almost hear the legend of Myrddyn's magic being told.

The wizard tapped me on my shoulder and I started to kick. Gradually we edged towards the northern bank. It was just a darker patch of fog at first but soon we could discern the foliage sprouting from its sides. A look over my shoulder told me that the other two were close behind. The log made a soft hissing sound as it slid against the reeds. We waited without moving until Aedh and Lann had joined us. We slowly clambered over the logs on to the bank. There were young oak trees lining the bank and we crawled beneath them to get a view of where we were.

To the left, about fifty paces away, was the Gwynedd end of the bridge. I could see there were guards there. The gatehouse of the fort touched the bridge and I could see the sentries on the top. The walls of the fort came towards us and there was another tower forty paces to the north of us. To the right I could see the glow of another Saxon fire. This would be the most difficult part of our quest. The men in the fort would be nervous and likely to fight first and ask questions later. In addition I was an enemy of their king. We had to tread very carefully.

The ditch around the fort ended at the gatehouse and so we would have to approach the sentries on the bridge. Myrddyn mimed him going to them and talking and us following. That made sense. If he approached alone and then three more warriors appeared they would suspect a trap. I tapped Aedh and Lann on the shoulder and we crouched as Myrddyn stood and began to creep towards the sentries. We followed, keeping our heads as close to the line of fog as we could. The closer we got to the bridge the thinner became the fog. Suddenly Myrddyn stood and spoke in the language of the sentries. "I am Myrddyn the wizard, and I am here with news of your king. I have three companions." We stood as one.

It could have been comical for the ten sentries looked in awe at the wraiths that appeared from the fog. Without my wolf skin, helmet and shield I was not recognisable as the Warlord and Myrddyn's fame was known throughout the land. I was no different from Lann Aelle beside me; save a little older. The leader of the sentries quickly recovered his composure and a spear was thrust at Myrddyn's throat. "I am Myrddyn the wizard. I appeared without you seeing me as did my companions. Do you not think, had I wished you harm, that I could have materialised inside the fort?"

"Dai, get their weapons."

I nodded to the other two and we handed over our swords to the man called Dai. His eyes widened when he saw Bear Killer. I still had a dagger in my boot but I hoped that I would not need it.

"Dai, you stay here. Gareth, come with me." We were prodded, none too gently in the back and pushed towards the gate. When we reached it our captor rapped on the gate and said, "Captain of the guard, I have four prisoners."

We heard the beam being moved from the gate and it creaked open. In the dim light we saw a wall of spears appear. "He says he is Myrddyn with news from our king."

"Return to your post and leave them with me."

I was familiar with the layout of the fort. It was identical to Civitas and I knew that we were being taken to the Praetorium. We had got further than I had expected and I hoped it was a good sign. The captain of the guard went inside the office and we heard the murmurings of a conversation. Then the door was opened and we were pushed inside. The commander of the fort was a squat and tough looking warrior. I seemed to remember seeing him many years ago when we had fought Iago. I had had my helmet on then and he would not have recognised me.

"I am Llewellyn ap Daffydd and I command here. Before I order your deaths tell me the story you told my men so that I may judge the truth."

"I am Myrddyn the wizard!"

"I should kill you now as a liar for I know my king will have nothing to do with you!"

"King Iago is dead!"

"You lie! This is a Saxon trick."

"To what end? Besides when did you ever hear of Myrddyn working for the Saxons?"

I stepped forwards, "Or Lann, the Warlord of Rheged."

He suddenly recognised me and his sword came out in a flash and pricked my neck."

"Why should I now not kill you and receive great honour from my king?"

"Because your king is now King Cadfan and he defeated his father in battle outside Wrecsam."

"You lie!"

"You know I am the Warlord. Has anyone ever heard me lie? Even my greatest enemies know that I speak the truth. But King Cadfan gave me something to prove that I speak the truth." I reached down into my pouch and drew out a golden dragon with a red ruby for an eye. "You know that this was worn around the neck of King Iago. If I have it then…"

I saw his shoulders sag and the sword drooped. "You speak the truth but I do not understand. Why are you here? Why risk death?"

"Because I am Warlord and we now have an alliance of three kings in Cymri. The men you command in here are too valuable to King Cadfan to lose. We are here to rescue you."

He laughed. "That is a good one. How? Will Myrddyn fly us out?"

"First of all there is to be an assault by the Saxons in force the day after tomorrow. The fort will fall. Of that I have no doubt. I am here to offer you and your men a way out."

Llewellyn sank into his seat with his shoulders slumped. He looked into my eyes. "The king is truly dead?"

I nodded. "I killed him in single combat."

He gave a rueful smile. "He always thought he was the greatest warrior in the land. He was foolish to take on Lord Lann, the killer of champions. He kept promising that he would relieve us but in my heart I knew that he would not." He sighed and then sat upright. "So tell me your plan and I will decide if I we escape or die at our posts."

"King Cadfan is waiting close to the bridge. My warriors are with him. Tomorrow morning we loose three fire arrows. They will then attack the bridge. When we see the standard of King Cadfan on the bridge then we cross and escape."

"As simple as that?"

"Can you see a flaw in it?"

"Will they be able to hold the bridge?"

"We just defeated King Iago and his army. I have seen their camps. There are less than three hundred close to the bridge." I pointed west. "There are more than fifteen hundred ready to attack from the west the day after tomorrow."

He looked at Myrddyn. "Can you use magic to help us wizard?"

He smiled, "I got us in here did I not. We crossed through their camps, and the river, to reach the fort."

He nodded, "Very well. There seems little alternative."

"How many men do you have?"

"One hundred and fifty fighting men and forty wounded. There are another fifty refugees."

"Any horses?"

He shook his head. "We ate them."

He looked at me to see if I was disappointed. I was not. This was all that I had expected. "We need everyone ready to leave as soon as we see the standard waved. Keep all of your soldiers on the walls but I want everything that will burn putting next to the north, west and east gates. We will fire them when we leave. The smoke will aid our escape and the flames will deter the pursuit from the north. We will burn the gatehouse before we cross the bridge."

"We?"

"My warriors and me."

"And I will aid you. You are a strange one, Warlord. You are putting your lives in jeopardy for an enemy."

"No Llewellyn, King Iago was my enemy never the people or warriors of Gwynedd. Remember he attacked us. I was his ally as I was his father's and now his son. The Emperor of Rome gave me the title of Dux Britannica. I swore an oath to protect this land and its people. My only enemy is the Saxon race."

We had much to do. We reclaimed our weapons and began to build our pyres. The mist hid dawn for longer than usual and we had to wait to make sure that our arrows would be seen. Llewellyn summoned one of his archers. He loosed the three arrows in succession. They arced towards the south. I wondered what the Saxons would make of that. They could do little about it now anyway. All the people and warriors who were not on the walls were gathered behind the southern gate close to the bridge. Llewellyn had his best forty warriors on the bridge ready to support his new king.

"Myrddyn, can we do anything about damaging the bridge?"

"Fire will weaken it. I will build a couple of pyres beneath the northern pillars. There is plenty of wood." He pointed at the crude huts first the Saxons and latterly the men of Gwynedd had erected. They were bone dry and would burn quickly. He ordered some of the defenders to follow him. Such was his power that they did so without question. I stood with Llewellyn and Lann by the bridge as Myrddyn and his men beavered away beneath our feet. The Saxons at the other end of the bridge were eyeing us suspiciously but we did not appear to be doing anything belligerent. It was a hiatus and I could feel the tension in the fort commander.

"How will we know when the King is attacking?"

I pointed to the men at the other end of the bridge. "I suspect they will form a shield wall but they will be worried about an attack to their rear. My men will be charging with the equites and it takes a brave man to stand up to a mounted, armoured man on an armoured horse. You have faced a wedge," he nodded, "imagine facing that on horseback. There will not be many of them but they will be led by the king and my son. I guarantee that they will clear a way to the bridge and then my shield wall will hold the enemy back until we escape."

"You are that confident about your men and the king?"

I said simply, "I trained them all; the men and your king. I have fought besides all of them and I know how good they are. Do not worry; your new king will forge and army ten times better than that of his father. He has a sound mind and a good heart."

"Meaning that Iago had a poor mind and a bad heart?"

"I have learned never to speak ill of the dead."

Our conversation was interrupted by a roar from the Saxon side and we heard the first clash of battle. It was easy for me to visualise as I knew what would be happening. The scouts would have cleared the sentries; the archers would have showered the camp with arrows and then the equites, led by those wielding long spears would have charged. Poor Llewellyn had no concept of that type of warfare. I saw the worry etched into his face.

As I had expected they formed a weak shield wall to stop our escaping. "Come Lann. Let us introduce the Saxons to Bear Killer."

"Yes my lord."

"You would attack them, just the two of you? There are twenty of them."

"There are twenty men looking over their shoulders. When I shout my war cry and we run at them they will think the whole fort is charging them."

Without further ado I drew my sword and we ran at the shield wall. "Wolf Warrior!"

I heard a roar from behind me and knew that Llewellyn and his men had joined us. I was correct only three men had the courage to stand against us. Bear Killer took one, my shield punched a second over the bridge and my borrowed sword killed the last. We held both ends of the bridge. I grinned as I turned to face Llewellyn.

"You did it! That was mad, glorious, but mad."

"You can start the fires and withdraw your men now. " I pointed down the road where the standard of Gwynedd fluttered above the charging equites. The Saxons were not ready for battle and few had mail. I could see them throwing themselves away from the hooves. "Come Lann, let us find Aedh."

Aedh was at the northern gate supervising the fiercest of the fires. The men were streaming down the stairs and joining the rest across the bridge. He pointed at the east gate, "We started those two fires first at the east and the west. It made the Saxons to the north head for the northern gate. It has delayed them."

I heard the crash of axes on the undefended gates but it was too late now; the flames had caught hold. Not only were the gates on fire but the walkways and some of the wooden ladders were burning. The building had wooden beams in their roofs and they were burning. Deva would need to be completely rebuilt.

"Time for us to go."

Llewellyn was waiting at the southern gate. "There are just us left. The rest have crossed the bridge."

"Aedh light the last fire." I turned and shouted, "Now Myrddyn!"

"You had better be quick then!"

The gates caught, it was open but we couldn't help that. We reached the top of the bridge and Myrddyn and his men scrambled up. "I would run Warlord! I used some Greek Fire mixture!" Behind us we heard the screams of anger as the first of the Saxons burst through into the fort. We ran on to the bridge. Lann, Aedh and I turned to see how far away the enemy were. They were racing towards the southern gate.

"Warlord! Run!"

Chapter 19

We sped to the middle of the bridge. Suddenly, just as the first of the Saxons approached the end Myrddyn's flames leapt into the air. There was a strange sound as though every wind in the world had blown all at once. The wall of flame leapt higher than a warrior on a horse and the three of us were knocked from our feet. Myrddyn raced to help me up. "I did warn you my lord."

I stood laughing, "Am I complaining? That is a good fire; now let us get back to Ruthin." We ran down the line of equites who withdrew behind us. I could see the squires were armed with bows and they were keeping away any of the Saxons foolish enough to show themselves.

Hogan had my horse for me while Pol and another equite each had one for Lann and Myrddyn. I was about to ask about Aedh when I saw that he was mounted and with his precious scouts. He inclined his head, "My men were ready Warlord!"

As I mounted I asked. "Have you an ambush site?"

"No Warlord but there is a marshy area with small lakes about four miles away. We will hold them there while the King and his people escape to Wrecsam. Mungo and Daffydd are preparing the defences now."

"Good."

I could see that we had caught the Saxons unawares. The men whose bodies littered the land around us were lightly armed. They were not the shield wall. Ardal had spoken true, the attack would come the next day but it would not be attacking Deva, it would be attacking Ruthin. We began to trudge down the road to safety. When we were a mile or so from Deva I asked. "Have we enough men in Ruthin?"

"We sent to Rhuddlan and Mungo's Burg. We have stripped them of defenders but King Arthlwys and King Cloten took their warriors that way home and they will garrison the fort at the Narrows until we return. Mona will be safe."

"Reading my mind son?"

"Lets us just say I know the way that you think."

"Well Aethelfrith and his Eorl Aethelward have fifteen hundred men. I hope Aidan is prepared?"

"He is. Brother Oswald sent over extra bolts and arrows while we were in Wrecsam. It seems he knows our plans better than we do."

"You need to keep your horsemen out of the fort. Take them to Rhuddlan. When they are rested you can harass their supply lines. They will be using ships."

"I ordered Daffydd to anchor off Rhuddlan. The Saxons are wary of the bolt throwers." He pointed in the distance; there we could see the shield wall. "Keep to the road. There are traps and marshes to the left and right. I will leave you the squires. We will take our horses and go along the coast road to Rhuddlan. It should confuse the Saxons. They will think we are fleeing."

"I will be glad when I am within Ruthin's walls." I knew that we had another fifteen miles to go and the last five would be over hilly ground.

"The squires have plenty of arrows. They might not be able to use them when riding but they can stop frequently and annoy them." He handed me Saxon Slayer and, after I had sheathed it he clasped my arm. "Take care, father."

"I will. And King Cadfan and his men?"

"We made sure they were safely on their way. He wanted to stay and fight as did his commander, Llewellyn, but I insisted. They were in no condition to fight."

"And are we?"

"There are a hundred warriors and fifty archers ahead of us. They are all desperate to avenge Garth and Miach. They are ready."

Mungo grinned when I reached him. "This will see how fit the men are. Fight run and fight some more!"

I waved to Hogan, Pasgen and Tuanthal who took their place to our left. When the squires arrived they lined up to our right. The archers were already behind the shield wall. "Now Mungo, no heroics. We want them to bleed all the way to Ruthin."

"Of course Warlord."

The Saxons had formed a crude wedge. I could see them as they ran along the road. That suited me for it would tire them out. As soon as they were two hundred paces away the equites suddenly galloped off towards the west. I knew there was consternation amongst the Saxon ranks for they halted, unsure of what to do. They did not know if the horsemen were riding to attack their flank. They had no way of knowing they could not charge again. There also appeared to be twice as many of them as each equite was leading a spare horse.

The Saxon leader compromised and detached a wedge to follow them. The rest came on. Suddenly the detachment set up a wail as they found the traps and the marshes to the west of the road. I doubt that any died but they were out of the battle at any rate. The rest came on. They tried to spread into a larger wedge but they found marshes to the east of the road and they were forced to keep a narrow wedge. When they were a hundred paces from us Daffydd shouted the orders to the squires and his men. A hundred arrows soared into the sky. They kept loosing until the sky was black with them. The front of the wedge was so badly cut up that the thirty warriors who reached us were no match for our well armed and well trained warriors. I did not have to unsheathe Saxon Slayer. The enemy halted.

Mungo grinned at me, "Now we can go." He waved at the squires who waved back. They formed a thin line before the Saxons as we moved along the road to Ruthin. We ran for five miles and then halted. We were not tired but I wanted the pursuing Saxons to be. The squires were enjoying themselves. Every time the Saxons ran to within fifty paces of their tormenting arrows they turned and rode out of range of the weary warriors. Aedh and his scouts were watching the Saxons and reporting to me.

"They are becoming weary my lord. There are about six hundred of them in the first group and another three hundred who are lagging behind."

"And they will have sent some by sea."

"True, Myrddyn. Aedh, send a scout to Aidan and warn him of our proximity." I turned to Daffydd. "You can best be used to ambush them close to the fort. Use the bushes and hedgerows close to the road. Five arrows each should do it and then join Aidan in the fort."

"Will be you be able to hold them off, Warlord?"

"We do not have to do that. We just have to draw them on to our walls and we can manage that."

It was late afternoon when Ruthin hove into view. The climb up the Clwyd hills was brutal even for my fit warriors. For the Saxons it must have been unbearable. The leader of the squires rode up to me. "My lord we are out of arrows and the horses are weary." He gave me a rueful look. "As are my men."

"You have done more than I could have hoped. Join the equites in Rhuddlan. My son knows what to do."

Aedh grinned at me. "We are not tired."

"I know and I want you to continue to watch them and keep us and my son informed. You have your instructions and your riders are the key to our victory. We will be within the walls and I need to know the best time to strike."

The open gates of Ruthin looked more welcoming than a fire on a winter's night. We were weary but we had evaded the Saxons and reached our lands without losing men. That was vital. The Saxons had closed to within three hundred paces of us by the time we reached the gates. When they saw the open gates they thought they had caught us. Daffydd and his archers rained their arrows on them and made them take shelter. Unfortunately for the Saxons the shelter they took was a bramble filled jungle and a trap filled open space. We had learned our lessons when we had ambushed the men of Gwynedd and we were now better prepared. By the time the gates slammed shut the Saxons had barely made the ditches. It was then the killing began. The bolt throwers did what they did best and cleared lines of Saxons. The javelins and stones hurled from the walls thinned out the mailed warriors and the pila of the warriors saw off any who made it across the death filled ditches. They wisely withdrew and surrounded our fort.

Aidan was pleased to see me. "I am in awe of the plan Warlord. I never thought that it would work as well as it did."

"Myrddyn is a clever man."

"And the Warlord is afraid of nothing so we make a good team. And now commander those of us who did without a night's sleep last night will make up for it now."

I must have looked more tired than I felt but Myrddyn was right and I fell asleep in a corner of the warrior hall. I was awoken by Lann. "The Saxon king himself is here my lord and we are surrounded." I began to dress and Lann helped me with my armour. "Are you sure that this will work my lord? There seem to be many of the enemy and they have circled the fort."

"Doubt nephew?" He could not see the plan that Myrddyn and me had concocted. We had gone over every detail working out exactly what the Saxons might do. So far they had done all that we had expected. "I am relying on the Saxons surrounding the fort. It will help us to defeat them."

I knew that the defences they had encountered thus far would not have thinned out their numbers. They had halted at the tree line once one or two of their men had fallen into the traps. I could see them now, in the first light of dawn, looking at the ground for obvious signs of traps. When the first frosts and snows came then the pits would be more obvious but it had rained recently and there was no sign where the traps were. They might have looked at the white stones dotted, apparently haphazardly around the trail but they would have had no idea that they were, in fact, distance markers for the archers and bolt throwers.

Aidan had every warrior and archer on the walls. As I peered out I could see few archers amongst the enemy ranks. Our men packed the walls but they had the protection of the wooden wall and the angled tops devised by Brother Oswald. It meant we could loose arrows and our men were protected from enemy missiles. This would, however, be the first time we had tried them.

I turned to Lann Aelle. "I think it is time we told them who we are. Unfurl the banner!" He was ready with it and he raised it. We had built a socket for it and he placed it there in the centre of the gatehouse.

The men saw it and began to rhythmically bang their shields chanting, "Wolf Warrior!" over and over. The two events seemed to inflame the enemy for they began to march forwards resolutely. They soon found the first traps and began to edge towards the trails leading to the fort. It was the signal for the bolt throwers and they carved a line of death through the serried ranks of warriors. They found that their shields were no match for the weapons which went through them as though they were parchment. Still they came on. Daffydd gave his signal and the arrows began to rain down upon the enemy. They were caught between the need to protect their front from the flat trajectory of the bolts and to protect their heads and upper bodies from the arrows. They ended doing neither. Finally the stones from the slingers crashed and cracked down on shields and armour. Each time a warrior fell another took his place but I could see the dents in the armour and the blood running from wounds. The Saxons were bleeding.

Once they reached the ditches they began to die as the traps in the bottom broke legs and ripped into unprotected groins. The warriors on my walls who had hitherto watched now joined in hurling their pila at those who managed to survive the traps and reach the last ditch. They tried for over an hour but each time they were repulsed. Finally we saw them withdraw and a gaggle of chiefs gathered around King Aethelfrith.

"Feed the men Aidan and give them water. This may not be over. Is there any word from the scouts?"

"No, Warlord, but it is early yet." He hesitated and then looked at the dead littering the four sides of the fort. "They are brave but this is pointless death. We are too well protected."

"They do not see a fort as well built and protected as Deva. They expected difficulty taking that Roman built fort but we look small and insignificant. They cannot believe that we are as strong as we are."

They attacked twice more and each time they were heavily repulsed. I think they tried as hard as they did because their king was watching. As the afternoon sun began to dip behind Wyddfa a warrior without sword or shield walked forwards with his hands held out.

"Should I kill him Warlord?"

"No Daffydd, he comes in peace let us hear his words."

He stood below the gate. He was a warrior who bore his battle scars and battle rings proudly. He had fought in the shield wall before. "I am Aella son of Aethelgirth and I am here to speak with Lord Lann, the Warlord of Rheged."

I removed my helmet so that he might see my face. "I am he. Speak."

He nodded. "I would like to have met you in battle for I have heard you are a fine warrior. Shall we try now?"

"If that was the reason you came here then I will have my archers end your life now. Speak the words your king gave you and then return to him."

I could see that I had annoyed him. "My king would speak with you. Do you give him safe passage?"

"I do. You have my word. He can bring one other but no more."

"Can he come armed?"

I laughed and tapped the bolt thrower next to me. "Of course!"

The king returned with Aella and they both had their swords strapped to their belts. "Lord Lann, you have fought me over the years and I admire you as an adversary. This bloodshed is pointless. Become my ally and rule this land for me. I promise that you will never be attacked by my men again."

I nodded and stroked my beard. "Your words are reasonable and deserve consideration." I looked towards the south and then smiled. "I have considered them. I would sooner ally with a snake for you know when he will strike by his hiss. You are a treacherous snake and I will not rest until you and every Saxon on this island is dead or fled back to their homeland. You do not know what truth is and I do not trust you. You have come like a thief in the night and stolen our land and now you say you will let us live? You are a fool. How many times have you bested me?"

He looked angry. "You fled Rheged!"

"And there is my answer. I fled my home but, even though outnumbered and encumbered with women and children you could neither catch me nor beat me. I even returned to rescue my brothers. In what life do you think you will ever defeat us?"

He became really angry. "In this life! I promise you there will be no quarter. I will slaughter every man in this fort and then do the same in all your others. Your family on Mona will become my slaves and I will make a footstool of that wizard Myrddyn's head."

Myrddyn looked down at him. "Brave words from a man with a handful of warriors."

The king gestured behind him. "There are two thousand men there ready to rip you and your wooden walls apart."

I laughed. "You were camped outside Deva for long enough so I am not afraid and it is nearer fifteen hundred not two thousand. You count about as well as you fight and now I think it is time to end this. Lann sound the buccina!"

Lann blew three blasts on the Roman horn. The two Saxons looked around fearfully. "What trickery is this? You promised us safe passage!"

"And you will not be harmed but your warriors are another matter and it is they who are now surrounded."

There was a roar from the east and the south as the armies of Cadfan and his allies attacked the rear of the Saxon line. Even as Aethelgirth faced that way there was the clash of steel from the north as Hogan led my warriors to fall upon the rest. "Go beyond the Dee and build forts King Aethelgirth because I am coming for you and you have my word on that!"

He shook his fist at me and Aella hurled an axe at my head. I ducked and when I looked up he had been pinned by a bolt and six arrows. The king ran as fast as he could.

I turned to Aidan, "Now captain, let your wolves loose!"

The garrison erupted out of the gates to fall upon a Saxon enemy attacked on all sides. They did as their king did, they ran. His advantage was that he was on a horse as were his bodyguard. The rest of his men were not so lucky. You could see their route home by the corpses and the feasting carrion. I do not know how many escaped but hundreds died. When we finally got around to burning the bodies the sky south of the Dee was black with smoke. The weapons we took ensured that the alliance had the best arms and armour and were secure for many years. The victory was all the sweeter for the fact that we barely lost a warrior and our frontier was safe for many years to come.

Epilogue

All of the armies gathered at the fort at the Narrows. The three kings and all of my leaders were present. My brothers and their families joined mine in a journey from Mona that was both joyful and a relief. We could not all fit inside the warrior hall; we gathered in the area between the halls and the gates. Prince Pasgen had two wagons tied together to make a platform as I addressed the assembled multitude.

"We have achieved a great victory and defeated the Saxons, a tyrant and the Hibernians. We have forged an alliance of kings to withstand the Saxon hordes. I, along with my warriors, am the guardian of that alliance. We will never fight amongst ourselves and I will lead our armies to reconquer the lands taken from us by the Saxon. Aethelgirth has scurried back to the north but Cearl will need to watch his borders, for Mercia has stolen much land from our people." There was a huge cheer. I took out Saxon Slayer. "We are here to show that our alliance is forged in steel and here, beneath Wyddfa I swear on this ancient sword, Saxon Slayer that I will accept the title given to me by the three kings, Warlord of Cymri and Britannia. I am Dux Britannica still!"

There was a great outpouring of cheers and celebration. Raibeart and Aelle both sat with me and our sons as we watched the nations of Cymri joined together, for the first time, as allies.

"How did you know that the armies had surrounded the Saxons?"

"The towers; the Saxons were so pleased to have captured them that they failed to destroy them. Aedh and his scouts killed the warriors who were guarding them. They signalled to me when all was in place. The attacks they had planned on Rhuddlan were halted when my five ships defeated their fleet. They had no answer to the bolt throwers. It meant that Hogan and his men could get to Ruthin even earlier than we had planned."

"But it was dangerous to draw him on after you. He could have caught you at any time."

"No, Raibeart, the men we trained all those years ago have just got better and better. These are now the new Roman Army. These are the legionaries and auxiliaries who conquered Britannia for Rome. This is the army which will reconquer the land for Britannia." I patted Saxon Slayer which lay across my lap, "This sword was part of that conquest and it continues that work."

Hogan knelt as did my brothers, "And we swear that we will fight for you, Warlord, and your powerful sword, Saxon Slayer, the sword which will save Britannia!"

The End

Glossary

Characters in italics are fictional

Name-Explanation
Aedh-Despatch rider and scout
Aelfere-Northallerton
Aelfraed-Saxon volunteer
Aelle-Monca's son and Lann's step brother
Aethelfrith-King of Bernicia and Aethelric's overlord
Aethelric-King of Deira (The land to the south of the Tees)
Aidan-Priest from Metcauld
Alavna-Maryport
Artorius-King Arthur
Banna-Birdoswald
Belatu-Cadros-God of war
Belerion-Land's End (Cornwall)
Beli ap Rhun-King of Gwynedd until 599
Bellatrix-Gallic Warrior
Bishop Stephen-Bishop of St Asaph
Caedwalestate-Cadishead near Salford
Caergybi-Holyhead
Civitas Carvetiorum-Carlisle
Constantinopolis-Constantinople (modern Istanbul)
Cymri-Wales
Cynfarch Oer-Descendant of Coel Hen (King Cole)
Daffydd ap Gwynfor-Lann's chief captain
Daffydd ap Miach-Miach's son
Dai ap Gruffyd-Prince Cadfan's squire
Delbchaem Lann-Lann's daughter
Din Guardi-Bamburgh Castle
Dunum-River Tees
Dux Britannica-The Roman British leader after the Romans left (King Arthur)
Erecura-Goddess of the earth
Fanum Cocidii-Bewcastle
Felan-Irish pirate
Freja-Saxon captive and Aelle's wife
Gareth-Harbour master Caergybi
Garth-Lann's lieutenant
Gawan Lann-Lann's son
Gawan Lann-Son of Lann
Gildas-Urien's nephew
Glanibanta-Ambleside
Gwynfor-Headman at Caergybi
Gwyr-The land close to Swansea
Halvelyn-Helvellyn
Haordine-Hawarden Cheshire
Hen Ogledd-Northern England and Southern Scotland
Hogan-Father of Lann and Raibeart
Hogan Lann-Lann's son
Iago ap Beli-King of Gwynedd 599-613
Icaunus-River god
King Ywain Rheged-Eldest son of King Urien

Lann-[1] Warlord of Rheged and Dux Britannica
Loge-God of trickery
Loidis-Leeds
Maeresea-River Mersey
*Maiwen-*The daughter of the King of Elmet
Mare Nostrum-Mediterranean Sea
Metcauld-Lindisfarne
*Miach-*Leader of Lann's archers
*Monca-*An escaped Briton and mother of Aelle
Morcant Bulc-King of Bryneich (Northumberland)
*Mungo-*Leader of the men of Strathclyde
*Myfanwy-*Lann's wife
*Myrddyn-*Welsh wizard fighting for Rheged
*Nanna Lann-*Lann's daughter
*Niamh-*Queen of Rheged
Nithing-A man without honour
Nodens-God of hunting
*Osric-*Irish priest
*Oswald-*Priest at Castle Perilous
Penrhyn Llŷn-Llŷn Peninsula
pharos-lighthouse
Phocas-Byzantine Emperor 602-610
*Pol-*Equite and Lann's standard bearer
Prestune-Preston Lancashire
Prince Cadfan Ap Iago-Heir to the Gwynedd throne
Prince Pasgen-Youngest son of Urien
*Radha-*Mother of Lann and Raibeart
*Raibeart-*Lann's brother
*Ridwyn-*Bernician warrior fighting for Rheged
*Roman Bridge-*Piercebridge (Durham)
Scillonia Insula-Scilly Isles
Solar-West facing room in a castle
Sucellos-God of love and time
Tatenhale-Tattenhall near Chester
*The Narrows-*The Menaii Straits
Treffynnon-Holywell (North Wales)
*Tuanthal-*Leader of Lann's horse warriors
Vectis-Isle of Wight
Vindonnus-God of hunting
*Wachanglen-*Wakefield
wapentake-Muster of an army
*Wide Water-*Windermere
Wyddfa-Snowdon
Wyrd-Fate
Y Fflint-Flint (North Wales)
Ynys Enlli-Bardsey Island
Yr Wyddgrug-Mold (North Wales)

---

[1] Lann means sword in Celtic

Historical note

I mainly used four books to research the material. The first was the excellent Michael Wood's book *"In Search of the Dark Ages"* and the second was *"The Middle Ages"* Edited by Robert Fossier. The third was the Osprey Book- *"Saxon, Viking and Norman"* by Terence Wise. I also used Brian Sykes book, *"Blood of the Isles"* for reference. In addition I searched on line for more obscure information. All the place names are accurate, as far as I know, and I have researched the names of the characters to reflect the period. My apologies if I have made a mistake.

The Saxons and Britons all valued swords and cherished them. They were passed from father to son. The use of rings on the hilts of great swords was a common practice and showed the prowess of the warrior in battle. I do not subscribe to Brian Sykes' theory that the Saxons merely assimilated into the existing people. One only has to look at the place names and listen to the language of the north and north western part of England. You can still hear anomalies. Perhaps that is because I come from the north but all of my reading leads me to believe that the Anglo-Saxons were intent upon conquest. The people of Rheged were the last survivors of Roman Britain and I have given them all of the characteristics they would have had. They were educated and ingenious. The Dark Ages was the time when much knowledge was lost and would not reappear until Constantinople fell. This period was also the time when the old ways changed and Britain became Christian but I have not used this as a source of conflict but rather growth.

Beli ap Rhun was king of Gwynedd at the end of the sixth century. Asaph was the bishop at the monastery of St. Kentigern (Aka St. Mungo) and they named the town after him. Julius Agricola swam horses and men across the straits between Wales and Anglesey four hundred years earlier and I thought that Lann could do the same. There is no evidence that Ywain succumbed to the Saxons but Prince Pasgen did rule, briefly in Rheged. The Bishop of the monastery of St Kentigern was called Asaph and he did become a saint. Bishop Asaph was the second bishop at the monastery and town which now bears his name. He did die at the end of the sixth century as did King Beli who was slain in battle with the Saxons. His monastery did survive quite well against raids by Saxons and the Irish. I have used Lord Lann as the protector of the monastery; it seemed as plausible a story as any.

King Iago did succeed King Beli and his son was Cadfan. I did not learn much about them when I researched other than when they died. I have given them their attributes as they fitted in with my story line. For all that I know King Iago was a good king but I couldn't resist casting him as the baddie! King Aethelfrith did capture Chester in 613 and King Iago died in the same year; the writings of the time say he was killed in battle. I have used the limited facts available to suit my story. Wales began to become united from the end of the Sixth Century. Eventually what was Gwynedd took over the whole of the lane from the Dee to the Severn and Offa had to build his dyke a century or so later to stop their advances.

Griff Hosker October 2013

Other books by Griff Hosker

If you enjoyed reading this book, then why not read another one by the author?

Ancient History

The Sword of Cartimandua Series (Germania and Britannia 50A.D. – 130 A.D.)
 Ulpius Felix- Roman Warrior (prequel)
 Book 1 The Sword of Cartimandua
 Book 2 The Horse Warriors
 Book 3 Invasion Caledonia
 Book 4 Roman Retreat
 Book 5 Revolt of the Red Witch
 Book 6 Druid's Gold
 Book 7 Trajan's Hunters
 Book 8 The Last Frontier
 Book 9 Hero of Rome
 Book 10 Roman Hawk
 Book 11 Roman Treachery
 Book 12 Roman Wall
 Book 13 Roman Courage

The Aelfraed Series (Britain and Byzantium 1050 A.D. - 1085 A.D.)
 Book 1 Housecarl
 Book 2 Outlaw
 Book 3 Varangian

The Wolf Warrior series (Britain in the late 6th Century)
 Book 1 Saxon Dawn
 Book 2 Saxon Revenge
 Book 3 Saxon England
 Book 4 Saxon Blood
 Book 5 Saxon Slayer
 Book 6 Saxon Slaughter
 Book 7 Saxon Bane
 Book 8 Saxon Fall: Rise of the Warlord
 Book 9 Saxon Throne
 Book 10 Saxon Sword

The Dragon Heart Series
 Book 1 Viking Slave
 Book 2 Viking Warrior
 Book 3 Viking Jarl
 Book 4 Viking Kingdom
 Book 5 Viking Wolf
 Book 6 Viking War
 Book 7 Viking Sword

Book 8 Viking Wrath
Book 9 Viking Raid
Book 10 Viking Legend
Book 11 Viking Vengeance
Book 12 Viking Dragon
Book 13 Viking Treasure
Book 14 Viking Enemy
Book 15 Viking Witch
Bool 16 Viking Blood
Book 17 Viking Weregeld
Book 18 Viking Storm
Book 19 Viking Warband
Book 20 Viking Shadow
Book 21 Viking Legacy

The Norman Genesis Series
Hrolf the Viking
Horseman
The Battle for a Home
Revenge of the Franks
The Land of the Northmen
Ragnvald Hrolfsson
Brothers in Blood
Lord of Rouen
Drekar in the Seine

The Anarchy Series England 1120-1180
English Knight
Knight of the Empress
Northern Knight
Baron of the North
Earl
King Henry's Champion
The King is Dead
Warlord of the North
Enemy at the Gate
Fallen Crown
Warlord's War
Kingmaker
Henry II
Crusader
The Welsh Marches
Irish War
Poisonous Plots
Princes' Revolt
Earl Marshal

Border Knight 1190-1300
Sword for Hire
Return of the Knight
Baron's War
Magna Carta

Struggle for a Crown England 1367-1485
Blood on the Crown

Modern History
The Napoleonic Horseman Series
Book 1 Chasseur a Cheval
Book 2 Napoleon's Guard
Book 3 British Light Dragoon
Book 4 Soldier Spy
Book 5 1808: The Road to Corunna
Waterloo

The Lucky Jack American Civil War series
Rebel Raiders
Confederate Rangers
The Road to Gettysburg

The British Ace Series
1914
1915 Fokker Scourge
1916 Angels over the Somme
1917 Eagles Fall
1918 We will remember them
From Arctic Snow to Desert Sand
Wings over Persia

Combined Operations series 1940-1945
Commando
Raider
Behind Enemy Lines
Dieppe
Toehold in Europe
Sword Beach
Breakout
The Battle for Antwerp
King Tiger
Beyond the Rhine

Other Books
Carnage at Cannes (a thriller)
Great Granny's Ghost (Aimed at 9-14-year-old young people)
Adventure at 63-Backpacking to Istanbul

For more information on all of the books then please visit the author's web site at http://www.griffhosker.com where there is a link to contact him. Or you can Tweet me at @HoskerGriff

Made in United States
Orlando, FL
02 March 2022